I'll
Be Home
for Christmas

BOOKS BY KAREN CLARKE

Karen Clarke

I'll
Be Home
for Christmas

Bookouture

Published by Bookouture in 2019

An imprint of StoryFire Ltd.
Carmelite House
50 Victoria Embankment
London EC4Y 0DZ

www.bookouture.com

ISBN: 978-1-78681-802-7
eBook ISBN: 978-1-78681-801-0

For Tim, with all my love

Chapter One

The last thing I wanted to see when I was supposed to be escaping Christmas was an oversized tree, trussed with tinsel and baubles and an angel with a startled expression stuffed on top. It was almost identical to the one I'd left behind, which had been up since November when my mother had declared it was 'legitimate to start Christmas'.

Also, why was it snowing, when it never snowed in this part of France? The Île de Ré proclaimed itself 'a Mediterranean island lost in the Atlantic' and when I'd visited my aunt, almost six years ago, the week had passed in an endless succession of cloudless blue skies – in March. I'd hardly expected tropical weather in December, but hadn't predicted snow the second I arrived. *Thanks a lot, global warming.*

Still, as I stared at the enormous pine tree dominating the café window, almost blocking the words 'Café Belle Vie' in gold letters on the glass, I had to admit it would make a good photo for the travel blog I was planning to launch, once I had some decent pictures… and had done some travelling. I fished my phone from my pocket and took a couple of snaps, liking the slightly blurring effect of the gently falling snow.

Beyond the twinkling tree lights were customers in the café – lots of them, chatting and laughing. I imagined inserting myself among them and being sociable. It was ages since I'd mingled with that many people, much less chatted and laughed. In fact, I wasn't sure I'd laughed at all since Gran's death, nearly eight months ago.

My gaze tracked a woman and child heading towards the entrance, the girl's eyes aglow as if she'd had a glimpse of Narnia. If she'd lived here all her four (five, six?) years, she might never have seen snow before.

'I want hot chocolate, Mummy, and a great big cake like this,' she said, voice carrying on the chilly, afternoon air, demonstrating the size with a pair of small gloved hands. 'Maybe *two* cakes.'

English.

'You can have some hot chocolate, but no cake,' said her mum with a smile in her voice. 'We'll be having dinner soon.'

'Can we have a snowball fight?'

'There's not enough snow yet, Holly.'

Holly? It seemed the universe was determined to remind me of Christmas at every turn.

I huddled into my pale blue furry coat – the one my friend Anna said made me look like Sully from *Monsters, Inc.* – as if I'd landed in Antarctica instead of a fishing village on the west coast of France, and imagined Mum saying, 'Go *on*,' as if coaxing Tess, our ancient Collie, into the garden on a rainy morning.

I hitched up my holdall, treading gingerly across the cobbles as the snow settled around me, glad I'd worn my old Doc Martens and allowed Mum to wind her woolly scarf around my neck before leaving the house that morning.

Entering the café behind the woman and her daughter, I was hit with a blast of warmth and two of my favourite smells: ground coffee and freshly baked pastry (the others being lemons, pizza and cut grass after rain), and my appetite rebooted. I hadn't eaten since breakfast, when Mum insisted I demolish a bowl of porridge to 'line my stomach' as though I was planning to drink my body-weight in gin, rather than heading to the airport to catch a plane.

Watching her dart around the kitchen in her ancient jeans and roll-neck sweater, I'd felt a rush of affection and almost asked her to come with me, but she'd been to Chamillon a few months earlier to attend her sister's wedding, and I knew she wouldn't want to leave the farm again so soon. Plus, she was helping organise the Christmas play at the local village hall and preparing to host the Bailey family Christmas at the farmhouse – which wouldn't be the same without Gran, and was the main reason I'd opted to give the whole thing a miss this year.

'It won't be the same without you, Nina, but your aunt will take good care of you,' Mum had said, pausing to massage my shoulders, her arms and hands strong from years of sheep-shearing. 'Just try to have a nice break.'

'I'll do my best,' I'd promised. I hadn't mentioned I was going to use the time away to try and get my travel blog off the ground, preferring to present it when I'd got some posts to share.

When he dropped me at the airport, Dad had wrapped me in a bear hug, almost crushing my ribs, as though I was embarking on an expedition fraught with danger. 'Sure you don't want me to sort the bastard out?' he'd said gruffly. 'It's not too late, you know.'

I'd breathed in his familiar scent of old barns and dried manure, overlaid with Mum's jasmine-scented shower gel, and considered his offer for a moment, imagining Scott's face as he turned to see Dad bearing down on him in his tractor… except, Scott had moved on and so had I, and I couldn't condone murder. Not even by tractor.

'Honestly, Dad, I had a lucky escape,' I'd said, wondering whether it would be better or worse to admit that my ongoing grief was more about losing Gran than Scott. 'It's in the past and I'm over it.'

He'd held me at arm's length, the soulful dark eyes my brother had inherited – mine were the same clear-grey on a good day as Mum's – searching my face for clues. 'Really?'

'Really,' I'd reassured him, affectionately taking in his everyday look of blue-checked work shirt tucked into old Levi's, worn with a leather belt and matching boots. He always looked out of place anywhere but the farm. 'I just want to escape for a week or so, that's all.'

'Your gran loved you, you know.' He'd always been able to see right through me. 'She wouldn't want you to be unhappy.' His eyes had filled, and I'd reminded myself she was his mother and he was still mourning her too.

'I know,' I'd said, pulling him in for another hug, unable to admit how responsible I felt for hastening her death.

'And you'll be all right on the plane on your own?'

'Dad, I'm thirty!'

'I know, but…' Blinking, he'd eyed a mop-haired man in a black coat and a red and gold scarf, scoping the area through little round glasses as he hoisted a rucksack out of a taxi. 'I don't want you sitting next to someone like *that*.' He jerked his head at the man, who gave him a startled look.

'Like a grown-up Harry Potter?' Some would say – specifically my older brother Ben – that Dad was overprotective, but I knew it killed him that he hadn't been able to prevent me from getting hurt; or do anything about it when I was. 'I'll probably just listen to a podcast, or some music on my phone.'

'You don't like flying.'

'Dad, I'll be fine,' I said. 'The flight's less than two hours.'

His face – leathery from years of farming in all weathers – had been mapped with worry as he squeezed my shoulders and said, 'I suppose you know what you're doing, love.'

*

Now, standing in the café, a babble of impenetrable voices competing with the whoosh of the coffee machine and clatter of crockery, I wondered whether I'd done the right thing, coming to stay at my aunt's. I'd considered accepting my friend Anna's offer to go with her to Spain and 'pick up men' (she hated Christmas), or take off on my own to a remote part of Ireland – both places would have been a good starting point for my blog – but worried being alone would give me too much time to think. To remember that this was the week I was supposed to get married, before I called off my wedding and effectively killed my gran.

'Nina!'

At the sound of my name, I turned to see my cousin Charlie weaving between tables and felt my spirits rise at the sight of his smiling face.

'Hey, Chuck!' I raised a palm in greeting and let him grab me in a gentle headlock and ruffle my hair with his knuckles. Charlie had always been my favourite cousin – I had loads on Dad's side; his three brothers had twelve children between them – but I was closer to Charlie as we had been more like brother and sister growing up.

'Heartbreak haircut?' he enquired, when I'd laughingly wriggled free and was attempting to smooth my short, tousled layers.

'You should have seen it seven months ago.' I grimaced, recalling the crop I'd replaced my shoulder-length waves with after cancelling the wedding. I'd thought it would make me look 'edgy' and I'd start wearing cute dresses with cowboy boots instead of my usual jumpers and jeans, or appear 'elfin' like Emma Watson had. Instead, I'd looked like a choirboy, and had to wear more make-up because I kept being asked for ID. 'I tried to spike it up a bit on top,' I said, fluffing my too-short tresses. 'Dad said it looked like I'd brushed it with a Brillo pad. I cried more about that than anything,' I added, which wasn't remotely true. I'd cried floods after walking in on Scott at the art gallery, his hand on his latest protégée's buttock (again) and hearing him say it was nothing (again), and had cried until I nearly made myself ill when Gran passed away shortly after.

Charlie's laugh was as warm and encompassing as I remembered – as if he was laughing with me, not at me. 'It's natural to want to reinvent yourself,' he said. 'After my last break-up, I grew my hair to my waist and dyed it pink.'

'Idiot!' I punched his arm, already feeling better than I had in ages. 'I was a bit of a cliché for a while,' I admitted. 'I didn't think I was the sort to react like that after a break-up.'

'You're only human, or so I've heard.' Charlie paused as I unwound my scarf, perspiring a little in the coffee-scented heat. 'I'm sorry about what happened,' he said.

'I expect my mum gave your mum all the gruesome details.'

'You know what they're like, especially when they get together.' He gave a comical wince. 'I'm sorry about your gran, too. I know you were really close.'

For a second, my eyes went swimmy and I had to keep them fixed on Charlie's nose. He pulled out a chair at the only free table and said, 'Sit down and I'll bring you a drink.'

'Where's Dolly?' Blinking, I unbuttoned my coat and looked around for my aunt. The last time I'd visited her presence had been obvious right away – she'd been on her hands and knees, her bottom in the air, attempting to coax a cat out from under one of the tables.

'Upstairs.' Charlie tilted his eyes to the ceiling, indicating the apartment above, where he and Dolly lived – or at least, where Charlie still lived. Dolly had moved into Frank's cottage on the opposite side of the harbour after their wedding. 'She's hunting for a Christmas CD to play for the customers.'

I eyed the heavily-decorated tree and array of holly garlands, the pine-studded wreaths on the walls, and a row of red Christmas stockings with furry white tops hanging from the wooden counter. 'What's with all the decorations?' I said. 'I was expecting... not this.'

Charlie grinned. 'Mum usually goes for a typically French theme – a tree with ribbons and candles and a star on top – but this year, she wanted to show the locals how the Brits do Christmas.' His gaze trailed mine. 'Looks like our living room in the nineties, but with a coffee machine, and customers and better flooring.' He cast an admiring gaze at the solid, maple boards beneath our feet.

'Looks like ours does now.' As I glanced at the little girl I'd followed into the café, standing behind her mum and staring in awe at some reindeer-shaped cookies, I felt a pang for my own childhood, when I'd believed in Father Christmas long after my brother revealed the man who delivered our presents on Christmas Eve was Uncle Hank – Dad's oldest brother, chosen for the task because he (literally) had the stomach for it. 'I thought I was escaping all this.'

'You always loved Christmas.' Charlie looked as though he was remembering too, when our families got together and everything normal was suspended in a magical bubble for a week. 'We thought you'd like it.'

'Oh, I do,' I said, feeling bad that I'd sounded less than enthusiastic. 'I mean... I would normally *love* it, it's just...'

'I know, I know.' Charlie rubbed a hand over his wavy, blondish hair. It had grown since I'd last seen him in person – Mum had lots of photos of him on her phone from Dolly's wedding – and he was sporting a close-cut beard, like most men in their early thirties seemed to do. He looked more mature and I supposed I did too, with the new lines I was certain I'd developed over the past few months. Catching sight of my reflection these days wasn't a pleasant experience. Mum had taken to carolling, 'Turn that frown upside down, Nina!' stretching her mouth into a grin with her hands until I couldn't help smiling back.

'We might have got a bit carried away,' Charlie admitted, pointing to a clump of mistletoe by the door. 'Mum didn't want your memories of Christmas to be tainted by that… by whatsisface letting you down.'

'That's kind of her.' I sloughed my coat off. 'But letting me down sounds a bit mild. Like air from a balloon.'

'Yes, after it's been popped by a little prick.'

My snort of laughter caught me by surprise. 'Good one, Chuck.'

'Happy to oblige.' His friendly brown eyes twinkled with good humour. 'Now, coffee or hot chocolate?'

'I'll have coffee and pastry, please. *Lots* of pastry. Can I help?'

'Absolutely not. Pain au chocolat?'

'Thanks, at least seven.'

Still smiling, he returned to the counter and I dropped onto the padded chair seat, some of the tension seeping out of my body, despite being surrounded by at least half of all the Christmas decorations in the world. Was that an inflatable Santa in the corner, with a bulging sack slung over one shoulder? It was, an adorable little black dog in a knitted Nordic sweater sleeping beside it, the owner – an elderly man with ruddy cheeks under a white beard – engrossed in what looked like a newspaper crossword. I thought about taking another photo, then decided to text Mum that I'd arrived safely instead. I'd just pressed send when I heard a blast of 'It's the Most Wonderful Time of the Year' followed by another familiar voice, calling my (extremely full) name.

'Nina Katrina Augustine Bailey!'

'Hi, Dolly!' I stood to receive my aunt's hug, which was as heartfelt and strong as ever and squashed the breath from my lungs. 'It's really good to see you,' I said, recognising her favourite Elizabeth Arden perfume beneath the vanilla-and-spice baking scents clinging to her clothes.

She pulled back and squinted as though bringing me into focus. 'You've lost weight,' she observed, which couldn't be true with the amount of comfort eating I'd been doing, which meant hardly any of my old clothes – the clothes I'd worn when I was with Scott – fitted me any more. 'I like your hair,' she said. 'You look like your mum when she was younger and it was still that nice chestnut colour.'

'Not like the member of a terrible boy band?'

'Silly.' Her brown eyes were shiny with tears and she yanked me close again, rocking from side to side. 'It's been too long, lovely girl.'

'Dolly, I'm sorry I didn't make it to your wedding,' I said, reluctantly breaking free. 'I just… I couldn't…'

'No need to apologise.' Gripping my hands, she tipped her head to one side, her apple-cheeked face wreathed in sympathy. 'Your mum told me everything that happened. Someone else's wedding was the last thing you needed, what with losing your gran on top.'

'It was selfish,' I said, pierced with guilt, not sure I deserved her forgiveness. 'Frank looks lovely, though. Mum showed me the pictures.'

Dolly waggled her hand to show off a narrow gold band nestled on her wedding finger. 'Never thought I'd wear one of these again,' she said. 'Did your mum tell you that Elle took the official photos?' Her face – softer and rounder than Mum's, but with the same crinkly-eyed smile and spiky lashes – melted into a smile. 'Charlie's girlfriend,' she added, in a way that suggested she'd never tire of saying those two words – at least until she could start saying *Charlie's wife*.

'She might have mentioned it once or twice.'

'Mum, I don't think Nina needs to hear about my love life.' As Charlie returned with two steaming mugs on a tray, and a plate of assorted pastries, I realised he had a shine about him I hadn't noticed at first. *He was in love.*

'I'm pleased for you,' I said. Charlie deserved to be happy. He'd avoided serious relationships, ever since his long-term girlfriend fell for my brother, eight years ago, causing a family rift that had lasted until they broke up, eighteen months later. I could still recall the heart-wrenching sound of Charlie's stifled sobs in the bathroom the night he'd caught Emma kissing Ben in the barn, drunk on champagne at Mum's fiftieth birthday party. 'Do I get to meet this amazing woman?'

He gave an endearingly bashful smile. 'She's in England at the moment, selling her house, but will be back for Christmas.'

'She came to Chamillon to look for her birth mother and found she had an aunt. Then she and Charlie fell in love so she's coming to live with him here.' Dolly seemed ecstatic to have someone new to impart this information to, and I couldn't help smiling at the look of mortified delight on Charlie's face.

'Mum,' he said, shaking his head as he placed the tray on the table, laughing when I picked up a pain au chocolat and took a giant bite. Bing Crosby was singing 'Let it Snow' and although several customers looked baffled, most were jigging their shoulders, getting into the spirit, and my toes itched to join in.

'They're adorable together,' Dolly continued, catching Charlie around the waist to give him a squeeze, her head only reaching his chest. Her hair was dark-blonde like his, but with a heavy fringe she'd had for as long as I could remember.

'Can't wait to see it for myself.' I picked up my mug to take a long drink of sweet, milky coffee, feeling the warmth spread down inside my chest.

'I wouldn't be surprised if wedding bells…' Dolly tactfully caught her bottom lip between her teeth while Charlie sucked in a breath.

'Don't worry, we're allowed to talk about weddings,' I said briskly, but my appetite had dwindled. I put down the half-eaten pastry and almost-empty mug and pinned on a smile. 'Would you mind if I went upstairs, Dolly? I'm pretty tired.'

'Of course I don't mind, love.' She and Charlie exchanged a look. 'I've put you in my old room, if that's OK.'

'Thank you.' I gave her a grateful smile. 'I'll see myself up, shall I?'

'Erm, hang on a minute.' Charlie touched my elbow as I bent to scoop up my things.

'What is it?' Straightening, I caught a glimpse of panic in his eyes. 'Chuck?'

'It's nothing, really.' He scratched his ear, then ruffled his hair – a sure sign it was *something*. 'Listen, Nina, I know you're here to get away from everything, and that you probably don't want to have to speak to anyone, apart from me and Mum.'

'Spit it out,' I said, unease swilling in my stomach. 'What's going on?'

Charlie swallowed hard and flicked a glance around the café, as if hoping for a distraction, but the staff appeared to have everything under control. 'It's just…' He pressed his lips together, a plea in his eyes.

'*What?*'

Dolly let out an exasperated huff. 'He's got a friend staying.'

I flipped my eyebrows up. 'What sort of friend?'

'Mum,' growled Charlie, signalling her with his eyes.

Dolly ignored him. 'A male one,' she said, smoothing the little black apron fastened around her waist. 'His name's Ryan.' She held my gaze, adding, in case I'd failed to understand, 'He's a man.'

Chapter Two

'So, this man… he's here?' I said, as though Dolly had announced that a serial killer was hiding out upstairs. 'In your apartment?'

Charlie nodded, moving aside to let the young waiter deliver mugs of hot chocolate to a table of women, fighting to be heard over the music. 'He's an old mate from home,' he said, and I instantly remembered him mentioning his best friend Ryan, who'd lived on the same street in Buckinghamshire when they were growing up. They used to be in and out of each other's houses all the time and I'd been vaguely jealous that I didn't have a best friend like that, because our home in Somerset was quite remote and none of the girls at my school were keen to hang out on a farm. 'He was supposed to get married this year too—'

'And you thought we'd have something in common?'

'Maybe a bit,' Charlie said, scrunching his nose. 'He called off the wedding at his stag do—'

'His *stag do*?' I cut in. 'Wasn't that a bit late to be having second thoughts?'

'It was… complicated.' He tugged his earlobe, clearly not comfortable giving away any details. 'He wanted to do what was best for the children, and—'

'*Children*?'

Dolly rested a placatory hand on my arm. 'Things have been difficult for Ryan and so Charlie invited him over on the spur of the moment.'

'Well, that's... nice,' I said, wishing I'd known. I hadn't envisioned a stranger staying here too, and the last thing I wanted was to make small talk with anyone.

'Ryan wanted some time away too,' said Charlie, as though reading my thoughts, which were probably plastered all over my face. 'He's got a writing deadline to meet, so he'll be busy with that.'

'I'll be busy too.' I thought of my blog, waiting patiently for me to post something on it. 'We probably won't even see each other.'

Dolly, distracted by the young girl Holly asking the man who owned the little black dog if he was older than Father Christmas, discreetly backed away.

'If you do, just don't ask him any personal questions, will you?' Charlie sounded anxious. 'He doesn't like talking about what happened.'

'You have my word.' I wouldn't have any trouble keeping *that* promise. 'Obviously, I'll be polite though,' I said. 'And I really appreciate you and Dolly letting me stay.'

'It's about time. You haven't been here for ages.' He bent and grabbed my holdall, testing its weight with a furrowed brow. 'Is this all you've got?'

'I'm travelling light.' I flung my arms out to demonstrate. 'I wasn't planning on attending any functions while I'm here.'

'Just as well,' he said, with a grin. 'We're not exactly known for our state dinners.' He weighed the bag again. 'You've obviously forgotten our Christmas pressies.'

I inwardly cringed. I'd decided to skip Christmas shopping this year on the grounds it was too Christmassy. Plus, Mum and Dad never knew what they wanted, and Ben had declared he'd found the woman of his dreams (lovely Lena) and didn't want anything else, so I'd taken him at his word. 'They're very *small* gifts,' I said. 'And I might not have bought them yet.'

With a knowing smile, he eased my bag over his shoulder and I followed him through the café to a soundtrack of 'Frosty the Snowman', pausing on the way to make a fuss of the dog, whose name, the owner informed me, was Hamish.

'*Ma femme était ecossaise*,' he said, translating in thickly-accented English as Hamish rolled onto his back so I could tickle his tummy. 'My wife, she was Scottish.'

'*C'est un beau chien*,' I replied, earning an approving nod. My great-grandmother Augustine had been French, and despite growing up in England she'd often lapse into her native language, so Ben and I had picked up the odd word and phrase. '*Nous avons un mouton appelé Tess.*'

'You just told Gérard you have a sheep called Tess,' Charlie said with a chuckle as I joined him in the kitchen, which smelt overwhelmingly of mince pies – the one pastry item I'd been confident of avoiding in Chamillon.

'No wonder he looked surprised,' I said. 'I meant sheepdog, though obviously we have sheep too.'

'I can't believe Tess is still going strong.' Charlie raised his eyebrows. 'Does she still bark to go out, then bark to come straight back in?'

'Yes, but she won't go out at all now unless Mum joins her.'

There was an old woman by the central worktop, vigorously dusting the mince pies with icing sugar, which rose in a cloud around her head, giving her a ghostly air. She returned my curious look with a fierce glare.

'Hi, Mathilde,' said Charlie loudly and with obvious affection. '*C'est mon cousin*, Nina.' Mathilde's heavily wrinkled face formed a sinister smile. 'She's a bit deaf,' he added. 'She and her husband used to own the café and Mathilde still pops in every week to help.'

I remembered now that Mum had likened Mathilde's presence at Dolly's wedding to that of a mafia granny, but said Dolly and Charlie were genuinely fond of her; had both adopted her as a grandmother replacement.

'She doesn't speak English, right?'

'Right,' said Charlie, but I got the feeling she'd understood every word as she beadily tracked our progress through the side door leading to the apartment, where I paused to look around. Since my last visit, the walls had been painted white to reflect the light from a narrow window on the landing, where a flurry of snowflakes was whirling past the glass. The sky had darkened and I remembered it was an hour later here than in England, making it late afternoon. 'I take it Auntie Serena and Uncle Rick are still enjoying farm life?'

'Always,' I said. 'I can't imagine Dad ever retiring, and Mum's had a new lease of life since opening the farm shop last year.'

'No plans to work there permanently, now you're living back at home?'

I angled a disbelieving look at Charlie's trouser-clad calves as he climbed the stairs. 'I'm not planning on staying forever, and can you honestly see me as a farmer?' I didn't wait for a reply in case he said *yes*. 'That's Ben's department,' I said. 'He's got the travelling bug out of his system and finally accepted his fate.'

'I bet your dad's happy about that.'

'Over the moon.' I was glad we could mention my brother without too much awkwardness. They'd made up before Charlie moved to Chamillon, after Ben begged his forgiveness, though I doubted they'd ever really be close again.

As Charlie pushed open a door off the landing, I looked past him, reminding myself of the layout. 'What about you?' he said. 'Have you decided what you want to be when you grow up?'

The tips of my ears grew hot with embarrassment. It was humiliating to be unemployed at my age. My job at the art gallery had ended with my relationship – not that it had been my perfect career choice in the first place. More a case of my boyfriend giving me a job because he didn't like me working in a pub.

'Almost,' I said, edging into the bedroom before Charlie's friend emerged and insisted on introducing himself. 'I've decided to start a travel blog.'

'Sounds very grown-up.' Charlie switched on the overhead light and placed my holdall on the bed underneath the window, which was covered by a marshmallow duvet. The cover was a lavish colour that made me think of peacock feathers, and matched the curtains at the window.

I threw my coat over a velvet-padded chair inside the door, admiring the arrangement of the room. Dolly had obviously taken my advice last time, about maintaining a functional and clutter-free space – in her bedroom, at least. 'I've been keeping my options open,' I said. 'Using some of the money Gran left me to try and figure out what I might be good at.'

'You didn't do anything with your introduction to beekeeping then?'

I tutted, wishing Mum and Dolly didn't regale each other with every tiny aspect of our lives during their Skype catch-ups. It was obvious that Dolly shared more with Charlie than Mum did with me, but that wasn't really surprising when they lived and worked together. Until eight months ago, I'd been living in Southampton with Scott – a long way from where I'd grown up. 'I didn't hit it off with the bees and got stung,' I admitted. 'Though I did end up with a thimble full of honey at the end of the day.'

'I bet that was useful.'

'I had it on a slice of toast.' I turned from the inky view of the harbour, which was partly obscured by snow, to see that Charlie had thrown himself on the bed, hands laced behind his head. 'It was delicious.'

'What happened to your dalliance with horse whispering?' His face was alight with amusement.

'It was equestrian psychology,' I said, affecting a haughty accent. 'And it was actually fascinating.'

'Not fascinating enough to make a living at?'

'Jobs like that are thin on the ground.' I tried not to sound defensive. 'Plus, I got kicked, which put me off. I had a horse-shoe shaped bruise on my thigh for a fortnight.'

'Ouch!' Charlie winced. 'Sounds like fate was trying to tell you something.'

'Well, I listened.' I perched on the side of the bed and tugged off my boots. 'No more bees and horses from now on.'

'You've still got your diploma in creative problem solving and decision making.'

I groaned. 'The worst diploma in the world,' I said, still mortified that I'd stuck it out, simply because I didn't know what else to do. I couldn't take the humiliation of going back home after university, and hung onto my bar job long after my friend Anna had started working for a firm of chartered accountants. 'I never did anything with it,' I added, focusing my gaze on the shaggy cream rug by the bed, even though Charlie wasn't the type to judge. 'I stayed at the old pub for ages.'

'Which was actually called The Old Pub.'

I glanced at him and smiled. '*So* unimaginative.'

'And which you transformed and made really popular, if I remember correctly.'

'Bit of a stretch,' I said, though it was true that the pub, stuffed down a side street in Southampton, close to the university, had been a bit of a dump. But it had paid my half of the rent and bills at the tiny flat I'd shared with Anna, and when I discovered some amazing furniture and old paintings in the pub's basement and suggested doing the place up, the landlord had given me the go-ahead, figuring he had nothing to lose when business was already bad. It had been the happiest week of my life – especially as it meant I didn't have to work behind the bar – and business had tripled. 'I really enjoyed it though.'

'You always liked moving stuff about,' said Charlie. 'Remember when you came to stay with us once, and you reorganised Mum's bedroom?'

'And she went mad with me, because she couldn't find anything, but then I showed her how I'd arranged everything on those shelves she'd forgotten were there.'

'She said it was unusual for an eleven-year-old to enjoy tidying up.'

Tidying up. That's what Scott had called it too, when I'd happily reshuffled the furniture in his townhouse after I moved in, to make the design more appealing. *For God's sake, Nina, stop tidying all the time. You're like a fifties housewife.*

'You probably saved that pub from closing down,' said Charlie.

'You might be right.' It was still my proudest moment.

'And then you met Scott.'

I sighed. 'And then I met Scott and thought I'd made it,' I said. 'Whatever "it" is.'

'Didn't you like working for him?'

'Maybe, at first.' I picked the skin around my thumbnail, uncomfortable at revisiting the past. 'I was never a very good fit for the gallery, though. It was boring a lot of the time, and he wanted me to wear little dresses and be all knowledgeable about art.'

'Pretty important if you're the face of his gallery, I suppose.'

I smiled. 'I suppose it wasn't an unreasonable request, and I did get quite interested in art. I used to borrow all these books from the library.' Which Scott had found 'charmingly old-fashioned' though I didn't say that to Charlie.

'I'd never have put you two together,' he mused, having met Scott once, at my twenty-first birthday party at the farm. 'He seemed a bit up himself.'

I gave a wry smile. 'You know, when he came into the pub with his friends the night we met and asked for my number, I gave him an extra three digits because I thought he was a pretentious tosser, but he rumbled me.'

'I bet he was impressed because you were "different".' Charlie made quote marks with his voice. 'I've seen those films.'

'I forgot you like a good romcom.' I didn't add that Scott had said meeting me had been like a 'lightning bolt'. It was the sort of thing he used to say in the early days that made me feel unique, before the novelty began to wear off.

'You were right about him being a tosser.'

'Shame it took me so long to realise.' My skin burned with shame. 'He just liked the idea of moulding the little farmer's daughter into a gallery-owner's wife.'

'He should have known he was messing with the wrong person.' Charlie nudged my elbow with his knee. 'Anyway, you came here,' he said. 'That was a wise decision, so your diploma hasn't been completely wasted.' I flashed him a grateful smile. 'So, what's with this travel blog you mentioned?'

For some reason, I felt a blush spread across my face. 'Oh, I... er... I thought that now there's nothing holding me back, I could do some travelling and post lots of lovely pictures of where I'm staying, the attractions, best places to eat and drink, and offer travel tips,' I said, fumbling with the words I hadn't spoken aloud to anyone, wishing I didn't sound so unconvincing – like an heiress, plotting how to fill her empty days by doing something expensive and superficial.

Charlie looked thoughtful. 'You were never that keen on travelling,' he pointed out carefully. 'I thought you found it stressful because you're scared of flying and terrible at packing, and you don't like being away from home.'

'You make me sound like a recluse.' I gave an airy laugh that didn't suit me. 'I've got much better at travelling,' I said. 'I'm fine on short-haul flights – I'm here, aren't I? And, I've got loads of good packing tips.'

'Such as?' He looked genuinely interested.

'Well...' I thought back to an article I'd read online. 'Tumble dryer sheets in your luggage to keep things smelling fresh, packing your straighteners in an oven mitt to protect them, and feeding your jewellery through a straw to keep it tangle-free.'

He gave me a level look. 'You've done all of that?'

'Of course not,' I said. 'I don't have any jewellery, or straws. Or tumble dryer sheets.'

He grabbed one of the pillows and pressed it over his face to stifle his mirth.

'Oh, shut up.' Laughing, I grabbed the pillow and whacked him with it. 'Those tips might be really helpful to someone else.'

'Straighteners in an oven mitt!' His eyes were watering. 'I'll have to remember that the next time I go on my hols.'

'Chuck!'

'Sorry, I'm sorry.' He made a play of straightening his face and looking serious. 'I'm sure it'll be a brilliant blog, but how are you going to make any money?'

'Once I'm up and running, travel companies will place ads on my site, and each time a reader clicks on it, I'll get paid.'

'You'll need a lot of readers, won't you?'

'Well, yes, but as long as I post regularly and target the right audience, it'll happen.' I spoke with more confidence than I felt, hoping that if I kept saying it, I'd start to believe it. 'I just have to work hard and be patient,' I added. 'I did a course, run by a travel blogger.'

I tried to recapture the burst of enthusiasm I'd felt after seeing Lily Ashworth on breakfast television talking about her blog, which detailed her experiences in sun-drenched places, and when I'd looked online and saw she was running a two-day course in London, I'd immediately signed up, telling Mum and Dad I was going to stay with Anna for a few days. Anna had been surprisingly encouraging – although, with hindsight, her exhortations to get away from the bloody rat race and start living the dream, *and once you've settled with a surfer hunk in Antigua, invite me to come and live with you* might have said more about her state of mind than mine.

'It's about time I got out of my comfort zone,' I said to Charlie, and saw a flicker of concern pass over his features. 'Don't worry, Gran's money will tide me over,' I added, aware how lucky I was to have options, even though I'd have traded every penny to have her back.

'You should go to Norway to see the Northern Lights, like you planned.'

'That was meant to be my honeymoon.'

'I know, but there's no reason you can't still do it,' he said.

I felt a familiar prickle of tears behind my eyes. 'Maybe,' I said, forcing lightness into my tone. 'I could go anywhere.'

'Remember, wherever you go, you take yourself with you.'

'When did you become wise?'

'It's always been in me, I've kept it hidden,' he joked. I had the sense he was on the verge of offering further advice, but instead, he twirled his hands like a magician and said, 'Anyway, you've made a good start with Chamillon. It's photogenic all year round, and there are plenty of attractions besides the café.'

'I know, I've been before, remember.' As I flashed him a smile, my gaze fell on a photo on Dolly's bedside table, of Charlie with his arm wrapped around a pretty, windswept blonde, their heads pressed close together.

'Is that Elle?' I reached for the picture and studied it under the light. 'She looks a bit like Marilyn Monroe.'

'Gorgeous, isn't she?' Charlie sat up and looked at the picture with such awestruck longing I felt another shot of envy. 'It was our first photo together,' he added.

'It looks like that ostrich is trying to eat your hair.'

'It was.' He chuckled. 'We were at a wildlife park, trying to find a rare species of goat for Elle's sister.'

'That sounds completely normal.' Tracing a finger over a plump cherub engraved on the edge of the frame, I added, 'How did you know? That Elle was the one, I mean.'

His forehead scrunched. 'I just liked her from the start,' he said simply. 'There was a connection. I don't know…' He rubbed his eyebrow. 'It's hard to explain, but I'd never experienced anything like it before.'

'Not even with Emma?'

He shook his head. 'Not even with Emma.'

'And Elle... she felt the same?'

'Obviously.' He rubbed his hands up and down his torso and made his eyes go smoochy. 'Who wouldn't want some of this?'

'That's disgusting!' I swiped him with the photo and he took it off me.

'I'm sure you don't want to look at this before you fall asleep, like Mum does.'

'I don't mind.' I took it back and propped it against the lamp, liking how happy they looked – even if it highlighted the fact that I wasn't, and probably never would be. 'I'm surprised Dolly didn't take it with her when she moved in with her new hubby.'

'Oh, she's got copies.' His grin grew wider. 'She took loads of us at the wedding, has hundreds more on her phone, and some we didn't even know she was taking.'

I laughed. 'I really am pleased for you.'

He studied me for a moment, his gaze frank. 'And I'm sorry that things didn't work out with Scott.'

'Don't be.' I flicked his elbow. 'Once Christmas is done with, I'll be ready to embrace my brand-new future.' I spoke in a film-announcer voice to lighten the mood and jumped when I heard a noise outside the room. 'What was that?' We listened for a moment, heads cocked. 'Is it your friend?'

The noise came again and Charlie sprang off the bed. 'Don't worry,' he said, after poking his head out of the door. 'It's only the heating coming back on. Ryan's got into a TV drama that's on around this time, so he'll be watching that.'

I pressed a hand to my chest, where my heart was racing through my heavy-knit sweater. 'He sounds like a bored middle-aged woman,' I said. 'Or a pensioner.'

'He's trying to improve his French.'

'How long is he planning on staying?'

'I thought you weren't interested.' Charlie spun round with a teasing grin, and I realised he was winding me up. 'Hey, do you remember Scream City?'

I gave a groaning smile, recalling the summer we'd spent trying to terrify each other, hiding then pouncing to see who could produce the most blood-pounding scream. My favourite method had been to stand behind the fridge door, so when Charlie closed it, I'd be standing there, staring, while he had favoured creeping up behind me when I thought he was elsewhere and tapping me on the shoulder. My cinema-scream had easily topped his chest-clutching, high-pitched squeal – especially as I'd invariably drop whatever I was holding.

'How could I forget?' I said. 'Remember when the postman heard me from the bottom of the lane and ran into the house, thinking someone was being murdered?'

'And your dad thought he was attacking me and punched him?'

'And the dog bit him on the bum and he tried to sue us.'

It felt good to laugh at happy memories – as if I was using muscles that hadn't been worked for ages.

'Listen, I'd better go down and help Mum,' Charlie said at last, wiping his shirtsleeve across his eyes. 'Make yourself at home and I'll see you after we've closed the café.'

'I thought you opened in the evenings.'

'Not in winter,' he said. 'No one wants to come out after dark, and there aren't many visitors around at this time of year.'

'I can't believe it's snowing.'

'First time in years.' He looked pleased, as if he'd ordered it especially. 'An Arctic front heading to Britain, that took a detour here.'

'It was raining when I left Gatwick.'

He turned in the doorway. 'Ryan's sleeping in my room, by the way, which has an en suite, so the bathroom's all yours. Well, it's mine too,' he said with a smile. 'I'm sleeping on the sofa.'

'Very generous of you to give up your bed.'

'The sofa's really comfy. And I know he'd do the same for me.'

Once Charlie had gone, I transferred the few items of clothing I'd brought from my holdall to the wardrobe, which still held several of Dolly's outfits – mostly going-out clothes, judging by a gold-velour jumpsuit and a couple of swishy skirts; one a violent pink, the other threaded with silver. According to Mum, Dolly and Frank enjoyed salsa dancing – a far cry from her days married to Charlie's dad (a serial cheater, who eventually left her for a younger woman), when she'd worked hard as a marketing manager for a big tech company, only letting her hair down (literally) on visits to the farm with Charlie, when she and Mum invariably wound up jiving after getting stuck into Dad's homemade craft beer.

There was a giant bar of Cadbury's Wholenut chocolate at the bottom of my bag – Charlie's and my favourite treat whenever he'd stayed at the farm – which I'd brought in case of emergency midnight hunger, and I stashed it in the drawer of the bedside cabinet.

After removing my jeans and jumper, I pulled on my favourite onesie, designed to look like a koala, with a white fluffy chest and an embroidered face and furry ears attached to a hood. About to slip into the kitchen and make a cup of tea, I hesitated. What if *he* was there? Ryan. It was one thing for Dolly and Charlie to see me in my nightwear, but a total stranger?

I appraised myself in the Hollywood-style mirror above the dressing table. The softly glowing bulbs cast a flattering light that evened out my winter pallor and created the illusion of cheekbones. My eyes looked smoky and mysterious and even my hair appeared thicker and shinier than usual – though still several inches shorter than I'd have liked. *Not bad for a koala.* I drew up the hood and waggled the ears, then brought up my hands and smoothed imaginary whiskers. Did koalas have whiskers? If I bumped into Ryan, he'd have to take me as he found me. If I'd wanted to skulk around, fully dressed and on edge, I could have stayed at home.

Edging out onto the landing, which was lit by shell-shaped sconces on the walls, I peered around. From what I remembered, Charlie's room was the next one along, and next to that was the bathroom. The kitchen was only accessible through the living room, which was a shame if *he* was in there watching TV. Drawing in a breath, I crept across the carpeted floor and listened for signs of movement behind the living room door, but it was impossible to hear anything above the sound of Kylie Minogue singing 'Santa Baby' downstairs, accompanied by some barking – either it was a brand-new version of the song, or Hamish was singing along.

Annoyed that I was dithering, I shoved open the door and strode inside and let out a sigh of relief. The room was empty. Empty of people, that is. Blinking, I looked around, taking in the sheer excess of... *stuff*. Dolly certainly hadn't confined her Christmas decorations to the café, or maintained a functional and clutter-free space in here. Although the floor-length curtains had been pulled across the window, and the overhead light was off, the room was brightly lit, thanks to about a gazillion golden lights adorning a six-foot tree in the corner with a heap of gifts underneath, wrapped in shiny, ribbon-tied paper.

Metallic foil stars dangling from the ceiling, reindeer cushions on the sofa, tinsel decorating the bookshelves and a lantern-studded garland stretching the length of the mantelpiece made me feel like I'd stepped into Santa's Grotto. There was even a bowl of plump satsumas perched on top of a pile of newspapers, and in case there was any doubt about the time of year, a series of wooden letters spelled out Merry Christmas on the wall above the fireplace. The room so desperately needed pulling together and given some *coherence* – some reorganisation – that it made my fingers itch. Still, I couldn't help a small smile when I recognised the battered nativity scene in the hearth that I'd made at school with toilet-roll holders, cotton wool and a shoebox, and presented to Dolly after she admired it.

Not wishing to linger, as nostalgia threatened to overwhelm me, I shot through to the tiny kitchen. At least Ryan was out. Hopefully, he'd taken himself for a walk – all the way to the airport.

I switched on the ceiling strip light and filled the kettle, comforted by the familiar routine. In spite of the ramped-up Christmas theme, I felt better for being away from home, as if anything might be possible. Maybe, in Chamillon, I'd finally evolve into the person I was supposed to be – Nina Bailey: independent woman and travel-blogger extraordinaire.

There was a box of my favourite teabags on the worktop, next to a mug with a Santa-hatted robin on the side (subtle, my aunt was not), and while I waited for the kettle to boil, I did a koala-dance, shuffling my feet along the floor tiles and jabbing my elbows in and out.

I'd read somewhere that koalas make an unsettling grunting sound that didn't fit with their cute appearance and tried to conjure something more appealing: a chirruping sound, clicking the roof of my mouth with my tongue and adding a whistle and some kittenish mewing as I opened the fridge for some milk. I found an opened carton and pulled it out, and when I closed the door, a man was standing there, staring at me, and I let out a blood-curdling scream and dropped the milk.

Chapter Three

'What the *hell*?' I stared at the man, who'd grabbed a hand towel and tossed it down to staunch the flow of milk. 'You could have killed me!' I pressed my fist to my chest, surprised my heart was inside and not bouncing across the floor. 'What were you *doing*, creeping in like that?'

'I'm sorry,' he said, calmly picking up the empty carton, seemingly unshaken by the bone-chilling strength of my scream. Hopefully, no one in the café had heard it over the blast of Snoop Dogg's 'Christmas in tha Dogg House.' 'There was a weird noise, so I came to investigate.'

'Noise?' My eyes ranged over him as he straightened and met my gaze. He was a few inches taller than me – maybe five ten or eleven – with a lot of dark curly hair, an unkempt beard and intense, forest-green eyes, and was wearing a loosely belted, navy dressing gown. 'What sort of noise?'

'I thought it was a cat.'

'A… a *cat*?' Blood surged to my cheeks. Had he heard my made-up koala impression? 'Why would a cat be in here?'

'One of the customers brings hers into the café. Delphine, she's called. The cat, not the owner.' His eyes held a glint of amusement. 'She escaped a few days ago and found her way up here. I almost sat on her. The cat, not Madame Bisset.' His voice was low and even, his accent similar to Charlie's. 'That's the owner's name.'

Snapping back to my senses, I swept my arm around, wishing there wasn't a paw-like mitten attached to the cuff of my onesie. 'Well, as you can see, there aren't any cats in here.'

'No,' he agreed, shoving the soggy towel around with his bare foot. Thanks to his swift reaction and the carton being half-empty, the spill had been contained. 'I realised it was you, making the weird noise, but didn't get a chance to speak before you saw me and unleashed that… noise.' Before I could dredge up an explanation, his gaze flicked up to my hood. 'I like the look,' he said, toying with the end of his beard, while I replayed my mortifying shuffle in lurid detail. Had he seen that too? 'It's very… Australian.'

I was surprised into releasing a laugh. '*Australian?*'

'Aren't koalas Australian?'

'Yes, but it's hardly a description.'

'Cuddly?'

I tutted, glad to feel my heartrate dropping back to normal. 'Never use the word cuddly to describe a female.'

'Even a female koala?'

'Anyway, you need talk.' I flicked my fingers at his dressing gown, which was admittedly quite stylish – thick and fleecy, with silky piping along the edges. I had a similar one at home in green. 'What have you come as?'

'I was about to take a shower,' he said, eyes still staring at my furry ears as though transfixed. I noted his skin was pale, like mine, and was reminded of a TV series, where the hero transformed into a werewolf when he was hungry. 'What's your excuse?'

'Stop focusing on my appearance,' I said, hypocritically. 'It's not normal.'

'My focus, or your appearance?'

'I mean, I don't normally dress like this.'

'Probably just as well.' His eyebrows lifted. 'How do you handle going to the loo?'

'The whole thing has to come off.' I glanced down, and only just stopped myself miming the action. *What was I thinking?* Not only was I having a conversation with a hairy male, I was practically discussing how I went to the toilet. 'I suppose you're Charlie's friend,' I said, to divert him.

'You suppose correctly.' He gave an exaggerated bow, which revealed a tunnel of chest hair and glimpse of abs. 'Ryan Sadler,' he said, and I realised he wasn't bowing, he was mopping up the milk. I watched with mild fascination as he crossed to the sink and rinsed out the towel, before tossing it into the washing machine. He obviously knew his way around the kitchen.

'You're the one who called off his wedding on his stag night,' I said, instead of asking whether he'd visited Chamillon before, like a normal person.

He turned, his expression cooling. 'Stag *party*, not night.' He pushed a curl off his forehead. 'Night implies the wedding was taking place the following day when, in fact, it was a month away.'

'Oh, goodie,' I said. 'That's *so* much better.'

He leaned against the sink and folded his arms. 'And you must be Nina, who called off her wedding, then cut up her ex's clothes and burnt his stuff.'

I gasped, even though – technically – that was exactly what had happened. *Bloody Charlie.* Or maybe Dolly had told him. Either way, I was hurt the information had been passed on and distorted. 'I had a very good reason for calling off my wedding—'

'So did I.'

'—and it was only a couple of shirts and some photos,' I bulldozed on, ignoring his interruption. 'And a wallet.'

'Oh, goodie,' he deadpanned. 'That's *so* much better.'

'Oh, be quiet.' Heat stung my cheeks. Truthfully, I regretted letting Anna talk me into taking revenge on Scott. She'd insisted it would be symbolic and make me feel better, but I wasn't really suited to acts of destruction. I'd felt guilty, hacking at his shirts with a pair of kitchen scissors and building a fire in the grate for the sole purpose of setting things alight.

He hadn't even noticed. He'd never worn the shirts, and the photos I destroyed weren't the most flattering – of me, anyway – and the wallet he'd thought 'too girly' had been empty.

'I could have done a lot worse,' I said, as Ryan appeared to be waiting for more. Anna had suggested all sorts of things: spray-painting *twat* on Scott's beloved car, switching his shampoo for hair removal cream, washing his clothes in glitter and kicking him in his 'junk' to name a few. (She'd become bitter after her boyfriend got his ex-girlfriend pregnant and married her.) 'He deserved it.'

'Of course he did.' Ryan's tone was flat, as if it wasn't worth arguing about. Whatever he'd been told, he'd obviously taken in the worst bits – about me – and formed an unflattering opinion. 'Do you want a cup of tea?'

'Sorry?'

'You were making a cup of tea before I came in and scared you.'

Thrown by the change of topic, and strangely unwilling to let it go, I was about to mount a defence when he said in a rush, 'Look, I don't want to talk about the past. I'm trying to focus on the future while I'm here and I'm sure that you are too, so…' His gaze swivelled to the kettle. 'Tea?'

'In case you've forgotten, I dropped the milk.'

'There's another carton.' I stepped aside to let him open the fridge, catching a scent of musky, warm skin combined with a tang of citrus peel that suggested he'd been at the satsumas before I arrived. 'I'd offer you some eucalyptus leaves, but they don't grow very well in this part of the world.'

A reluctant smile tugged at my lips. 'Luckily, I'm a new breed of koala that only drinks tea, and occasionally wines and spirits.'

A grin softened his face – the top half, at least. I couldn't see much beneath his beard but a glimpse of straight, white teeth. He stuck out a hand. 'I'm Ryan, good to meet you, Nina. Shall we start again?'

We shook hands. 'Sounds good.'

'I'm ashamed to say that until quite recently, I thought koalas were bears,' he said, crossing to the kettle and switching it back on. Beneath the hem of his dressing gown, his calves were muscly and coated with dark hair – much like my own.

'Most people do.' I watched him take a clean mug from one of the cupboards and toss a teabag in. 'It's because they're cute, I suppose.' I winced. It sounded as if I was implying that *I* was cute, which blatantly wasn't true.

He turned, the belt of his dressing gown loosening further, presenting a shadowy view of his chest. 'My nephew put me straight after my sister and family moved to Australia last year. Apparently, koalas are more aggressive than a crocodile and have the smallest brain-to-body-size ratio of any mammal.'

My smile slipped. 'Is that a dig at me?'

'What?' He paused in the act of reaching for the milk.

'Forget it.' I yanked my koala hood down so fast, my hair flattened to my scalp with static. 'I don't want any tea,' I lied, backing towards the door, annoyed with myself for almost letting my guard drop. 'See you around.'

'What just happened?' He sounded bemused. 'You don't think I meant…? Hang on…'

But I didn't look back as I hurried through the grotto-like living room, swearing as I tripped over a lead trailing across the floor from a laptop on the two-seater dining table by the window. As I slammed into the table, the laptop screen leapt to life, revealing a document with the words **Chapter One** typed in a fancy script, and underneath, a series of words written in gigantic font.

If Grace Benedict doesn't find a case to solve REALLY SOON I'm F***ED!!!!!!!!!!!! ARGHHHHHHHH!!!! SHOULD HAVE KILLED HER OFF. I don't even like her any more. Why the hell did I give her a bloody parrot?????

An impressive array of angry and sad emojis followed – as well as one of a mischievous-looking parrot. A parrot called… called Buddy, who'd helped Grace solve a case. *Grace Benedict*. A beautiful detective with a troubled past, who played the cello, wore sharp suits and fastened her hair up with pencils.

'What do you think you're doing?'

I whipped round to see Ryan approaching at speed, his dressing gown flapping open. My gaze became trapped in his jersey shorts, which were black and extremely snug, as he dived for his laptop and slammed it shut, knocking over an acrylic, light-up polar bear in the process.

'That's private,' he snapped. He was breathing heavily.

Dragging my eyes from his nether regions, I shot him a furious frown. 'I tripped over your stupid charger.' I pointed to the trailing lead. 'I didn't know your computer was going to come on.'

He tracked the cable, which had become detached from his laptop. 'I'm sorry about that,' he said sheepishly. 'There's no socket near the table.'

'I'm fine, thank you for asking.'

He looked concerned. 'Are you?'

'Yes,' I said grudgingly.

'Oh.' That seemed to throw him. 'Well... good.'

The music downstairs had stopped and in the silence that ensued, I realised I was breathing heavily too – probably from the shock of nearly falling over. I straightened my shoulders in an effort to regain control and said, 'You're R.A. Sadler,' more accusingly than I'd intended. 'You wrote *The Midnight Hour.*'

Ryan winced, as though I'd reminded him of something traumatic he'd rather forget. 'I thought you knew that already.'

'It came to me just now, when I read what you'd written—'

'I *knew* you had.'

I threw him a look.

'—that my mum mentioned a while ago that Dolly told her an old friend of Charlie's had written a book and got it published.' *Too many words.* 'I didn't make the connection before,' I added.

'I wasn't suggesting you *ought* to have known, only that...' Ryan's words trailed off, as though finishing the sentence was too much effort. 'You haven't read the book then?'

'Actually, I have.' I rewound to my first night home after leaving Scott. I'd been nursing swollen eyes, a thumping headache and a sense of failure in my childhood bedroom, and Mum had brought me a novel with a cup of hot chocolate, to 'take my mind off things'. It had always worked in the past; everything from Enid Blyton and Roald Dahl, to Meg Rosoff and Dad's *Hitchhiker's Guide to the Galaxy*, but it was only Mum's enthusiasm about this book by 'Charlie's friend' that had stopped me tossing it out of the window. Surprisingly, I'd found myself engrossed to the point where I'd stayed up all night reading. 'It was… good,' I said.

Ryan hiked up an eyebrow. 'You should write that up for *The Times*.'

I gave him a chilly smile. 'OK, it was *very* good.'

Above his beard, his cheeks flushed. I wouldn't have had him down as the type to seek cheap reassurances, but then again, I'd only just met him. 'I know it's *good*,' he said, with a flash of frustration. 'I've got the awards to prove it.'

I wasn't exactly surprised, recalling the way that the gripping storyline and clever writing had transported me from my misery for several hours. 'No one likes a show-off,' I said, instead of congratulating him.

He gave a mirthless laugh. 'Believe me, I'm not showing off.' He still had a hand on the laptop lid, as if to stop it springing open and spilling words on the floor. 'If anything, I'm starting to wish it had sunk without a trace.'

'What?' I was taken aback by his vehemence. '*Why?* It was brilliant, the way you described Grace.' I perched on the arm of the sofa to make my point. 'You really know how to write women. I honestly thought R.A. Sadler was a woman,' I said. 'And Buddy the parrot was hilarious, the way he swore all the time and kept impersonating the neighbour, and then it turned out the neighbour was the murderer all along and Buddy had been trying to help Grace…' I stopped. I was on the verge of gushing. 'You're telling me you'd rather you *hadn't* written a bestselling murder mystery?'

He thrust a hand through his hair, seeming unaware that his dressing gown was open, showing his underwear. *At least he was wearing pants.* 'I know I must sound like an ungrateful idiot, but what with everything that's happened this year, I'm struggling to get going with the next book and I've already missed one deadline.'

'I gathered it wasn't going well.' I glanced at the laptop. 'You wish you'd killed Grace off.'

He nodded and pushed out a sigh. 'I never meant her to feature in the next book, but my agent—'

'Hell*oooo*!' Before he could finish, Dolly burst round the door, eyebrows disappearing into her fringe. 'How are you two getting along?'

I sprang to my feet and Ryan pivoted to face her, stiff as a soldier on parade.

'Hi,' we said simultaneously, as she bustled over and straightened the acrylic, light-up polar bear and gave him a pat on the head.

'Look at the pair of you.' Her eyes were as twinkly as the lights on the tree as they darted between Ryan and me. He fastened his dressing gown belt and I yanked the zip on my onesie up to my neck. 'You both look like you're ready for bed!'

Chapter Four

I woke the next morning to the muffled sounds of the café below and buried myself deeper beneath the duvet, keen to cling onto sleep. When I'd first moved back home, Mum had taken to charging in first thing with a mug of coffee and a list of jobs to get me 'out of my pit'. She was a firm believer in the power of *doing* rather than *thinking* and, to be fair, she'd had a point. It had been hard to wallow when there was straw to bale, and sheep were lambing and the pigs needed mucking out. Not to mention helping in the farm shop, which had proved a runaway success with people flocking for miles to buy freshly-laid eggs, and home-grown produce and catch up on local gossip.

'You've got a job here, if you want it,' Mum had said hopefully, during that first week, harbouring visions of us running the shop together, like Charlie and Dolly at the café, but we'd both known it wouldn't work. Apart from anything, Mum – like Dolly – was terrible at delegating, and it turned out I had a knack for putting customers off, even when they'd come prepared to spend.

'What on earth did you say to Mrs Danvers?' Mum asked, when her wealthiest and most regular client had fled the shop empty-handed, her lips drawn in an unforgiving line.

'She asked what was in the jar of pickled rhubarb and I told her it was rhubarb that had been pickled.'

'For goodness sake, Nina.' Mum had called Mrs Danvers to apologise, and to offer her two free jars as compensation. 'She thought you were taking the mickey,' she said, when she'd finished stroking Mrs Danvers' ego, but I wasn't. I just hadn't known that pickling rhubarb involved cider vinegar, water, sea salt, sugar, pink peppercorns and cloves. Who did, apart from Mum?

'You could have asked,' she said.

I'd apologised, and Mum had sighed.

Then I'd tried rearranging the shop so the displays were less haphazard, but Mum put everything back, preferring the element of chaos, and that's when I'd embarked on a series of courses in my quest for a career.

Flipping over in bed, I pulled the duvet higher, but sleep was slipping away as the day seeped in, and I wondered what Ryan was doing.

After Dolly's loaded comment, we'd caught each other's eye, and there'd been a moment when we might have laughed or made a joke, if we'd known and liked each other. Then Ryan had murmured something about taking a shower and left the room with his laptop under his arm and Dolly had given me an innocent smile and said, 'He's lovely, isn't he?'

I'd immediately suspected that she was planning to set us up. Now that Charlie had apparently met *The One*, she needed an outlet for her matchmaking tendencies. 'She won't be able to help herself,' Mum had warned, but with a hopeful air that suggested she wouldn't mind Dolly finding me a nice Frenchman to settle down with. I hadn't taken much notice. The idea of meeting someone new – never mind *liking* them – had seemed ludicrous.

'It's a bit too soon to say,' I'd said cagily. 'He's Charlie's friend, so I suppose he must be OK.'

She'd studied me for an uncomfortably long moment, as though trying to work something out, then instructed me to help myself to food and get a good night's sleep. 'I was going to invite you for dinner and to meet Frank, but we'll leave it for another day,' she'd said, before blowing a kiss at a photo on the wall of her with the film star Jay Merino, who'd made a film, featuring his serial character Max Weaver, on the island earlier in the year and was now in a relationship with Charlie's close friend Natalie. (The Mum/Dolly grapevine had gone bananas the week *that* happened.) 'Have a good night's sleep and I'll see you in the morning.'

Assuming she was talking to me, not Jay Merino, I'd watched her retreat with my face moulded into a smile, then retired to my room, where I'd flopped on the bed and tried for a while to think of a name for my travel blog. After popping back out for a bowl of soup and a chat with Charlie, while Ryan took a walk to 'think about his book', I'd taken a shower, before settling down and instantly falling asleep.

Now, I debated whether to get up or have a lie-in, but before I could decide, the door creaked open and a hand grabbed my foot through the duvet.

'ARGH!' I jerked free and rolled over to see Dolly, standing at the end of the bed with a steaming mug, a fragrant scent of coffee filling the room.

'Wakey, wakey, rise and shine!' She placed the mug on the bedside table and lovingly tweaked the photo of Charlie and Elle, before crossing to the window and pulling the curtains back.

'Morning.' I squinted against the brightness flooding in. 'What time is it?'

'Time to get up,' she announced cheerily.

I cowered as she approached, clutching the duvet to my chest as if she might be about to rip it off, and she sat on the side of the bed and patted my knee. 'I thought you might need a wake-up call.'

'Thanks.' I sat up, ruffling my hair into place with my fingers. It became unruly after being in contact with pillows – even ones with silky covers like Dolly's. 'Is it still snowing?'

'It's stopped for now, but there's more on the way.' She picked up my hand and pressed it between both of hers. 'Now, I know you've come here partly to get away from everything,' she said. 'I want to say properly how sorry I am about your gran, I know how hard it is.'

I nodded. Mum and Dolly had been extremely close to their grandmother, Augustine – Mum had even given me her name as one of my middle names. She'd stepped into the breach when a car crash killed their parents, and they'd always been fiercely protective of her.

'Gran was only hanging on to see me married, and I let her down,' I said.

'Now stop that.' Dolly bounced my hand. 'She wouldn't have wanted you to be unhappy.'

'It's just the look on her face, when I told her the wedding wasn't happening…'

Dolly tutted. 'Oh, love. Now listen to me. Augustine used to get a look on her face,' she said. 'It was every New Year's Eve, and I know she was thinking about that man… the one she wished she'd married. Grandmothers know better than anyone – you only marry the right one. They have a sixth sense for this sort of thing, I promise you.'

'Dolly, you don't know that's what she was thinking.' I'd heard the story before – a supposed lover that Augustine had been secretly pining for, based on a throwaway comment she'd made after one too many gins one Christmas. It had set Mum and Dolly wondering whether she'd ever really loved their grandpa. Something about a ship, and the power of first love. Augustine had refused to acknowledge it the next day, and never spoke of it again, but Dolly occasionally poked at the subject, like a fire just before it goes out.

'Well, if I misinterpreted that look, then so did *you* with your gran,' she said, and I knew I'd lost the argument – if that's what it was – before it had even begun.

Dolly dusted herself down, as if getting rid of non-existent flour. I smiled at her, thinking of the café downstairs, filled with home-baked treats. 'Now,' she said, giving me a beady look, 'I don't think it's healthy for you to stay cooped up in here all day.'

'Oh no, I wasn't planning to,' I said. 'I'm going to use the time here to get my… um… things off the ground.'

She cocked her head, her fringe falling to one side. 'Things?'

'I, er…' I'd planned to be vague about my plans until my blog was established, when I could point people towards it and impress them, but realised that being vague made me sound both wishy-washy and too mysterious. Plus, I'd already confided in Charlie, which made it real. 'It's a travel thing,' I mumbled.

'Hmm?' She let go of my hand and cupped her ear. 'Sorry, love, I didn't hear you.'

'Travel blog,' I said loudly, trying not to squirm. Why did it sound so *silly* spoken aloud, when in my head it seemed such a brilliant idea?

'Travel blog?' Dolly sounded startled, as though I'd sworn, but quickly recovered. 'Does your mum know?'

'If she did, you would too,' I said wryly.

Dolly gave an affectionate eye roll. 'That sister of mine was never any good at keeping secrets,' she said, and I didn't like to point out that Mum would have said the exact same thing about Dolly – usually followed by the words, *but that's a good thing, because keeping secrets is bad for your well-being.* 'Which is probably a good thing, because keeping secrets is bad for you,' Dolly added.

I tried to hide a smile. 'It's not a secret... well, I suppose it is, but I don't want to get Mum and Dad's hopes up, in case it doesn't work out.'

'Oh, I'm sure it will,' said Dolly, suddenly beaming. 'You can do anything, if you put your mind to it, and Chamillon's a great place to start.' She patted my arm. 'Now, get up whenever you're ready and come down to the café for breakfast.'

She rose and left the room, leaving the door ajar, and I leapt out of bed to close it. I didn't want Ryan looking in – my morning hair wasn't fit for viewing.

I leaned against the door, considering my options. I didn't fancy climbing back under the duvet, and all the talk about my plans had left me not so much fired up as unsettled. I straightened the bedding and plumped up the pillows, then padded barefoot to the window with my coffee. Peering at the view, I couldn't help a sharp intake of breath. From my last visit, I remembered lush vineyards and poppies in cornfields, sand dunes and salt marshes, long white beaches, and yachts sparkling in the harbour. I'd thought Chamillon was pretty, but a place best enjoyed in summer, yet under a covering of snow it had taken on an almost magical quality.

'It's beautiful,' I breathed, then looked round, embarrassed in case someone had overheard. Blowing steam from my mug, I returned my gaze to the street below. There were plenty of people about, as though drawn from their beds by the unusual weather, their faces ruddy with cold, smiling as they called out greetings, and I cleared a patch on the window where my breath had misted the glass so I could see better. I put down my mug and picked up my phone to snap a photo, but as I clicked, a seagull hurled itself onto the ledge outside, filling the frame with its open beak and a beady eye.

I waited for it to move so I could take another – more appealing – shot and sent the picture to Ben, adding *This is Steven. He likes fish, doughnuts and martial arts. (Steven Seagull – Seagal, get it?) X* It was an old gag, from a time when my brother never got jokes, even when they were explained to him in detail. He was probably helping Dad with the cows right now, I reflected, or maybe they'd finished and were tucking into an enormous breakfast.

The thought of food made my stomach growl. Deciding to leave the picture-taking until after I'd eaten, I dressed in clean jeans and one of my chunky sweaters – the sort Scott would have said didn't 'do me justice' (he'd preferred outfits that clung, which had required a reduction in carbohydrates that I'd never been comfortable with), pulled on my socks and boots and headed to the bathroom. Coming out, I paused on the landing, hearing voices from the living room. The door was ajar and I clearly heard Charlie say, 'I'm really sorry, mate, I don't know what to suggest.'

I sidled closer, even as the words *curiosity killed the cat* and a saying about eavesdroppers never hearing any good of themselves popped into my head.

'… just wish she'd stop calling,' Ryan was saying as I hovered outside the door and held my breath. 'I could hear Lulu asking for her daddy in the background, and Jackson has started wetting the bed.'

'It's not fair of Nicole to put that on you,' Charlie said grimly. 'You need to put your foot down and tell her to leave you alone.'

I inched closer, curiosity brimming over.

'I just can't help wishing that I hadn't got involved in the first place.' Ryan sounded wretched. 'I wasn't even sure I was ready to be a husband, let alone a father.'

'Well, you know my feelings about that.' Disapproval had leaked into Charlie's voice. He generally saw the good in everyone – unless he'd drastically changed – but I wondered whether his own dad walking out had coloured his feelings about Ryan leaving his children.

It certainly coloured mine. The time to decide you didn't want daddy duties was *before* having children, not after.

'You promise you won't discuss any of this with your cousin,' he went on and I stiffened. 'I feel bad enough as it is, and I don't fancy having to defend myself to her.'

I bristled. I wasn't intending to discuss *anything* personal with him, and no defence would make a difference anyway – I simply wasn't interested in hearing his reasons or excuses.

'Mum's the word.' I imagined Charlie pretend-zipping his mouth, but then he added, 'Sorry, that was a stupid thing to say under the circumstances.'

At the sound of Ryan's chuckle, my hackles rose. 'Nina seems nice on the surface,' he said, 'but she's really jumpy and, like I said last night, I caught her looking at my laptop.' As Charlie started to speak, he continued, 'It's just, after Nicole, I've had enough of high-maintenance women.'

I stifled an outraged gasp. I was anything *but* high-maintenance. I'd barely asked anything of Scott, other than he be faithful to me – although maybe that's where I'd gone wrong. I'd been *too* forgiving.

'Nina's not like that,' Charlie said. 'She's actually really cool.' *Thank you!*

'You haven't seen her for a while,' said Ryan. 'She seemed to be a bit unstable—'

I rapped loudly on the door and entered the room to meet Charlie's startled gaze. 'Good morning.' I fixed him with my sweetest smile. 'Can I please say something?'

'Er... of course you can, Nina.'

My gaze shot to Ryan, standing by the Christmas tree in his dressing gown. 'If we're going to be sharing this apartment, I suggest you find somewhere else to gossip, where I can't hear you,' I said. 'Or, better still, don't gossip about me at all.'

Charlie immediately apologised, but as Ryan began to speak, I rounded on him.

'Obviously, we've both been through a lot, but how dare you call me unstable and high-maintenance to my cousin when you don't even know me?' I blasted. 'You of all people should know better than to judge a book by its cover.' Ryan stared at the floor, head shaking slightly – whether in denial of my words, or because he felt bad, was hard to tell. 'Charlie and Dolly are my family.'

'They're like family to me too,' he mumbled.

'Yes, but my *actual* family,' I said hotly. 'If you're going to hang around here causing trouble, maybe I'd be better off staying with Dolly.'

'Nina, you don't have to do that,' Charlie said, putting his hands up. 'Honestly, it won't happen again.'

I turned to him. 'Why did you tell him about me cutting up Scott's shirts and burning his wallet?'

'What?' He rose off the sofa – a vivid orange in daylight – and took a step towards me. 'I *didn't* tell him.' His eyes were clear and his words had the ring of truth.

'Oh,' I said, deflated. 'It must have been your mum, then.'

'I doubt it.' His eyebrows pulled together. 'Mum wouldn't discuss something like that with anyone outside the family.' His eyes flicked past me. 'No offence, Ryan.'

My gaze moved back to Ryan, who was rubbing a hand over his beard and looking shifty. 'Actually, neither of them told me.' He flashed Charlie an apologetic look. 'I overheard you and Dolly talking about it yesterday morning,' he confessed. 'It was just before I came into the kitchen for a couple of croissants.'

'Right.' Now Charlie looked uncomfortable. 'Sorry, Nina, it was just that your mum had told Dolly about it and we were saying how unlike you it was to react like that—'

'For God's sake!' I threw up my hands. 'It was hardly anything, just a few photos in the fire that weren't even very good. I had my eyes shut in most of them.'

'I thought it was pretty funny, to be honest.' A smile nudged Charlie's mouth. 'You could have done a lot worse.'

'See!' I swivelled back to Ryan. '*You* shouldn't have been eavesdropping,' I said, ignoring my rampant hypocrisy. 'And you definitely shouldn't have used what you heard against me.'

'I wasn't eavesdropping, I just happened to overhear a conversation.' He shoved his hands in his dressing gown pockets, as if resisting the urge to strangle me. 'There's a difference.'

'Oh well, excuse *me*.' I'd definitely been eavesdropping.

'But, you're right,' he said, unexpectedly. 'I shouldn't have said anything, and I shouldn't have judged you by your cover. I'm sorry.'

'Well... OK.' Flustered, I turned to Charlie, who'd picked up a Christmas card and appeared fascinated by the snowy woodland scene on the front.

'From our old neighbour, Dorothy,' he said into the strained silence that followed Ryan's apology. 'She sends one every year, with all the local gossip.'

'I remember her.' Ryan's tone lightened, presumably thinking he was forgiven and keen to move on. 'I was at your house once when she came round to complain about the neighbour on the other side, sunbathing in the nude.'

'God, that's right.' Charlie's grin was nostalgic, and his expression invited me to join in. 'The next time it was sunny, we climbed out onto the garage roof to try and get a look, thinking she meant Georgia Cavendish, but it turned out to be her husband.'

'And Dorothy was looking at him out of her bedroom window.'

'Through a pair of binoculars.'

I made a half-hearted attempt to join in with the laughter. At least Ryan's laugh was nicer than the sound of his annoyingly calm voice, putting me right on the difference between *overhearing* and *eavesdropping*. Or asking Charlie not to discuss his personal life with me because I was obviously *unstable*.

'Right, I'm off to work,' Charlie said, putting the card back on the mantelpiece. 'Coming down for breakfast?'

Ryan's forest-dark gaze slid to me and away, as if seeing something in my face he wasn't sure of. 'I'll probably grab something later,' he said, rubbing his fingertips through his hair. 'I'm not hungry right now.'

'Count me in, I'm starving.' As I followed Charlie out of the room, I turned, sensing Ryan was watching, but he was eyeing his laptop on the table as if it had teeth and might bite him. 'Good luck with your writing,' I said pleasantly, and slammed the door behind me.

Chapter Five

At the bottom of the stairs, Charlie turned and eyed my outfit. 'At least you're not dressed as a marsupial,' he said with a grin. 'I might treat myself to a giraffe onesie. Elle would love that.'

'Or, she'll realise she's made a mistake and stay in England,' I joked, feeling better already for being out of Ryan's orbit. *High-maintenance.* The insult still stung.

'There you are!' Dolly looked up from rolling out dough, a dusting of flour on her forehead, her beam so wide her eyes were in danger of vanishing. 'Go through and order some food,' she said, wiping her hands on her apron before handing a tray of cinnamon swirls to a woman in an identical apron with neatly parted hair scooped back in a ponytail.

'Can I do anything to help?'

Dolly shook her head as if the suggestion was outrageous. 'Celeste will bring you whatever you want,' she said, adding something in French to the woman that I interpreted as *This is my niece, look after her.* Celeste nodded and flashed me a dimpled smile as she left with the tray of swirls.

'Just make yourself at home,' said Dolly as I sidestepped the young waiter I'd seen the day before, who was transporting a stack of plates to the sink, while another male – surely his brother, judging by their matching hair – efficiently unloaded the dishwasher. 'Find a nice table, or even sit with someone, if you want to. We have lots of people your age come in, so you won't be lonely.'

By *people* she probably meant eligible young men. I wouldn't have been surprised if she'd invited a few in, especially to meet me. 'Thanks, Dolly,' I said, with a smiling shake of my head. 'I don't think I'll be lonely, though.'

Charlie winked at me as he picked up a half-eaten croissant and dropped it in the bin. 'Just don't ask her to cook anything, Mum, or she'll drive our customers away.'

Dolly leaned over and swiped Charlie's arm. 'I'm sure Nina's come a long way since the day of the fire.'

'*Why* do you still call it that?' I gave a groaning laugh. 'All I did was put some toast on the highest setting by mistake and a bit of smoke came out. No one needed to call the fire brigade.'

'I think it's the fact that you *literally* burn toast that's funny,' said Charlie, grinning. 'And the firemen were sympathetic in the end.'

'Thanks for that reminder.'

He inclined his head. 'You're welcome.'

'Shouldn't you be going to the bank?' Dolly gave Charlie a mock-stern glare. 'Make sure you wrap up warm, it's brass monkeys out there.'

'I'm a grown man,' he said good-naturedly, giving me a little salute as he moon-walked out of the kitchen. 'Gotta go, buffalo.'

'See you soon, racoon.'

Dolly laughed indulgently. 'You two,' she said. 'It's like the old days.'

Smiling, I made my way into the bustling café and immediately felt underdressed among the customers, who all appeared to be wearing festive jumpers. Dolly must have ordered a job lot for her 'British Christmas' assault. The waiter was trying to hand one to a striking middle-aged woman with a laptop bag, who seemed utterly mystified – as if he was handing her a bag of dog poo.

'*Qu'est-ce que c'est?*' She held up the garment, which was styled to look like a Santa jacket, with white pom-poms down the front and a black, knitted belt around the middle, and inspected it closely. '*Très bon.*' She handed it back with a polite smile before drifting to a nearby table and shaking off her mustard ankle-length coat.

The waiter approached me, the sweater over his shoulder. 'Hello, I am Stefan, and you are Nina.'

'I am,' I confirmed, returning his cautious smile. 'Hi, Stefan.'

'*C'est le pull Noël.*' He pointed to a chalkboard on the counter where a matchstick couple were wearing Santa sweaters under today's date. *Three days before my non-wedding.* 'I do not have a pullover for today, but my *maman* is making one with wool.' He mimed knitting, holding imaginary needles so close to his face, I wondered whether his mother was short-sighted. 'I will put it on tomorrow, if it is ready.'

'You could wear that one.'

He held out the rejected Santa sweater. 'It is for a lady,' he said. 'You would like it?'

'Thanks, but I'm warm enough just now.' I smiled to show there were no hard feelings. It was impossible not to appreciate his fine manners, even if I was jealous of his luxurious hair and thickly-lashed eyes, which were the colour of dark chocolate. A pair of sleek-haired females at the table closest were vying for his attention, laughing too loudly, then looking to see if he'd noticed. I would have been too, at their age. 'I'll have a black coffee and a pain au chocolat, *s'il vous plaît.*'

He inclined his head and darted to the huge, chrome coffee machine squatting behind the counter, its handles and dials reminiscent of an

aeroplane cockpit. Not that I'd ever been in an aeroplane cockpit. Cups
and bowls were arranged haphazardly on top and I itched to move them
to the shelf that ran along the length of the wall, where they'd be easy
to reach and would look more attractive.

Also, decanting the tea and coffee into labelled jars wouldn't go
amiss – pretty and practical – and the empty jug on the side could double
as a spoon-holder. Cutlery was spilling across the worktop, taking up
valuable space, and I rejected the idea of taking a quick photo for my
blog. The Café Belle Vie may serve the best coffee and pastries on the
island, but the counter area needed a bit of tweaking to make the grade.

''ello, Nina.' The woman – Celeste – had finished serving a man
with a nose so red, I couldn't help thinking of Rudolph, and turned her
attention to me. 'If you go to that table over there, I shall bring your
order.' She spoke slowly, as though experimenting with her English.
'It has a… *belle vue.*'

I looked at the table she was pointing to, which was by the window
overlooking the snowy harbour. '*Merci.*' I weaved my way there, ducking
round the fairy-lit tree, offering a cheery *bonjour* to the smiling faces
tilted to greet me as I passed. No handsome strangers, as far as I could
detect, just some curious but friendly glances, as if the customers had
been primed for my visit by Dolly and were keen to make a connection.
She'd always had a way of drawing people in; of making them care
about her life and the people in it – which had made it all the harder
to understand why Charlie's dad hadn't hung around.

It's not you, it's him, I'd heard Mum consoling her on the phone. *Even
if he'd married Madonna, or… I don't know, Mother Teresa, he wouldn't
have stuck around. It's not in his nature, Doll.*

Sinking onto one of the bistro-style chairs, I took my phone
out of my pocket and checked the photos I'd taken of the café the

day before, my heart sinking when I realised they were wonky – I must have tilted my phone by mistake. I fiddled with the editing buttons and accidentally chopped the first picture in half. Sighing, I decided to leave it until later, and turned to admire the view instead. It looked even more like a Christmas card, with snow-topped boats in the harbour, and rosy-cheeked cyclists passing in brightly-coloured bobble hats and scarves. A pair of children were scooping snow off the railings opposite and shaping them into balls, reminding me of epic snow fights at the farm in winter when Ben and I were children.

I took a couple of pictures through the window and imagined posting them with the caption *Plenty to do in Chamillon, even when it's snowing!* Would anyone care? If they wanted to come to Chamillon, wouldn't they just look online? Or was I self-sabotaging – finding reasons not to pursue the travel blog idea in case it failed?

I didn't want to think about that right now. The café was warm and snug, the hum of chit-chat and laughter soothing, and I propped my chin on my hand, tuning in to a conversation at a neighbouring table. I could just make out that the occupants were discussing the weather, remarking how unusual it was to see snow. It was almost like being in England – except that they sounded delighted. I smiled to myself and felt an expansion inside, as if my organs had shifted slightly and made themselves more comfortable. Outside, one of the children caught my eye and waved, and I waved back and drew a smiley face in the condensation blooming across the window.

My coffee arrived the traditional French way: treacle dark in a bowl, topped with creamy milk, accompanied by a warm pain au chocolat that smelt like being inside a chocolate fountain and I concentrated on my breakfast, savouring every mouthful.

I was dabbing at pastry flakes with my fingertip, when I felt something nudge my leg beneath the table and looked down to see Hamish, wagging his pointy tail. 'Hello, gorgeous.' I stooped to rub my cheek on his wiry head. 'I love your little legs, and your beard's fantastic,' I fussed, tugging at the straggly fur around his muzzle. 'You could give any hipster a run for his money with this.'

Hamish looked quietly pleased by the compliment and I kissed his nose before lifting my head to look for his owner, trying to remember the man's name. *Gérard*, that was it. He was easing himself down at a nearby table, propping up a wooden walking stick that I hadn't noticed yesterday. Not that I'd noticed much, beyond the extravagant Christmas décor.

Seeing me looking, he lifted a hand in acknowledgement, and I threw him a smile and gently prodded Hamish in his direction. 'Go and look after your master,' I said, but the dog settled down at my feet and rested his head on my boots.

Gérard gave an extravagant shrug, as if to say *what can you do?* before turning to greet the staff. I felt ridiculously flattered that Hamish had chosen to stay, his head pleasantly heavy on my feet. There was a cat on the premises too, extravagantly furry and ginger, curled on the lap of an elderly woman wearing vivid lipstick, and I guessed it was the cat that had escaped upstairs, the one Ryan had almost sat on.

I relaxed back in my chair and sipped the last of my coffee, and jumped when Charlie breezed in and sat down opposite me, snowflakes melting in his hair.

'It's snowing again,' he announced.

'Really?' I eyed the top of his head. 'I thought you'd got dandruff.'

'Hilarious.' He rubbed his hair with both hands. 'Listen, I wanted to give you a heads-up,' he said, unzipping his padded coat as he leaned closer. 'Mum might be up to her matchmaking tricks, in case you hadn't noticed.'

I groaned. 'Ryan, I suppose.'

'What?'

'What?'

Charlie sat back, face bright with cold. 'What made you think of Ryan?'

'I don't... I didn't...' I stuttered. 'I just thought... yesterday, she seemed to be... the way she was looking at us, it seemed...'

Charlie started laughing. 'Just winding you up. Of *course* I'm talking about Ryan,' he said. 'She can't help herself, and we both know that nothing will stop her from trying.'

'It won't work.' It came out forcefully. 'This isn't one of those films where we start out hating each other, then end up passionately kissing and falling in love.' My face fired up as the word *love* seemed to hover between us in flashing neon pink letters surrounded by golden stars.

'I'm sorry he was such a jerk earlier,' Charlie said. 'You were right to call him out. It's not an excuse but he's been through—'

Hamish interrupted what he had been about to say by springing onto Charlie's lap.

'Don't worry about it.' I pushed aside my plate, then moved it back again, trying to hold Charlie's gaze. 'I'm sure now we've cleared the air, we'll get on just fine.'

'Look, I'm hardly expecting romance to blossom, even if Mum is.' He sounded vaguely disappointed, and I hoped it was because his friend had been so rude about me.

'Anyway, moving on,' I said. 'Have you got any tips for places I can photograph for my blog?'

'You're in the best place already.' He looked around the bustling café. 'But if you *insist* on going elsewhere,' he said, smiling as he did a dramatic eye roll, 'you should try eating at Chez Phillipe. It's the best restaurant in Chamillon. Plus, I can show you round the island sometime if you like – if Mum can spare me.'

Dolly was behind the counter, craning her neck in our direction. Her fringe had separated – a sign she was working too hard. 'I don't think she can,' I said.

Charlie looked round. 'It's probably time for Stefan's break.' He put Hamish down and rose, picking up my empty coffee bowl and plate. 'What are you going to do?'

'Go out and explore on my own,' I said, infusing the words with a determination I didn't quite feel. 'My blog's not going to start itself.'

He looked at me for a moment, as if weighing up how to respond, then a customer caught his attention. He gave me a quick smile and said, 'I'm so happy you're here, Nina,' and hurried away.

I stood up, preparing to leave, and saw Gérard beckon me over with a jerk of his head.

'*Bonjour*,' I said, drawing up to his table as he reached for his stick and began struggling to his feet. 'Are you OK?'

'Gérard, be careful!' Dolly materialised, as if she'd sensed him struggling, and pressed him gently down. He submitted with a resigned shake of his head. 'He shouldn't be here at all when his leg's playing up,' she said to me. 'It's an old injury that flares up now and then.'

'I'm sorry,' I said, as though it was my fault.

'It's a shame, as he normally walks Hamish along the beach on his way home.'

Hearing his name, Hamish sat up and cocked his head and Gérard spoke in French, waving his hands as he protested that he was perfectly capable of walking his dog.

'Doesn't he have any family?' I said, careful to include Gérard. There was nothing worse than being talked about as if you weren't there.

'His wife died a few years ago, and his son and family live in Scotland,' said Dolly, before he could speak. 'It's just him and the dog at home.'

'I suppose it won't do him any harm to miss a walk for a day. The dog, I mean.'

Dolly looked down at Gérard's leg, sticking out an angle. His flannel trousers had ridden up, revealing a strip of red-and-blue stripy sock. 'I suppose so,' she said doubtfully.

'I guess I could take him for a walk. Hamish, I mean.' The words were out before I could stop them and three pairs of eyes swivelled hopefully towards me.

'Did you hear that?' Dolly said to Gérard. 'My niece has offered to walk Hamish.'

'*C'est très gentil.*' He pulled a handkerchief out of his jacket pocket and passed it over his eyes. 'Very kind.' He reached out a veiny hand and wrapped it around mine. 'I cannot thank you enough.'

'It's no trouble,' I said, surprised by his strong reaction. Maybe he wasn't used to people doing him favours. 'I'll just go and get my coat.'

'Hurry,' said Dolly, and three minutes later, I found myself outside the café, an icy wind blasting my cheeks and a little black dog straining at the end of a lead.

Chapter Six

Hamish was keen to get going, practically dragging me along. The cold was a shock after the warmth of the café, and although it was no longer snowing, I was glad of my furry coat.

'Hang on,' I said, breath fanning out in a puff of white as I tugged on the blue woolly hat that Dolly had pushed into my hand as I left the café.

Gérard had explained that Hamish knew the route and would lead me back to his cottage, so I let the dog direct me round the back of the café to a lane that wound down to the beach, where I remembered hanging out on my last visit.

It wasn't long after Dolly had bought the café before Charlie came out to join her, and I'd felt a bit lost as Scott was supposed to have been with me, but insisted on staying behind to deal with a problem at the gallery (or so he'd said).

The weather had been glorious then; brightly-coloured hollyhocks clustered along the lane, the stretch of beach littered with visitors wearing shorts and flip-flops. Today, my boots crunched along snow-covered ground and the flowers had drooped beneath a thick white blanket. On the beach, the sparse tufts of seagrass among the low-lying dunes were tipped ice-white, and the sand looked as if it had been replaced with icing sugar.

'Isn't it pretty?' I said to Hamish, but he'd paused to snuffle about and didn't reply as I looked around, breathing in the salted scent of the sea. Above, the sky was a clear, denim-blue that coordinated with the sea, where a breeze was pushing frilly-edged waves to the shoreline. 'Bit cold for a paddle,' I concluded, recalling how I'd wandered for miles at the water's edge last time, the sea washing over my feet, and ended up with sunburn. *No chance of that today.*

I dug my phone out of my coat pocket and awkwardly framed the scene one-handed, wishing it didn't look so ordinary through the lens. A filter would make it stand out, I decided, snapping away, trying to avoid a cluster of fighting seagulls at the water's edge.

As I tucked my phone away, Hamish darted forward all of a sudden, almost yanking my arm from its socket, and although Gérard had maintained he could be let off the lead, I decided not to. I didn't want him running off, or starting a fight with another dog, however friendly he seemed.

There were a few people about; a bunch of teenagers trying to walk in each other's footprints and taking selfies; a family in matching scarves cycling the path alongside the beach; a woman with a little boy, attempting to build a snowman and another dog walker, huddled into a Sherpa-style coat with his head down, hands thrust into his pockets, coming towards us. The small white dog trotting neatly at his side was barely visible against the snow, and exceptionally well-behaved compared to Hamish, who'd begun pulling at his lead and barking with excitement.

'Don't be silly,' I ordered, without much conviction, while he jumped up and down as though his legs were spring-loaded. Crouching, I tried to draw him to my side, willing the dog walker to pass quickly before there was a scene, but Hamish squirmed out of my grasp and shot forward, dragging me flat on my stomach. 'For God's *sake*!'

Still gripping his lead (how could he be this *strong*?), I managed to scramble to my hands and knees and crawl forwards, ice-cold wetness seeping through my jeans, to where Hamish was now cavorting – there was no other word for it – with the little white dog. It was on its hind legs, pawing the air in front of Hamish's face, its tongue startlingly pink against all the whiteness, giving it a smiley expression that Hamish seemed to like.

My gaze shifted to the boots beside the dog; dull, black leather, the toes gritty with snow and sand, the laces not fastened properly, and I stared for a moment, hoping they'd move away and leave me to my humiliation. They stayed put, and I realised with a sag that I was going to have to get up and take control – especially as the canine cavorting had taken on a flirty quality, with bottom-sniffing and yelping from both parties.

'Hamish!' I implored, tugging his lead – *it was far too long; how did Gérard cope?* – remembering this sort of caper was why my parents preferred to follow the female bloodline with the sheepdogs at the farm. Hamish flicked me a look that suggested he'd forgotten my presence, before resuming his ungentlemanly behaviour. 'Could you please call off your dog?' I said as I pushed to my feet, brushing snow off my coat, wondering why the owner was just standing there doing nothing – though, to be fair, his dog was now sitting down, seeming faintly amused by Hamish's antics. '*Appelez votre chien, s'il vous plaît.*'

'Nina!'

My head jerked up. 'Ryan!'

'Are you OK?'

I gawped, as if I'd spotted an octopus. 'I'm fine,' I said, adjusting my hat, which had slipped over my brow, and wishing he hadn't seen me lying at his feet. 'What are you doing here?' *Outdoors and fully dressed*, I nearly added, clocking the dark jeans and jumper beneath his coat. 'You look like you should be leading an expedition up Everest.'

'I was bored, so thought I'd come out and steal a dog.'

'Ha, ha.' I couldn't take my eyes off him, despite the fact that Hamish's prancing was jerking my arm around. 'You look…' *really good*. His beard had been drastically pruned so the outline of his jaw was visible, as were his lips, which were… nice. *Very* nice. The sort an author might describe as luscious. 'You look different,' I said, more aggressively than I'd intended. 'Better, I mean. Than before.'

'Thank you for that amazingly generous compliment.' He looked self-conscious, as if he'd rather I hadn't said anything at all.

'I take it you don't go for the tortured-writer look?'

'Judging me on my appearance?'

I prickled at the reference to our conversation this morning, deciding not to mention that he looked a bit like Jon Snow from *Game of Thrones*, but without a massive fur hanging around his shoulders. 'I suppose I was.'

'Fair enough.' A glimmer of warmth entered his eyes, which appeared greener in daylight, probably due to the snow around us highlighting all the colours. Everything about him seemed brighter and more detailed: the texture of his hair, the fine lines at the corners of his eyes, which suggested he smiled a lot – though I'd yet to see the evidence – and even his skin looked less pale, a trace of colour on his cheeks from the bracing air. 'Dolly told me I was starting to look like Hagrid from *Harry Potter*, so I thought it was time for a trim,' he said, as if compelled to explain as he ran a hand over his chin.

'And did she also tell you to buy a pet?'

His mouth turned up as he started to smile. 'This is Bon-Bon.' He eyed the dog at his feet rather warily. 'She's a girl and she's not mine. I'm walking her as a favour.'

'*Bon-Bon?*' I smirked. 'No wonder you weren't keen to call her off.' I squatted to stroke her silky head. 'A favour for whom?'

'Whom?' Ryan's voice was lightly mocking. 'Get you, grammar girl.'

'Get you, walking a dog called Bon-Bon,' I hit back.

Ryan squatted, his jean-clad leg knee brushing mine. 'She belongs to a woman in the village. Her usual dog walker's away today and she asked Dolly if anyone could help.'

'And she suggested you?'

'Yup.' He nodded, and I caught a whiff of whatever he'd used in the shower and that same, warm skin scent from the day before. 'That was quite a tumble you took.' He gave up trying to pat Hamish, who was only interested in trying to get Bon-Bon back on her feet. 'Are you sure you're OK?'

'I'm perfectly fine,' I said, wishing he hadn't brought it up. 'This is Hamish, by the way. He's a boy and I'm also walking him as a favour.'

'For whom?'

'One of the customers.' I was determined not to smile, unwilling to draw him in. 'An old leg injury flared up, so Dolly volunteered me for dog walking services.'

'Nice of her.'

'Of me, you mean.'

'I mean, it was nice of Dolly to volunteer our services this morning.'

Catching something in his tone, I shot him a look. 'What do you mean?'

'Well, it's a bit of a coincidence, don't you think?'

I recalled Dolly hustling me out of the café, almost as if there was somewhere I needed to be. 'You think she intended us to bump into each other?'

He lifted his eyes to meet mine. 'Let's just say, she knew what time Bon-Bon was being dropped off this morning.'

'Right.' I wasn't even surprised. Hadn't Charlie warned me his mum was on the matchmaking trail? Mum had warned me too, and it had been clear when Dolly had caught us together the day before, she'd been imagining us as a couple. 'I think it's just something she does,' I said, embarrassed that Ryan had noticed it too as it meant that – however briefly and unwillingly – he must have considered my potential partner qualities, and found them as lacking as I'd found his. 'Don't take it personally.'

'I won't,' he promised, returning his hands to his pockets as he straightened.

'Good. Well… I'd better go,' I said, just as Hamish sat down with a frustrated sigh. 'I've got stuff to do.'

'Of course you have.' I couldn't work out whether he was being sarcastic or not. Perhaps he thought I had endless time at my disposal, while I worked my way through a trust fund. He gave a low whistle to attract Bon-Bon's attention and she sprang to her feet, giving him an adoring look. 'See you later.'

'Maybe.' I tried to restrain Hamish, who was keen to follow his four-legged friend, but before I could make the first move, Ryan turned and hurried along the beach towards the café with little more than a nod in my direction. Either he really needed to warm up, or couldn't wait to escape.

Hamish looked dejected as he watched them go, but swiftly rallied when the little boy further down the beach gave up on his collapsing snowman, and ran over to make a fuss of him. Ten minutes later, we were outside a row of fishermen's cottages and Gérard was waiting on the doorstep to greet us.

Chapter Seven

I watched Gérard lead the way inside after Hamish, who'd bolted straight to his water bowl in the kitchen, no doubt dehydrated from the exercise – and from drooling over Bon-Bon.

'How's your leg?' I asked, wondering whether Dolly had invented the 'old injury' story to get me out of the café and close to Ryan. Would Gérard have gone along with it? It seemed a bit unlikely, and I felt guilty for doubting him when I spotted his pronounced limp. (*Too* pronounced?)

'It is improving, *merci.*' He paused to grip the back of a wooden chair positioned by a small round table in the centre of the stone-flagged kitchen. The table had been polished to a gleam, a cut-glass bowl of fruit in the centre reflected in the surface, and I was impressed by how clean and tidy everything looked, even though the room was small enough to feel crowded. 'I am trying not to…' Gérard's bright blue eyes scrunched up as he sought the right word, white eyebrows meeting in the middle. 'Not to rely on *ma canne.*' He jabbed a finger at his stick by the door, tossed aside in a way that suggested a love-hate relationship. 'My Maggie, she would 'ave said, "It's a slippery slope, Gérard."'

His uncannily accurate accent made me smile, and I remembered his wife had been Scottish – which explained why his English was good.

'I understand, but it's important to know when you need a helping hand,' I said, recalling how fiercely independent Great-Grandma Augustine had been.

Even after she came to live at the farm, due to her failing sight and dodgy hips (she refused to enter a hospital, terrified she'd never come out), she'd insisted on 'doing her share'. Luckily for us, it had mostly involved her life-long passion for baking – a skill Dolly had inherited, but bypassed Mum and me.

'You don't want to have a fall,' I added now to Gérard. It had been Augustine's worst fear.

'It is nothing.' Gérard waved a gnarly hand and shuffled in soft moccasins to an old enamel kettle with a wooden handle perched on the shiny stove. Picking up a box of matches, he said, 'You English, you like to 'ave a cup of tea,' in that funny, hybrid accent. 'It was Maggie's favourite *boisson*. I learnt to love it too.'

'Oh… well, thank you.' Although I'd planned to take some more photos before returning to the café to work on my blog, it didn't seem right to just leave. Especially as he'd lit the gas beneath the kettle with a flourish, and was placing two floral china cups on matching saucers in a way I guessed his wife used to do. Instead, I eased off my boots and wiggled my toes, embarrassed that my socks were bright pink and patterned with yellow bananas. 'Were you married a long time?'

'Almost 'alf of a century,' Gérard said. 'We were *trés heureux*. Very 'appy.' A blanket of sadness seemed to settle around him and I felt bad for asking.

'*Je vous envoie mes condoléances.*' I wasn't sure it was appropriate at this stage to offer my deepest condolences, but he nodded as if appreciating the sentiment. Turning, his craggy face creased into a smile.

'I 'ope you will find such *d'amour, un jour*.'

'One day,' I agreed, wondering how he knew that I hadn't already found *such a love*. Probably because Dolly had told him, as she seemed to treat her regulars like beloved family members.

I removed Dolly's hat and scruffed up my hair, then wriggled out of my coat. It was hot with the old-fangled wood-burning stove pushing out heat. Hamish had settled beside it, already dozing off, and I glanced around, taking in the traditional wood-beamed ceiling where an old-fashioned light-shade hung. There were lots of rustic cupboards lining the walls, and shelves laden with cookbooks, jars and a collection of wooden utensils. Everything was orderly and well-cared for, and I guessed he had someone to help look after the place.

'I will make food.'

'Pardon?' I turned to see Gérard with a knife in his hand, preparing to hack into a loaf of bread that seemed to have appeared out of nowhere.

He pointed to a block of aged-looking cheese with a rind. '*Fromage.*'

'Oh, er…' It didn't appear to be a question, and the fresh air had given me an appetite so I nodded. 'That would be lovely, thank you.'

'Go, sit down. I will bring a tray,' he said, but when I made to pull out a chair at the table, he shook his head.

'*Non, non*, not 'ere.' He pointed the knife to a door leading off the kitchen. 'In there.'

It sounded like an order. I wondered whether Gérard had once been in the armed forces. He certainly looked forbidding, brandishing the knife and glowering from under his eyebrows, but there was a trace of anxiety in his expression too. 'It is a little…' He waved his arms and I took a step back to avoid being pronged with the knife. 'I 'ave a lot of *des choes*,' he concluded. 'Possessions.'

'OK.'

'You will need to make a space.'

'Right.' *Wouldn't it just be easier to eat in the kitchen?* Hamish whined, but when I looked down, he was sleeping, paws twitching as though dreaming he was chasing Bon-Bon up the snowy beach. 'I'll go through then,' I said, stepping around Gérard, who'd turned his attention to the stove where the kettle was starting to whistle. 'Sure you don't want a hand?'

He waved me away as he switched off the gas and I pushed open the door and stepped inside a living room so different from the traditional, homely kitchen it was like entering a parallel universe; one filled with chaos and darkness – and lots and lots of clutter. There were newspapers – heaps of them, stacked in random piles – and cardboard boxes stuffed with pictures and paintings, some with clothes spilling out, and there was fabric piled on the furniture: two armchairs and a sofa, pushed against the walls as if better to accommodate the mess. The curtains were pulled across the window, but a finger of light spilled through a gap where they didn't quite meet, highlighting a jumble of photos and ornaments all higgledy-piggledy on the dresser, as if Gérard had started to rearrange them and lost heart. There was no dust that I could detect, just stuff on every surface, and definitely no room to sit down.

Make a space, Gérard had said. Instructed, almost. My fingers twitched with a life of their own and before I'd had time to think it through, I'd rolled up my sleeves and started shifting things. First, the newspapers became one pile instead of five and I transported them to the furthest corner, out of the way of the fire – even though the grate was empty, they were an obvious fire hazard.

After depositing armfuls of fabric into a wooden chest beside the dresser (perhaps Maggie had been a seamstress), I tucked the spilled clothes into their respective boxes before stacking them neatly by the newspapers, pausing to look at a black and white photo of a newly-wed Gérard and Maggie, which was lying on the floor. They were beaming for the photographer on the steps of a church, confetti raining around them, joy evident in their faces. Gérard was easily recognisable, even in a snooker-player suit with short dark hair and no Santa beard – something about the brightness of his eyes – while Maggie was tiny and twinkly in a fussy dress with ruffled shoulders, her copper hair styled in a beehive.

I placed the photo in the centre of the stone mantle above the fireplace, switching some candlesticks and a trailing plant to opposite ends, and draped a gold locket I'd spotted in one of the boxes around the frame. *Much better.*

I crossed to the window and whipped open the curtains, blinking as daylight streamed in, and turned to study the room. The floorboards were visible now, bare apart from a big rug in earthy tones, and I knelt in front of the fireplace and placed some logs in the grate from a basket in the hearth. There was a box of matches and the fire didn't take long to catch, the dancing flames throwing out instant warmth. Not that I needed warming up. All the exertion meant I wished I wasn't wearing a thick jumper, but the room still didn't look quite right. Squinting, I eyed the array of furniture – no television, I noted – trying to imagine where Gérard would sit, then heaved the solid sofa round to face the armchairs and plumped up the chintzy cushions that the piles of fabric had been hiding. After arranging a soft, blue knitted blanket along the back of the sofa, I positioned a fifty-pence shaped table, previously buried beneath a pile of crime novels – now gracing the bookshelf under the window – between the armchairs and placed a lamp on top. *Perfect.* A matching table looked just right beside the sofa and would serve as a holder for Gérard's tea – or coffee – as well as his newspaper and a pen for his crosswords.

Casting a critical gaze around, I hummed an off-key version of 'Rockin' Around the Christmas Tree' and noticed a couple of faded patches on the whitewashed wall where pictures had once hung, the hooks still in place. Dipping into one of the boxes, I tugged out a pretty watercolour in a pale-wood frame, its amateurish quality suggesting it had been Maggie's work – that and her name painted in the corner. The picture was of pastel-coloured boats on the sand, waiting for the tide to come in, a heron nearby in a puddle of seawater, the sky a luminous wash of pearly pink and grey. I instantly recognised Loix, having cycled there on my last visit, meandering through the salt marshes that covered the island. I'd been struck by the atmosphere, which had seemed eerie and otherworldly, full of the pungent smell of iodine.

Still humming, I hung up the painting and found another, of a church with a black-and-white steeple rising up from sunflower fields. It had to be Ars-en-Ré – one of the island's prettiest villages (apart from Chamillon) – the steeple was a landmark for boats entering the bay, and I'd stopped off there to have crêpes and cider at a touristy café.

I hung that painting too and stood back to admire the effect, feeling a deep sense of satisfaction that they were where they were supposed to be – as was everything else in the room, discounting the newspapers and boxes, now partially hidden by the dresser. I couldn't resist taking a couple of photos on my phone and, as I did, I noticed something on the floor where the sofa had been: a handful of letters, slipping from a loosely tied strip of faded pink ribbon.

Putting my phone down, I crossed the room and crouched to pick them up, the pieces of paper yellowed with age, soft with handling and clearly cherished. Love letters, probably. I'd never seen any in real life – they belonged to novels and movies – and there was something irresistible about them. One had unfolded and I couldn't resist a quick peek at the sloping handwriting in faded black ink, neatly spread across the page. My heart gave an odd little leap when I saw the name *Augustine* at the bottom, followed by four neat kisses.

Augustine. My great-grandmother's name. Apparently, it wasn't that common in France.

My darling William… There was something oddly familiar about the handwriting, and I realised with a jolt that I'd seen it before – on old birthday and Christmas cards, and the backs of photos Mum had kept in a shoebox down the years.

My eyes skittered over the words, the odd sentence leaping out.

So wonderful to be in your arms again… how can I bear to be apart from you… can't wait until we're together again, my love…

It was written in English, but that wasn't surprising as Augustine had grown up in England and was writing to someone called William. If it was my Augustine, which every cell in my body was telling me it was. Someone who *wasn't* my great-grandfather Charles, who Charlie had been named after.

I checked the top of the letter for a date, but there wasn't one, and almost leapt out of my skin when I heard a sharp intake of breath. Turning, I saw Gérard in the doorway, holding a tray of cups that were rattling on their saucers, and shot to my feet, the letter fluttering to the floor.

'You made me jump,' I said. *How much time had passed since I'd left him in the kitchen?* 'Here, let me take that.' I moved over and took the tray from him, worried he might drop it, though I felt pretty shaky myself. 'What do you think?' I followed his wide-eyed gaze around the room, my mouth trapped in a smile as I took in his reaction. 'Doesn't it just feel… *right*?' I said, filling the stunned silence. '*Maison heureuse, esprit heureux.*' I hoped it translated as *happy house, happy mind*, but when Gérard remained quiet, reality swept in and I clattered the tray onto the table at the side of the sofa.

'Gérard, I'm *so* sorry. *Je suis désolé.*'

His hands were still poised as if holding an invisible tray and I was terrified he might be about to collapse. The only signs of life were his eyeballs darting from the sofa to the wall, to the blazing fire in the grate, and across to the towering pile of papers in the corner.

'Gérard?' Panic rose. *What had I done?* He must be a hoarder and didn't hoarders take comfort from being surrounded by clutter, even if it made no sense to anyone else? And I'd come along – a virtual stranger – and unthinkingly stripped everything back, most of it belonging to his beloved wife. I'd pushed everything away, as though it meant nothing, and his precious newspapers had probably been in some sort of order I hadn't understood, or maybe he'd been saving the crosswords and now… 'I'll put it all as it was,' I said, backing away, hands up as though to ward off an attack. Not that he looked capable of attacking me. If anything, he seemed to have entered a state of shock.

'Stop!'

I froze. Gérard had turned to stare at the paintings on the wall, one arm outstretched as if to stroke them. 'How did you know?' His eyes came to life as they rested on me, a mix of bewilderment and happiness in them that made my heart soar. 'There was so much, I did not know how to do it, where to start, so I left it all here.' He gestured towards the boxes. 'I thought… I thought it would be simple after Maggie was gone, that it would be a good thing to reorganise, to *évacuer* but… I…' He tapped his temples and worked his fingertips through his snow-white hair, his expression becoming anguished.

'You became overwhelmed.' Understanding mingled with hot relief. 'It was easier to leave it all?' I mimed a muddle with my hands and he nodded, mimicking the movement.

'*Le chaos*,' he said, looking around again with an expression of childlike wonder.

'*Exactement.*'

He flung his arms out to the side. '*C'est magnifique!*'

'You really like it?' I wanted to clap my hands, but was worried I'd got it wrong.

'*Oui.*' He nodded, a wisp of hair drifting out like a cobweb. 'Maggie would say, you're a bonnie lassie.' I grinned and shook my head, embarrassed. 'You 'ave a gift.'

'Oh, I wouldn't go that far,' I said, a wave of pleasure washing through me. It was like waking from a nice dream and discovering it was real. 'I just tidied up a bit, that's all.'

He moved forward and stroked the knitted blanket on the sofa, his gaze returning to the paintings. 'It is like Maggie is with me, but not...' He shuffled his hands around and clamped them to his head, making his mouth turn down.

'Not too overpowering?' Gérard would have made a good mime artist. 'You don't want it to look like a shrine?'

He pointed, like a contestant on *Give us a Clue*. '*C'est tout!*' he said, eyes shining. 'You 'ave 'it the nail on the 'ead.'

I smiled, recognising Maggie's influence once more. '*Merci.*' I executed a bow to hide my flushing face. 'I'm happy you like it, but there's still some clearing up to do.' I nodded at the newspapers and boxes, their presence like an itch I couldn't reach, a guilty flush racing through me when I spotted the disturbed letters on the floor. 'Gérard, I'm sorry, I wasn't snooping, they were behind the sofa and—'

He waved a dismissive hand, and I guessed he'd been given enough to absorb for one day. 'They are of no use to me,' he said a little sadly. 'Maggie, she kept them. They belonged to William, her *papa*.'

My heart lurched. 'Maggie's father?'

Gérard nodded. 'It was… *une affaire de coeur*.' He placed a hand on his heart. 'Maggie, she found the letters after he died. She liked the…' He pursed his lips and waggled his fingers, searching for the sentiment.

'The romance?'

'Ah, *oui. Le grande passion*.'

Blimey. It all sounded a bit *Brief Encounter*. In fact, hadn't that been Augustine's favourite film? I dimly remembered Dolly saying how they'd sometimes watch it together on Sunday afternoons and how her normally pragmatic grandmother would come over all nostalgic.

'Was Maggie's mother not William's grand passion?' I asked as a thought occurred to me. *Did he and Augustine have an affair while married to other people?*

'He did not talk about such matters.' Gérard spoke gravely. 'He was a private man, so quiet, but I think he and Maggie's *maman*, they were 'appy together.' His eyebrows dipped. 'Maggie was very surprised to find the letters,' he added. 'He did not ever speak of another *amour*.'

'Could I… would you mind if I borrowed them?' I glanced at the letter I'd discarded. 'I find them fascinating.'

Gérard raised his shoulders. 'They are of no use to me,' he said and then he smiled. 'You may do as you wish with them, *ma chérie*, after what you have done for me.'

When I'd scooped them up and clumsily retied the pink ribbon – half-hoping I was mistaken and it was another Augustine altogether – he gestured grandly at the tray. 'Maybe we go to the kitchen now.' He cast a loving glance at the sofa, as if he'd forgotten what it looked like without layers of fabric heaped on top. 'We do not want to be messy in 'ere.'

I hid a smile, suddenly ravenous, as I carefully tucked the letters under my arm, picked up the tray and followed him out to the kitchen. After transferring the letters to my coat pocket, I sat at the table with Gérard, watched closely by Hamish, who'd woken up and was hopefully sniffing the air.

A simple lunch of fresh bread and cheese, washed down by strong tea from a china cup, had never tasted so good. Every now and then Gérard would look at me and chuckle, shaking his head as he delicately sipped his tea, and I smiled back, while Hamish tracked our every mouthful. I pushed the letters to the back of my mind as Gérard talked a bit about Maggie – her dressmaking skills and her love of Scotland, where they'd met when he was twenty-one on a visit to the Scottish Highlands – and his granddaughter Jacqueline, who had a gift for painting, like her grandmother.

'I think she will be happy to come here now.' His face was lit with anticipation. 'It has not been easy for her to see our home like this, and I…' He put down his cup. 'I would not let her help, like a stubborn old goat.' *Another Maggie-ism.* 'My *petite fille*, she will come to play now.'

Play was an odd word – his granddaughter had to be an adult. Maybe something had got lost in translation. 'That's good,' I said, feeling as if I'd engineered some sort of family reunion, as well as opened a possible can of worms with the discovery of the letters. 'You really need some Christmas decorations.' His granddaughter would appreciate them, even if Gérard wasn't keen, but he gave an eager nod.

'Maggie, she always went… *à la mer.*' He mimed a diving action. 'Overboard?'

He smiled. 'Jacqueline will help,' he said. 'We will decorate together. But I wonder, if you have time, if you would also have a little tidy-up of my spare bedroom, so my granddaughter can sleep over.'

Walking back to the café much later, I still had a smile on my face, in spite of the cold and the fact that I'd left Dolly's hat behind, but the rustle of letters in my coat pocket had a sobering effect. I might have unwittingly done Gérard a favour, but I'd also (probably) uncovered an affair between his father-in-law and my great-grandmother – the romance Dolly had wondered about, and one that could change everything she thought she knew about Augustine.

Chapter Eight

'Nice walk?' Dolly poked her head out of the kitchen as I came through the back door, stamping snow off my boots. 'You've been gone ages.'

'I stayed and had some lunch with Gérard,' I said, deciding not to mention I'd 'bumped' into Ryan – or the letters I'd found. Face-to-face, it suddenly seemed too far-fetched to be true. I needed to read them properly, search for clues.

'Did you see anyone else while you were out?' She sounded deliberately casual and I wondered whether Ryan had sidestepped the question too.

'There were a few people on the beach.' I kept my voice vague, jumping when Mathilde suddenly emerged, fastening a cape at her throat like someone from a Dickens novel. I moved aside as she pushed her feet into a pair of pointy black boots and threw me a suspicious stare, before lighting up in a smile when Charlie materialised in his padded coat.

'Time to escort you home, Madame Bouvier?' he said, crooking his elbow for Mathilde to hold, and she gave a girlish giggle at odds with her crow-like appearance. 'Nice walk?' he said to me, but Mathilde was clearly keen to get going and yanked him outside with surprising strength. 'Talk later,' he called, as Dolly gave them a wave and pushed the door shut.

'What's her problem?' I said.

'She hasn't quite forgiven me for not keeping her grandson on.' Dolly made a face. 'I gave him a job here in the summer, but we didn't need him after the season ended.'

'I thought she was going to put a curse on me.'

'I think she's given that up now.'

Sometimes, it was hard to tell whether Dolly was joking.

'How was Gérard?' she said.

'He seemed fine.' I was aware of her scrutiny and wondered whether I looked different. I'd never been very good at hiding my feelings. 'I left the hat you lent me at his cottage.'

'He phoned,' she said.

'About the hat?'

'And to tell me what you did.'

'Ah.' I fiddled with the cuff of my jumper and wondered whether everyone in the village now knew I'd tided Gérard's front room. I'd almost forgotten what village life was like after living in a city for several years. Though our farm was several miles from Appleby, the nearest village, the residents had a good working knowledge of our business, and Mum and Dad knew a surprising amount about theirs.

'Oh, he was over the moon, love.' Dolly clasped her hands beneath her chin. 'You've made his year, never mind his day.'

'Oh?' I gently stepped back, unused to so much praise. 'Well, that's nice to know. Did he say anything else?'

She cocked her head. 'Such as?'

'Oh… nothing.' I blinked. 'I think Hamish enjoyed his walk.'

Dolly smiled. 'So did Bon-Bon,' she said. 'Ryan came down for a bite to eat and said he was planning to write this afternoon.' It was clear she couldn't resist mentioning his name. 'You should pop up and say hello.'

'Hmm?' I tried to pull my mind away from William and Augustine. 'Isn't Frank helping out today?'

Unfazed by the change of topic, Dolly said, 'He's doing some DIY,' with a note of pride in her voice. 'He's not just good with his hips.' She swivelled her own, and I hoped she was referring to their salsa activities. 'He's pretty good with a tool.'

'Just the one?'

'Silly.' She swiped at me playfully. 'He's making me a walk-in wardrobe.'

'Frank sounds great.'

'He is.' She said it with heartfelt sincerity. 'You will come over for dinner this evening, won't you?'

'Of course!' I smiled. 'I want to meet the man who's made my aunt so happy.'

She winked and patted my arm, just as Stefan called her from the kitchen. 'I'd better get back to work,' she said with obvious eagerness, and I made my way upstairs, thinking how lucky she was to be doing a job she loved.

Television voices floated down the landing and I hovered for a moment outside my bedroom before making my way to the living room and sticking my head round the door.

Ryan was at the table near the Christmas tree, tapping away at his laptop. The tree lights had been set to flash on and off in an annoyingly random sequence, but he was completely engrossed and didn't seem bothered. The television was on too, and I wondered how he could focus with it so loud, an anguished-looking couple arguing and gesturing wildly.

As I made to close the door, he turned and stared in an unfocused way, as if in the grip of a dream. 'What are you doing?' he said, seeming to come back from wherever he'd been. *Amazon*, I noticed, glancing at the screen.

'Just wondered what all the noise was about.' I gestured at the TV. 'I think they can hear it from space.'

'Sorry.' He rose and rotated his shoulders as though they'd stiffened up. He looked strong and capable in jeans, and a cable-knit jumper a shade darker than his eyes – as though he should be outdoors, chopping wood. 'I like it being on, it helps me concentrate.' He stretched his arms over his head, and I slid my eyes away from a glimpse of lean stomach where a trail of black hair led beneath the waistband of his jeans. 'I was doing a bit of online Christmas shopping.' Lowering his arms, he gave me a half-smile that did something odd to my insides. 'It's not a bad show, actually.'

'Hmm?'

'The show.' He nodded at the television screen, where the couple were now kissing as though their lives depended on it. 'It's about the residents of a working-class neighbourhood in Marseille. A bit like *Neighbours* or an upmarket *EastEnders*.'

'And you can understand what they're saying?'

'Hardly a word.' He sat back down, fingers absently stroking his laptop keyboard. 'But it's pretty easy to work out what's happening.'

'OK, well, I'll leave you to it,' I said.

'You can come in, if you like.'

'No. I mean, thanks, but I've got stuff to do.'

'What sort of stuff?'

Turning back, I thought I detected a sceptical twist to his mouth.

'Oh, you know. Checking my bank account to see how much money I've got and planning more revenge on my ex… that sort of thing.' I threw him a syrupy grin as I pulled the door shut, hoping his laptop would melt and he'd be forced to go back to England.

*

In my room, I removed my coat and took the letters out of my pocket, then sat on the bed to read them with an uneasy mix of guilt and anticipation. It felt wrong to be reading words meant only for William, even with Gérard's blessing, but surely if he'd meant his affair to remain a secret forever, he'd have destroyed them.

The letters weren't long, but it was clear the relationship was punctuated with absences, as it appeared that William had been a radio operator in the Navy, away for long stretches of time. *I think of you at sea, so handsome in your uniform, and can't help wishing that you were here with me.* Any doubts that it might be a different Augustine dissolved when I read the words, *I am writing from the bedroom overlooking the church, and the sky is as blue as your eyes.*

It was definitely the house in High Wycombe, where she'd grown up after her parents moved to England; the house she inherited after they died and where Dolly's mother was born. Augustine had lived there through her married life and beyond, until it became too difficult for her to live alone and Mum brought her to the farm for her final years.

I dream of you, the smell of you, the touch of your hands. Never did I think I could feel like this, she'd written in rather flowery language, clearly in the throes of first love. Unless she'd met William *after* she was married, and realised she didn't care that much for my great-grandfather after all.

I checked all ten letters for dates, but apart from one dated *24 July* in the corner, there was nothing to indicate the year, and frustratingly little about her life and daily routine to give a hint of which decade they were in. She talked about a busy period at the department store where she'd worked for many years that had made her feet ache – *if only you were here with your magic fingers!* – and the sentence *I made your favourite seed cake, thinking of you and wishing you were here to eat it.* made me sit up straight.

It was a reference to her love of baking, but according to Dolly, she'd been making cakes since she was old enough to hold a wooden spoon. There were some other interesting snippets, but nothing that suggested any particular time frame. She mentioned a friend called Jean, who'd had a 'bust-up' with her husband and thrown all his clothes out of the window. *I simply cannot imagine feeling such anger towards you, my darling. You only ever make me smile, make me come alive, and without you by my side the world is pale and uninteresting.* It was so hard to reconcile the distant memories I had of brisk, no-nonsense Augustine, always with her hands in a bowl of flour – or so it had seemed at the time – insisting Ben and I talk to her in French (though Mum said she'd rarely spoken her native language when she and Dolly were growing up), with this passionate woman, pining for her lover. There were no references to children, or a husband, or anything clandestine... until the last letter I picked up.

Charles is a good man and I haven't heard from you in so long, William. I need to talk to you about something and I don't know what to do. Please, please, write if you can.

It was such an impassioned plea I found myself looking on the back of the letter, as if there might be more, then reread the rest, checking I hadn't missed a mention of my great-grandfather before.

What had she needed to talk to William about? Did she want to end their affair because she'd met my great-grandfather, or was she planning to leave Charles for him? Had William replied? Perhaps he'd fallen for

Maggie's mother and had done the old-fashioned version of ghosting Augustine – simply not bothering to reply to her letters, hoping she'd get the message. Maybe she'd married Charles on the rebound, then spent her marriage pining for William. And what if the something she'd wanted to talk about was that she'd fallen pregnant – either with Dolly, or Mum?

I had so many questions flying around my head, but I couldn't ask Dolly for answers she might not have and that would make her doubt everything she thought she knew about her beloved grandmother. And Gérard had told me his father-in-law never talked about the past, so it was unlikely he knew anything either.

I knew I should let it go, but it was such a coincidence, finding the letters so unexpectedly and so far from home – it felt like it meant something, and Gran's favourite saying drifted across my mind. *Perhaps it was meant to be.* But for what purpose, if I couldn't share them with Dolly?

Deciding I should sleep on it, I slipped the letters into the drawer of the bedside cabinet and picked up my notepad – the one where I'd neatly written the rules for setting up a travel blog, and hadn't looked at since.

1) Be real
2) Be useful
3) Be unconventional
4) Be yourself
5) Be honest
6) Be an expert

The seventh was a deviation from all the 'be's'.

Don't start a travel blog before you've travelled.

I sighed, and looked at the rules again through narrowed eyes. It had all seemed so simple when I was doing the course, brainstorming ideas with the other participants, scribbling things like *Off the beaten track. Be reckless!! Intimate travelogue? Tips and tricks and hacks! Diary??* and underlined in capitals *BE UNIQUE.* I tapped my teeth with my pen and tried to recapture the enthusiasm I'd felt, but half an hour later, all I'd written was 'cultural differences?' and developed a nagging headache. I'd think about everything later, I decided. After I'd had a nap.

Chapter Nine

'Come in out of the cold, Nina,' Frank greeted me, wrapping a paw-like hand around mine and shaking it firmly as I stepped inside the cottage with a bunch of flowers I'd picked up from the florist's in the village. His Yorkshire accent was a surprise, even though Mum had told me he'd lived in Whitby before moving to Chamillon permanently. 'It's good to meet you at last.'

'You too.' He was instantly recognisable from the wedding pictures Mum had shown me on her phone: medium height and build, with a gentle, friendly smile and dark, sparkly eyes. It was easy to see why Dolly had chosen to marry him – he was the opposite of Charlie's dad, for a start.

'I ate a clock yesterday,' he said.

I'd been about to unwind my scarf with my free hand. 'I'm sorry… what?'

'I ate a clock,' he repeated with a very Dolly-like wink. 'It was pretty time-consuming.'

I smiled. 'Nice one.'

'That's his little icebreaker.' Dolly appeared at his side, looking unusually glamorous in a fitted black dress, her hair crimped into little waves. 'Ooh, are those from Dee's?' she asked, taking the flowers from me and burying her nose in the petals. 'The florist next to the gift shop,' she added, when I looked at her blankly.

'Oh, yes. They caught my eye, and I thought you'd like them.' I draped my coat and scarf over a wooden coat stand by the door, while Dolly handed the flowers to Frank to admire.

'How did your photo session go?' she said, and I remembered I'd said I was going to take a few pictures before coming over, determined to get some material for my travel blog.

'Great!' I shoved my fingers through my hair. 'I'm sorry I'm a bit late, I got carried away.' After I'd been to the florist, I'd taken a slow walk in the twilight, along the snowy beach, and the colours of the setting sun and the wintery scene were stunning. Unencumbered by Hamish, I'd managed to take a few shots, and got so wrapped up in the view that I'd lost track of time.

'You're here now, that's the main thing.' Dolly gave me one of her bone-crushing hugs, then stepped back and eyed me up and down. 'What's this?' she said, noting the silvery, swishy skirt I was wearing with my Doc Martens.

After a quick shower, I'd been loath to put on the jeans and jumper I'd been wearing to meet Dolly's new husband, so I'd wriggled into the skirt from her wardrobe, surprised to find it fitted. 'I hope you don't mind.' I gave the fabric a self-deprecating tweak. 'This is a pyjama top,' I confessed, brushing my hand down my dusky pink velour top. 'But I thought it went well with the skirt.'

'I'd never have thought to wear black tights with it, either.'

'They're actually leggings.'

'Well, you look lovely, and I really like that top with the skirt.' Dolly circled me, like a judge at Crufts sizing up a Dalmatian. 'It looks better on you than it does on me.'

'Nonsense,' said Frank, who looked like a fifties Chicago-style gangster in his black, pinstriped trousers, with red braces and big-collared shirt. 'Though you do look lovely,' he amended.

'The top makes the most of your bust.' Dolly did a shoulder wiggle. 'You take after me and your great-gran,' she said. 'Your mum doesn't have a lot going on in that department.'

'Dolly!' I tapped her hand away, my heart seizing at the mention of Augustine. 'The size of a bosom does not maketh the woman.'

Frank, eyes pinned to Dolly's chest, looked as though he vehemently disagreed but wisely kept quiet.

'Doesn't maketh the woman.' Dolly chuckled and squeezed my arm. 'You always were my favourite niece.'

'I'm your *only* niece,' I said, smiling. It was impossible to be mad with Dolly, even if her views on women's attributes were outdated. 'I like your light.' I pointed to a modest chandelier hanging from one of the ceiling beams. 'And your decorations.' The entrance was hung with tiny fairy lights and there was a holly wreath on the door. 'It's very subtle, for you.'

'I'm putting my own stamp on the place.'

Frank nodded his approval. 'It needed a woman's touch,' he said with obvious pride, still holding the bouquet like an Olympic torch. 'I didn't even have curtains when we met.'

Dolly gave him a loving hug. 'Come on,' she said to me. 'I hope you're hungry.'

'I know I am.' Frank patted his admirably flat stomach. 'I've been starving myself all day.'

'He means he was working upstairs and forgot the time,' Dolly corrected. 'He's been installing the shoe shelf in my walk-in wardrobe.'

'How many pairs have you got?' I imagined Oprah Winfrey's closet, with footwear in every style and colour invented. She even had a television in there – I'd seen a picture in a magazine at the dentist's.

'I've a pair for dancing, and two pairs for work that I alternate so my feet don't get smelly.'

Probably not a problem Oprah would ever encounter. 'I can't wait to see it,' I said.

As Dolly pushed open the door to the living room, I was buffeted by a mouth-watering smell of roasting meat, and the sound of Charlie's voice above a background of throbbing salsa music. He was pleading with someone to tell him what they wanted for Christmas.

'I normally buy joke gifts, in case I get it wrong,' he was saying. 'I bought Natalie a coaster with *Sweet dreams are made of cheese* on it last year and I don't even know why.'

'Hi, Chuck,' I said, waving like the Queen as I followed Frank and Dolly through.

He grinned and mouthed Elle, pointing to his phone.

'He's talking to his girlfriend,' said Dolly, in the way I imagined someone might say *I've won four million on the lottery.* 'Now, sit yourself at the table, love.'

'Don't you want a hand?'

'Everything's under control.' She gave Frank an affectionate smile. 'I've got my little helper.'

He rolled his eyes and heaved a sigh, but I could tell he was loving being married to Dolly and didn't mind one bit.

As they headed to the open-plan kitchen area, and Charlie continued his conversation with Elle – 'There's no point me trying to surprise you, because you'll end up with either a singing hot water bottle, or a trip somewhere you've never wanted to visit' – I looked around. The décor was a soothing palette of creams and golds, the furniture unexpectedly light and modern; a long, mink-coloured sofa beside a light oak sideboard; a copper lamp in the corner throwing out golden light and an oval, cloth-covered dining table opposite the kitchen. The only clue to the time of year was a medium-sized fir tree by the curtained window, tastefully adorned with little red bows and pine cones.

The whole effect was surprisingly elegant, compared to the apartment. The rattan basket of logs by the open fire was perfectly positioned, and a gallery of framed photos on the wall were placed at the perfect height to draw the eye without clashing. Even the cushions on the sofa were just right – not too many, and in spicy shades that added a touch of colour to the room. It was just how I would have done it, and the flowers, which Frank had neatly arranged in a jug, added a flourish to the dining table.

Feeling my shoulders relax, I crossed to admire them, resisting the urge to break out a few moves to the salsa beat pulsing through hidden speakers, knowing it wouldn't end well. Instead, I sat on a linen covered dining chair and checked my reflection in a silver knife handle, glad that my hair looked pleasantly tousled, and not like I'd stuck my head in a microwave.

Charlie was telling Elle he'd be happy with socks for Christmas as he could never find a matching pair, or Michelle Obama's autobiography, and I twisted my face into a gurn to make him laugh, just as the door opened and Ryan came into the room.

My features froze.

'Nina?' He seemed unsure it was me. 'Are you OK?'

I adjusted my features, suddenly dry-mouthed. 'What are you doing here?'

'It's the second time you've asked me that today.' He closed the door and ploughed a hand through his hair. 'I just nipped to the bathroom.'

'I meant, why are you *here*?' I gestured at the room.

'I invited him,' said Dolly, transporting a plate of crisp-skinned duck breasts to the table and plonking them down. 'I thought it would be nice for us all to eat together.' She nodded at the chair next to mine. 'Sit yourself down, Ryan.'

He hesitated, and I couldn't tell whether he didn't want to sit next to me, or wasn't certain I'd want him to, but Dolly whipped out the chair beside mine so he didn't have much choice.

'You look different,' he said as he sat down, clocking the skirt I was wearing, and I saw Frank swing a wide-eyed glance at Dolly. 'It's nice, but not as striking as the koala outfit.'

Frank's eyebrows shot up.

'Thanks,' I said, hoping Ryan would think it was the heat from the kitchen making my face look flushed. He was still in his jeans, but had swapped his jumper for a green and black plaid shirt. 'You look like a country and western singer.'

'Just the image I was going for.' He pretended to strum a guitar, then stopped as though embarrassed. 'How do you feel about salsa?' he said as an energetic trumpet solo rose to a crescendo.

'Too fiddly.' I forced a smile. 'I'm sure I'd fall over if I tried to dance.'

'You'd be fine, as long as you had the right partner.' Dolly's bright eyes encompassed us both for an embarrassingly long second, before she returned to the kitchen, where Frank rattled dinner plates out of the cupboard and pretended not to listen.

Ryan cleared his throat and shunted his chair up to the table. His elbow brushed mine and we jolted apart. 'Have you been here all this time?' I said.

'Charlie dragged me along after closing the café.' He nudged his fork a fraction closer to his placemat. 'Listen, Nina, I wanted to apologise properly for being such an arse.' His eyes grazed mine. 'I'm not usually so judgemental. I don't know what I was thinking.'

He seemed so genuinely remorseful that it didn't feel right to bring up the word *unstable*. 'Thanks,' I said, something inside me loosening its hold a little. 'For the apology, I mean.'

'Fresh start?'

I held his gaze. 'Fresh start,' I agreed, pretending I couldn't see that Dolly had frozen in the act of spooning buttered parsnips onto a serving dish as she strained to overhear.

Before either of us could speak again, a tinny female voice cut through the air.

'Let me say hello to them.'

Charlie had put his phone on speaker and was advancing towards us. 'Elle wants to meet you.' He twisted his phone and zoomed in on our faces like a crazed cameraman on a reality show. 'Say *hi*!'

'Chuck, for God's sake!' I tried to dodge the face onscreen, but it was too late. 'Hi, Elle!' I cocked my head in what I hoped was a friendly fashion. She looked lovely, her blue eyes peering out of the camera; blonde-haired, freckled (*so* many freckles) and smiley. 'Commiserations on dating my cousin.'

She giggled. 'I've heard a lot about you,' she said as Charlie moved the phone so that Ryan appeared next to me in the corner of the screen, his dark head close to mine. 'All good, I promise.'

'That's a relief,' I said. 'He's missing you a lot, been crying into his pillow.'

'Shut up, Nina,' Charlie said, adding to Elle, 'And this is Monsieur Sadler, bestselling author, ex-skateboard pro and—'

'I know, I've met him already,' she said, laughing. 'Hi, Ryan.'

Ryan raised his palm. 'Hi, Elle.'

'I hope you're feeling better,' she said, her voice warm with sympathy. I wondered for a moment whether he'd been ill then remembered that, like me, he'd called off his wedding earlier in the year, and (unlike me) hadn't seen his children since.

He lowered his eyes to the table, masking his expression. 'I'm good, thanks.'

Charlie drifted the phone across to where Dolly was doling more vegetables into a bowl and Frank was pouring sauce from a pan into a jug. Dolly blew a kiss and called, 'See you soon, sweetheart, we miss you,' before Charlie rotated the screen back to his face.

'Your cousin's gorgeous,' we all heard Elle say warmly. 'She and Ryan look really good together.'

Charlie jabbed at the phone with an exaggerated wince and turned away, telling Elle he had to go and would speak to her later. 'Sorry about that,' he said, dropping onto the chair opposite me, not sounding sorry at all, as I blushed scarlet. 'Now, where's the grub, I'm starving.'

Chapter Ten

The awkward beat of silence that followed Elle's comment was broken by Dolly and Frank, bringing over the food and pouring wine, and by the time we'd loaded our plates the atmosphere had relaxed, partly due to Dolly and Frank and their involuntary salsa shimmies, as the music continued to play.

'We're training for a competition in February,' Frank explained, once they were seated and were helping themselves to food. 'I think we've a good chance of winning.'

I smiled. 'You must be really good.'

'It's great exercise.' Dolly made it sound as though she sat around all day with her feet up. 'Releases lots of endorphins.'

'I've always wanted to go swimming with them.' We groaned at Charlie's joke – apart from Frank, who chuckled appreciatively.

'Were you really a skateboard pro?' I asked Ryan.

'Yes, he was,' said Charlie, before Ryan could open his mouth. 'He got hooked after playing Tony Hawk's… on PlayStation,' he elaborated, seeing my blank expression. 'I was rubbish, but Ryan was really good. He got to championship level and won a couple of trophies.'

I turned to look at Ryan, who'd been about to put a roast potato into his mouth. 'I was UK good,' he said modestly, lowering his fork. 'Not like world championships or anything.'

'Still sounds impressive to me.'

'He could crouch down on the board and do all sorts of flippy things,' said Dolly, pouring port and cherry sauce over her duck breast. 'I remember him practising outside our house because the pavement was on an incline, and loads of girls lining up to watch.'

'It definitely made him a girl-magnet,' agreed Charlie.

'He was fifteen, but already handsome.' Dolly's smile was nostalgic. 'When I saw him going by on his hands, legs in the air, I swear one of the girls nearly fainted.'

'One *did* faint, when I tried the same move and fell badly, remember?' Charlie pulled a face. 'You thought I'd broken my neck.'

'Oh, that was awful.' Dolly shuddered. 'I'd called 999 before I realised you were faking it.'

'I wasn't faking it!'

'You were milking it,' said Ryan, and I turned to see a smile curving his mouth. 'You wanted that girl, the one with plaits, to give you the kiss of life.'

'That's rubbish,' Charlie protested, but his ears had turned red.

'I remember you telling me about that,' I said. 'You made it sound as though you'd been at death's door.'

Ryan laughed. 'Sounds about right.'

'Did she give you the kiss of life?' asked Frank, a napkin tucked into the neck of his shirt like a cravat. 'Or was she the one who fainted?'

'She probably fainted afterwards,' said Ryan. 'He'd just eaten a packet of pickled onion flavoured Monster Munch.'

'Gross,' I said.

Charlie joined in the laughter and the conversation flowed easily after that – mostly reminiscing about the past. He had an easy rapport with Ryan that came from being childhood mates and there was no shortage of stories.

'Remember when you went through that phase of wearing a trench coat and a fedora, because you wanted to be a film-noir detective, but you looked like Inspector Gadget?' Charlie chortled at the memory, and Ryan reminded Charlie that he used to sometimes mispronounce words, like trickle treat instead of trick-or-treat, and once said his mum's favourite drink was Peanut Grigio.

Dolly dissolved into laughter. 'He used to think it was Lost Angeles,' she said. 'Which actually kind of makes sense.'

'And doggy dog world, instead of dog-eat-dog.' Ryan was laughing too, covering his mouth with the back of his hand. 'He'd said it to… surprise, surprise… impress a girl.'

'I tried to make out she'd misheard me,' Charlie said sheepishly.

'I used to say expresso instead of espresso until I was about twenty,' I admitted. 'Not that I went around saying it a lot.'

'There wasn't much espresso drinking on the farm,' said Dolly to Frank. He seemed to be enjoying the back and forth, though I noticed his eyes never strayed far from Dolly.

'It must have been fun growing up on a farm.' Ryan slid me a sideways look, just as I was thrusting a broccoli spear into my mouth.

'Mmmhmm,' I managed, adding once I'd swallowed it almost whole, 'It had its moments, I suppose. Lots of fresh air, animals, chores. OK, the chores weren't always fun, especially in winter, and we didn't have holidays because of… well, farming, and there was a lot of poo, but we didn't know anything else when we were little.'

'I loved staying there,' said Charlie. 'Those were my holidays.'

'Me too.' Dolly nodded. 'I'd never imagined my big sister becoming a farmer's wife – she was a bit of a glamour puss, liked her manicures – but she turned out to be a natural.'

'The farm has been in my dad's family for generations,' I said, in case Ryan wasn't just pretending to look interested. 'But the farming gene seemed to skip me and I wanted to go to university.'

'Where did you go?'

'Southampton,' I said. 'I thought that's where real life was happening.'

'Was it?' He was frowning a little, as though trying to picture me there. Either that, or he'd got indigestion.

'Well, there were definitely more people than animals.' I recalled the shock and exhilaration of 'being away from home', anonymous in a city that didn't smell of manure, but of something earthy and vital – with a hint of pizza and exhaust fumes in the part where The Old Pub was. 'I didn't really miss the farm,' I confessed, thinking fondly of the flat I'd shared with Anna, where the cat downstairs used to lie in wait and scratch our ankles. 'I suppose there was too much going on to think of home.'

Ryan looked like he wanted to know more. 'I guess we take things for granted when we're children.'

'Ryan had a textbook childhood,' Charlie said easily. I knew he didn't resent it; that he'd been treated like part of their family growing up. I suddenly remembered him telling me once that his best friend's dad was much nicer than his own – not because Charlie's dad had been horrible, he just hadn't been around much when Charlie was growing up.

'Mum could be a bit bossy, being a teacher,' Ryan said, helping himself to a heap of parsnips. 'I didn't always appreciate that, and Dad wanted me to be an architect like him.'

'He never rebelled though, because he was a good boy.' Charlie's tone was mischievous as he jabbed his fork at Ryan. 'The worst thing you ever did was stick your tongue out and go cross-eyed during school photos.'

'Every. Time.' Ryan sounded proud. 'That's why there aren't any school photos of me after primary school.'

'Nina once tried to keep a sheep in her bedroom,' Charlie said.

'What?' Ryan's eyes widened as he took a sip of wine.

'I got too attached,' I explained, laughing at the look on his face. 'I couldn't bear the thought of Lamby going off to market.'

He almost choked. 'Lamby?'

'Lamby, Piggy, Cowabunga,' I said. 'I wasn't very imaginative with names.'

'She turned her wardrobe into a sort of stable, with straw and everything,' said Charlie.

'I'd fed her with a bottle since she was a baby.' I felt the need to add some context. 'Her mother had died, poor thing.'

'That's pretty sad.'

'Then her dad caught Lamby roaming around on the landing one night and nearly had a heart attack.' Charlie's shoulders shook with laughter. 'Can you imagine, going for a wee in the night and seeing a sheep?'

'I got to save her though,' I pointed out, aiming a kick at him under the table. 'She didn't go off to market, did she?'

'Only because you threatened to run away,' Dolly chimed in. 'That was a lovely summer, the sun shone every day, but it wasn't too hot.'

'My great-gran Augustine lived with us too for a while, when I was little.' I glanced at Dolly, hoping she'd take the bait.

'Oh, yes, she loved it there, especially as your mum let her bake all the time.'

'My mum was no good with cakes,' said Ryan. 'She makes a good lasagne though.'

'How old was Augustine, when she got married?'

'Young, by today's standards.' Dolly pursed her lips. 'She was twenty-six, and it was 1930 – good times, by all accounts, between wars. She worked in a department store.'

'And your mum was born in…'

'Nineteen-thirty-two.' Dolly never seemed to find any topic odd or uncomfortable, and I knew she'd be happy to chatter on for hours about Augustine. 'My parents died in a car crash abroad,' she said to Ryan. 'They'd gone on holiday together for the first time in years, because my sister and I were all grown up, and some silly old man on the wrong side of the road drove right into their car.'

'That's awful, I'm so sorry,' said Ryan.

'Augustine was an absolute rock.' Dolly's voice was nostalgic. 'It must have been dreadful for her to lose her daughter, but we never saw her cry after the funeral.'

'She was amazing,' I said, tucking the date of Augustine's wedding to the back of my mind as I turned to Ryan, keen to move away from talk of funerals and the risk of Dolly getting upset. 'So, have you always been a writer?'

'Actually, yes,' he said. 'My first words were "once upon a time".'

Charlie sniggered.

'Funny,' I said. 'You should have been a comedian instead.'

'God, no.' Ryan grimaced. 'I could never put myself out there like that.'

'My grandfather was a comedian.' Frank dabbed at his chin with his napkin. 'It's where I got my funny bone from.'

'He *is* very funny,' Dolly confirmed and Charlie and I swapped smiles.

'I'm actually an accountant,' Ryan said. 'Or I was, until the book took off, and at the rate I'm going, that's what I'll be doing again in a few months' time.'

'I'm sure you won't have to, once you've decided what your story's going to be about.'

'Did he tell you he's got writer's block?' Charlie sounded surprised.

'I might have accidentally seen a document I shouldn't have.'

'Ooh!' Dolly looked thrilled.

Ryan threw her a sheepish smile. 'I actually have a case for Grace, my main character, to solve, but feel like there's something missing. And I don't see a place for the parrot in this story, but readers seem to love him.'

'You have to keep him in because he adds humour,' I said. 'Maybe he could just take a back seat this time.' I rested my elbows on the table. 'What you need is an adversary for Grace. Someone who's her opposite.' I was warming to my theme. 'Maybe another detective, who keeps getting in the way. A new partner, perhaps.'

A series of expressions passed over his face, and I couldn't tell whether he was giving it some thought, or wondering who I thought I was, telling him what to write.

'Maybe,' he said at last, turning his head to get a clearer view of me – probably not advisable in my current, pink-faced state. 'An adversary.' He nodded, his gaze becoming distant, as if a scene was playing out in his head. 'I actually hadn't thought of that.'

'Nina's very creative when she puts her mind to it,' said Dolly, as though I was seven years old.

'First I've heard of it,' murmured Charlie and I kicked him under the table again.

'Ow!'

'Just remember to credit me in the acknowledgements,' I said to Ryan.

'Remember your first book signing, when our old English teacher came, and said she was surprised you hadn't acknowledged her because she was the one who spotted your talent?' said Charlie.

Ryan gave a rueful smile and took a sip of wine. 'Shame she never mentioned it at the time.'

'Does your book have a title yet?' I quite fancied brainstorming ideas, and was almost disappointed when he nodded.

'*The Rising Dawn.*' He lifted an eyebrow. 'The publisher decided on a time of day theme, after *The Midnight Hour.*'

Charlie grinned. 'Well, you've plenty of scope with twenty-four hours in the day.'

'How about *A Late Lunch Break* for book three?' I said, gratified when everyone laughed – Frank a little too heartily.

'*A Minute Past Noon* for book four,' Charlie offered, and Frank almost choked into his napkin.

'So, what do you do for a living?' Ryan asked me, once Dolly had suggested *An Afternoon Nap* and the hilarity had settled.

'She breeds unicorns,' said Charlie, still in a silly mood.

'That would actually be an amazing job.' I thought of my travel-blog plan, and was wondering how to describe it in a way that sounded interesting, when I heard a ringing phone.

'Can't Elle leave you alone?' I joked to Charlie, but he shook his head.

'Not mine.' He was looking at Ryan. 'Must be you.'

'Sorry,' he murmured. He leaned forward and tugged his mobile from the back pocket of his jeans. 'It might be my agent,' he said. 'She warned she might call to see how I'm getting on.'

'You'd better take it.' Dolly passed an excited smile around the table. 'How exciting to have an *agent.*'

'Probably calling to massage his writer's ego,' Charlie said. 'Apparently, last time, she told him to stop whining like a brat and write like a mofo.'

I melted into giggles, then stopped when I realised Ryan wasn't answering his phone, but was staring at the screen with a look on his face poised somewhere between sorrow and irritation.

'What is it?' I asked, at the same time as Charlie spoke.

'I thought you were going to block her number.'

I fell silent, realising he was talking about Ryan's ex.

'It might be about the children,' he said, just as the call cut out, and I caught the name *Nicole* on the screen, and an image of a woman with tumbling, sun-kissed hair, cuddling a pair of young children with the same grey eyes and dimpled smile as hers.

'What are their names?' I said as Ryan stuffed the phone back in his pocket, even though I already knew from my eavesdropping session at the apartment.

For a moment, I thought he wasn't going to answer. 'Jackson and Lulu.' His voice was terse and he didn't look at me.

'How old are they?'

'Three and eighteen months.'

'They look really cute.'

'They are.' His words stuck to the silence that had fallen. The music had stopped, and Frank's hands were suspended over his dinner plate, as if to continue eating would be disrespectful.

After a moment's hesitation, Ryan pushed back his chair and got to his feet. 'Thanks for a lovely meal, Dolly, but I think I'll head off now,' he said, with what sounded like forced brightness.

Disappointment sliced over Dolly's face. 'But you haven't had dessert.'

'I need a bit of fresh air.' He softened the words with a smile that didn't quite reach his eyes, and I wondered whether he was planning to call Nicole in private. 'Charlie can have my share.'

'Don't worry, mate, I will.' Charlie stood and slapped his friend on the back and after the door had closed behind him, sat back down, biting his bottom lip.

I looked at my plate, questions swirling in my head, unsure what I had done wrong, and jumped when Dolly clattered her cutlery down. 'Frank, let's give them a demonstration,' she said, holding out a hand.

'Now?' He threw her a tender smile. 'Shouldn't we at least finish eating?'

'We can have a little break before pudding.' She leapt up and fiddled with the music player, and once the beat had resumed, waggled her fingers at him. 'Come on,' she implored. 'Let's show them how it's done.'

Frank valiantly rose with a playful twitch of his eyebrows as Dolly framed a pose, arms ready to receive him. 'You know I can't resist you.'

Charlie groaned and muttered *please, no*, but as they began twirling and foot-flicking on the honey-coloured floorboards, stepping forward and back and rotating to the beat with effortless ease, it was difficult not to be impressed and clap along. Or rather, I clapped along and tapped my feet, while Charlie watched though his fingers, a smile pulling at his mouth. Not for the first time, I admired Dolly's ability to rescue a situation – or at least create a diversion.

'Bravo!' I cheered as they executed a final twirl and dip, Dolly's head alarmingly close to the floor, Frank puffing a little too hard, and I felt the warmth of an evening spent with people wrap around me, and the cloud that had hovered over me for months, lifted.

Chapter Eleven

I was literally shaken awake the next morning from a dream about a moonwalking snowman, to see Dolly's face looming over mine. 'A customer wants a word with you,' she said without preamble.

'Wha—?' I struggled upright, rubbing sleep from my eyes, with a feeling of déjà vu as I watched her cross to the window and open the curtains. 'What time is it?'

'Just gone nine.' She turned to look at me, hands braced on her hips. She was wearing a lipstick-red jumper with parading reindeers on the front, as well as her usual work apron, trousers and chunky black trainers.

'What's with all the jumpers?'

'It's to get my customers in the mood for Christmas; they're starting to warm to them,' she said. 'I thought you'd like a lie-in after your exertions last night.'

I grinned, remembering our dance session. 'Thanks,' I said. 'It was a really lovely evening.'

She smiled. 'Come on, love, she's waiting.'

'Hang on.' I sat up straight as her words sank in. '*Who* wants to talk to me?'

'A customer.'

I frowned. 'About what?'

'I don't know, love.'

'Who is it?'

'I told you. A customer.'

'Male or female?'

'Female.'

'And you don't know who she is?'

'Of course I know, but her name won't mean anything to you.'

'Why does she want to speak to me?'

'I don't know, love.'

'Didn't you ask her?'

'I haven't got time for twenty questions, Nina.'

'I do have plans today.' I made a show of glancing at my notepad, when all I could think about were the letters in the bedside drawer. I wanted to do a bit of research on Maggie's dad and check out a few dates. 'Oh, and I'm going to Chez Phillipe for dinner this evening,' I said, remembering Charlie's recommendation. 'So I can recommend it on my blog.' The word *blog* felt clumsy in my mouth – almost like a swear word. 'Would you like to come with me? I'd love to treat you to dinner.'

'That would be lovely,' Dolly said, and patted my leg through the duvet. 'See you downstairs.'

I hurriedly pulled on my jeans, a fresh jumper and my boots. Sticking my head out of the bedroom door, the only signs of life I could detect were from the café below, where the clash of crockery competed with the hiss of the coffee machine and muted voices.

Perhaps Ryan was still sleeping. He'd been in bed when Charlie and I returned the night before, and we'd crept around with theatrical care so as not to wake him, shushing each other in exaggerated whispers while I helped Charlie make up his sofa bed.

As I headed to the bathroom, I wondered whether Ryan had called Nicole back and spoken to his children. They must be missing him, and it wasn't their fault he no longer wanted to be with their mother.

Brushing my teeth, it hit me that I might actually like him if he didn't have so much baggage. He was Charlie's best friend, so couldn't be all bad, and there was no denying he was attractive.

I paused, lips foaming with toothpaste.

Where had that come from? Ryan wasn't my type – at least, he was the total opposite to clean-shaven Scott, with his swept-back blond hair and piercing blue eyes. *As useless as a concrete parachute*, Dad had joked after meeting him, when Scott had managed to work in a quote from Henri Matisse – *Derive happiness in oneself from a good day's work* – but Dad measured most people on how useful he thought they'd be around the farm.

Admittedly, Scott had looked out of place, clambering from his shiny Maserati in a suit, still bronzed from our recent trip to Florence, where he'd focused on showing me the contemporary art scene, and I'd tried not to yawn too much, but I'd liked that he was so different to the boyfriends I'd had before. (I was certain to this day that Matt Devlin in Year Six had only asked me out to get a go on Dad's tractor.) Obviously, I knew there was more to attraction than appearances, but someone with Ryan's complicated personal life could never be a contender.

I banished an unexpected image of him, atop a bale of hay with an armful of lambs, and another of him shirtless with a scythe, *à la* the actor from *Poldark*.

I glanced at myself in the mirror. I looked flushed, dazed and wide-eyed and thought about slapping myself. Instead, I spat and rinsed, combed my hair with my fingers and headed downstairs.

*

As I entered the café, I nodded hello to Stefan behind the counter, attempting to keep a straight face when I spied his hand-knitted sweater, which had two woolly sprigs of mistletoe stitched to the front, on either side of his chest. From a distance, they looked like nipple tassels. 'Nice,' I managed, indicating the jumper, and his shy grin melted my heart.

'I couldn't bear to tell him,' Dolly murmured, coming over with a tray of empty mugs, which she deposited on the counter. 'Now, come and talk to Jacqueline.'

Jacqueline? The name sounded familiar for some reason. As Dolly led me to a corner table, I recognised the woman I'd followed into the café the day I arrived, sitting with her daughter, Holly.

'Here she is!' Dolly announced, as if introducing a mid-grade celebrity. 'This is my niece, Nina Bailey.'

Charlie, who appeared to be having a violin lesson from an elderly man with mad-scientist hair, looked over and grinned and I gave him a wave.

'Hi, Nina.' The woman rose with a friendly smile. She wasn't much older than me, with a wavy, highlighted bob that suited her face, and tiny Christmas baubles as earrings. 'Nice to meet you.'

Holly was finishing a cup of milky hot chocolate and had a foamy moustache. 'I like cats,' she announced, looking up at me with serious brown eyes. 'But that one scratchted me.' She pointed an accusing finger at Madame Bisset, sitting at the next table with a ball of purring fur on her spacious lap.

'Scratched,' her mother corrected. 'And you did pull its tail,' she pointed out, sweeping a strand of hair behind her ear. It was thick and shiny, like my hair was before I butchered it.

'And we couldn't find a scratch, could we?' Dolly said kindly. 'I think Delphine was just telling you that she wanted to be left alone.'

Holly propped her elbow on the table and rested her head on her palm. 'I want cake.' She seemed keen to switch topics now she'd been caught out.

'You've just had a croissant.' Jacqueline indicated the crumb-scattered plate in front of her daughter. 'You won't have any room for lunch if you eat some cake,' she added in an easy, maternal way.

Holly stuck out her bottom lip and swivelled to face the window, arms tightly folded across her chest. Her dark hair was a mass of curls I imagined were a nightmare to get a comb through. 'I don't want to talk,' she said. 'I want to see Grampsy.'

As we traded smiles – Jacqueline's apologetic, Dolly's sentimental, mine knowing (Dolly was *definitely* imagining her first grandchild) – I wondered whether I was going to be asked to look after Holly while her mother went Christmas shopping, or had her hair made even thicker and shinier. I hoped not. I had nothing against children (or thick, shiny hair) and hoped to have both myself one day but – right now – childcare in particular wasn't on my agenda.

The thought brought me back to Ryan, and for a split second, I thought I saw him through the window, wearing his big coat, but when I looked closer, all I could see were people streaming past with drinks in cardboard cups, breath clouding the air. The snow was melting, dripping off guttering and turning to slush underfoot, but no one seemed to mind.

'... what you did at the cottage.'

I realised Jacqueline was speaking and quickly tuned back in. 'Sorry?'

'I was saying, I've seen what you did at Grandpa's cottage yesterday.'

'Grandpa?'

'Jacqueline is Gérard's granddaughter,' Dolly explained, her *keep-up* tone softened by a smile. 'She and Holly are over from Scotland for a Christmas visit, staying in a guest house in the village.'

Things started slotting into place. Jacqueline, spoken in a French accent, meant I'd assumed Gérard's granddaughter was local, but she must have grown up in Scotland with his son – her voice had a faint, Highland lilt – and the *petite fille* he'd referred to was Holly, his great-granddaughter.

'He let you go through my grandmother's things.'

Jacqueline's words made my heart seize. 'I'm so sorry,' I said, growing hot. 'I know I shouldn't have done it, I got carried away, but I... he didn't seem to mind.' I threw Dolly a pleading look – not sure what I expected her to say – but her face was impassive. 'If I'd known... or he'd mentioned you were here,' I turned back to Jacqueline, 'I would never have interfered, I—'

'Oh no, don't get me wrong.' Jacqueline seemed bemused by my guilty bluster. 'I wanted to thank you,' she said, a smile creasing her eyes, which were a bright, sparkly blue – like Gérard's. 'We've wanted him to sort out that room for ages, but he just seemed stuck, as if he didn't know where to begin. He would get cross and tell me off if I tried to help.'

'So, you... you don't mind?'

'*Mind?*' Her enviable hair swayed around her jaw as she shook her head. 'I can't tell you how grateful I am.' She drew me into an unexpected hug. 'You did an amazing job, Nina.'

'Oh.' I awkwardly patted her cashmere-clad back and wondered what perfume she was wearing. It made me think of the old-fashioned strawberry bonbons Gran had had a weakness for and my throat tightened. 'Well... thank you,' I mumbled as Jacqueline let me go and sat back down, wondering whether I should mention taking the letters.

Holly turned, her eyebrows gathering. 'You did a tidy for Hamish.'

'Did I?'

'He's taken up residence in *Grand-mère*'s favourite chair, now it's been stripped of clutter,' said Jacqueline, picking up her cup of coffee with neatly manicured hands. 'Honestly, Nina, it's going to make a massive difference to us this Christmas.' Her smile grew. 'Dad's even agreed to come over for a visit, and he hasn't been for a while, and my husband's flying out to join us on Christmas Eve.'

'Wow, that's… it's amazing, I'm so pleased,' I said, deciding not to mention the letters for now. 'Thank you for being nice about it.'

Even before she added, 'You could get paid for doing that sort of thing,' the thought had planted like a pip in my head that I wouldn't mind hearing such positive feedback on a regular basis. How lovely to do something for people that made them feel better – and something so simple too. Simple for me, at least. Clearly not for Gérard, or for a lot of people once their possessions took over, or had hung around so long they no longer made sense or gave comfort.

'It's just tidying up,' I said, pretending not to hear Dolly's dramatic tutting.

'Margot's asked if you'd do her,' she said.

'Pardon?'

'Our resident writer.' Dolly said it as though I should know who Margot was. 'She finally sold her romantic space-fantasy series a few months ago and has bought the house two doors down from Gérard's.'

'He told her you'd helped him out,' Jacqueline elaborated, leaning to help Holly into a cute tartan coat. 'She's moved in this week.'

'The place is a mess and she asked if you'd pop round and organise a couple of rooms.' Dolly looked incredibly pleased with herself.

'I highly recommended you,' Jacqueline added.

Clearly the Chamillon grapevine was even busier than the one back home. 'That's very kind of you, but—'

'She'll pay you,' Dolly cut in. 'She won't be expecting you to do it for nothing.'

'Oh, I… no, that wouldn't be right.'

'She's recently reunited with her son.' Jacqueline seemed as determined as Dolly to persuade me. 'He's lived in America with his dad for years, but he's coming over tomorrow and she'd like to get the place in shape before then.'

'Tomorrow?'

Dolly gripped my arm. 'She really needs you, love. She's having a book launch here tomorrow evening, so won't have time for much else.'

'*Needs* me?' I looked at Jacqueline, but she was absorbed in persuading Holly to put on her hat because it was cold outside. 'I'm sure her son won't care what her house looks like if he hasn't seen her for years.'

'No, but Margot cares.'

I narrowed my eyes at Dolly. 'You've already told her I'll do it, haven't you?'

'Of course not.' She feigned a look of wide-eyed injury. 'I just said I'd mention it to you, and that you'd pop round once you'd had breakfast.'

My mouth fell open, but nothing came out.

'Margot was really impressed with Grandad's front room,' Jacqueline offered. 'I think it would make her day if you helped her out.'

I knew I was cornered, but there was a definite tingle in my fingertips at the thought of placing things in their rightful space. Or maybe Dolly's grip was cutting off my circulation. 'It sounds like I have no choice.'

Dolly's hand fell away. 'You always have a choice, Nina.'

'No, it would be my pleasure. I'll go round after I've had breakfast.'

'Great!' Dolly squeezed my shoulder – I'd be bruised all over at this rate – and another big smile lit up Jacqueline's face.

'We'd better get going,' she said, holding out her hand to Holly, who pulled her bobble hat over her eyes and stuck out her tongue. 'We're going to the guest house to pack our things and then we'll head to *Grand-père*'s and surprise him.'

'They've been staying at Marie Girard's guest house,' said Dolly. 'Elle's aunt.'

'That's nice,' I said politely.

'Grampsy!' Holly clapped her hands, then tripped over the chair leg because she couldn't see where she was going. Watching Jacqueline carry her out, I was happy that their Christmas was on track, and hoped they would help Gérard put up the decorations.

Once I'd had some coffee, and a pain au chocolat fresh from the oven, while Dolly made herself scarce (probably worried I'd change my mind), I retraced my steps to Gérard's street. It was almost a surprise to see cobbles emerging, but a couple behind me were talking about the snow that was due to fall later on. 'More than this area's ever seen,' the man said glumly. 'We might as well have stayed in England.'

'You don't get a view like this where we live,' argued his female companion, and I had to admit the village was even prettier than I remembered, the colours more vivid against the backdrop of snow still coating the rooftops and clinging to the masts in the harbour.

I took a couple of pictures, taking care to frame them properly, wondering whether to book a boat ride around the island and write up the experience on my blog, but almost immediately spotted a tourist board declaring all trips were cancelled due to the weather. I felt a small ping of relief, seeing the ocean heaving in the distance. Dry land attractions were preferable at this time of year.

I carried on walking until I reached Margot's house, which was easy to spot as the blue front door was standing open, and a pair of burly removal men were heaving an ornate wardrobe inside.

'Hello?' I stepped into the hallway, where taped-up boxes were lined against the wall. The removal men – actually, now I was closer, I realised the burlier one was a woman – were halfway up the stairs, and I recognised a couple of swear words among the huffing and puffing. 'Margot?'

'Ah, you are Dolly's *nièce préférée*!' said a husky voice, and I turned to see the woman who'd rejected Stefan's Christmas jumper at the café the day before, wafting from a room at the end of the hall, absently trailing her fingers along the wall. She had pale smooth skin and high cheekbones, hinting at good genes, and wore a dreamy expression, as though her thoughts were more thrilling than anything in front of her.

'I'm her only niece,' I said with a smile, wondering whether Dolly would ever ditch that old joke about me being her favourite. 'And you must be Margot.'

'*Oui, oui.*' She nodded vaguely, then her perfectly round, brown eyes focused properly on me. She took my elbow and spun me to face the open door, as if she needed to see me in broad daylight. I tried to make my features more appealing, crinkling my eyes and lifting the corners of my mouth as she scanned my face.

'I 'ave never written about a woman who looks like you.'

'I'm not typical leading lady material,' I said. 'More faithful sidekick.' I tried to think of the appropriate French word, but she seemed to understand.

'Often, *le copain* is more interesting.' Her smile was whimsical. 'They like to kick down ze doors.'

'That's true.' I performed a karate-chopping motion with my hands and pulled a fierce face that made her laugh warmly. 'Congratulations on your new books,' I said, not quite remembering what genre Dolly had said they were.

'*Merci.*' Margot dipped her head in a gracious acknowledgement, her piled-up, dyed-blonde hair sparkling with accessories. 'I 'ave been talking to your friend about *le métier*,' she said, with a flutter of elegant fingers as footsteps pounded along the landing above. 'The craft of writing.'

I'd barely processed her words when the furniture handlers thundered downstairs and shot past, with a nod in Margot's direction, followed by another set of footsteps. They stopped abruptly as the owner clocked my presence, and I didn't need to look to know who it was. 'Hi, Nina.'

I turned to see Ryan, holding a painting almost as tall as he was, and for the third time in twenty-four hours said, 'What are *you* doing here?'

Chapter Twelve

'That's starting to sound like a catchphrase.' Ryan descended the last few stairs with the painting in front of him, so only his face and fingers were visible around the frame.

'A pretty rubbish one.' I avoided his gaze, cheeks prickling with heat. 'Not very catchy.'

'And it only seems to apply to me.' It was hard to discern his frame of mind from his tone. 'Dolly volunteered me to help move some furniture for Margot.'

'That was nice of her.' Our eyes collided. In the light from outside, his were a clear sea-green. 'She volunteered me to help make the place look nice.'

'She's obviously in a volunteering mood.'

'Obviously.' I fixed my gaze on the painting, where a chisel-jawed man, and a woman with waist-length hair, were holding each other in a gravity-defying clinch on board a spaceship. 'Nice picture.'

'It is the cover of my novel, *Tempêtes de Pluto*,' said Margot, casting it a passionate glance, as though it was a lover. 'Storms of Pluto,' she translated, though I'd roughly guessed the title. 'Do you not think he has a look of Zac Efron?'

I caught Ryan's startled gaze and swallowed a giggle. 'The American actor?'

'Of *course*.' Margot feigned a swoon, pressing a hand to her chest, where a silver heart necklace nestled in her floaty scarf. 'I find him *so* handsome.'

'I suppose he looks a *bit* like him.' I half-closed my eyes, trying to see the figure through her eyes, but her imagination was clearly more vivid than mine.

'I hope he will play Luc in the film.'

'There's going to be a film?'

'My agent is very hopeful.'

'Well, that's great,' I said.

'She's been giving me some writing tips.' Ryan's voice had lightened. 'I need to develop a more disciplined routine.'

'*Très important.*' Margot wagged a finger, a smile on her pink-glossed lips. 'Every morning, I go to the Café Belle Vie, and I will not leave until I have written two thousand words.'

'Sounds like a plan,' I said to Ryan.

'I'll definitely give it a try.' He sounded sincere – even though he'd written a bestselling book and probably didn't need tips. 'Where shall I put this, Margot?'

'Oh…' Margot looked at the painting, then peered at the door behind him. 'I think, in the dining room, *s'il vous plaît.*' As he lifted the picture and turned, his eyes briefly meeting mine, Margot glanced at a bracelet-like watch on her wrist.

'Now, I must go.' She wrapped herself in her mustard-coloured, ankle-brushing coat, and swept her laptop bag off the nearest packing box. 'I am excited to see what you do,' she said to me, eyes straying to the street outside, where the delivery van was revving away. 'It will be a wonderful surprise for when I return.'

'Wait.' I watched her glide to the doorway, the heels of her brown leather boots barely making a sound on the floorboards. 'You're leaving?'

Pausing, she looked at me over her shoulder. 'You do not need me to watch you.'

'But I don't know what you want where.' I'd confused her, judging by the frown that crossed her forehead. 'I'll need guidance.' I mimed opening boxes, moving furniture and hanging imaginary pictures. 'You tell me what you like.'

'*Non, non.*' A vague shake of the head. 'You do like you did for Gérard.' She nodded encouragement, eyebrows raised. 'Everything here is what I want to keep, but I am not knowing where to make it go.' She smiled. 'You decide and make me a nice surprise.'

'Well, if you're sure?' I preferred to work without interference, so didn't bother mounting an argument.

'I trust you,' she said. '*Aidez-vous à des rafraîchissements.* Coffee, tea.' She nodded at the door she'd come through earlier, which must be the kitchen. '*Je reviendrai dans deux heures.*'

Back in a couple of hours.

After she'd gone, I closed the door, shivering in spite of my coat. The cold had crept in from outside and the radiator on the wall didn't seem to be throwing out much warmth – unlike Gérard's house, which had been boiling. Hugging myself, I entered the front room, which was bright with light from the street, and in a tidier state than Gérard's had been – perhaps because Margot hadn't been living here long, and must have had a clear-out before the move.

All the furniture was clumped in the centre of the room, the rest of it cluttered with partially unpacked boxes, but as I looked around, I could easily see how things needed to be arranged to make the most of the space.

I wondered what Ryan was doing and jumped when he appeared in the doorway, blowing on his hands as if to warm them up. 'I don't think the heating's working.' He glanced about, not looking directly at me. 'I might go and have a fiddle with the boiler.'

'Fiddle away,' I said, matching his businesslike tone. The weight of last night's phone call from home sat between us, but I was reluctant to bring it up. What could I even say? *Sorry you have a family you don't want to talk to?* Hardly appropriate. And both he and Charlie had made it clear he didn't want to talk about his children. 'What else do you have to do?'

'Help you move any furniture you can't manage yourself.' He buried his hands in the pockets of his jeans; a different pair, in midnight blue, worn with a dark, hooded top. 'I'm at your disposal,' he said.

'Thanks, but I'm capable of moving furniture around on my own.'

'That's what I thought.' He leaned against the frame, eyes sweeping over me. I was half-expecting a joke about koalas, but all he said was, 'In that case, I'll just check out the boiler and get back to the café.'

'You're not staying?'

'Well, I do have a book to write.' His tone was dry. 'And you've just told me you don't need my help.'

'No offence,' I said. 'It's just that I'm stronger than I look.'

'I didn't say you weren't.'

'By saying you're at my disposal, you're implying I don't look strong enough to move a bit of furniture about.'

'If you're saying you *are* strong enough, I believe you.'

'Good, because I am.' *I wasn't.* I had very little upper-body strength, and while I could certainly shift the odd piece, I couldn't manage a wardrobe. Hopefully, I wouldn't have to. 'Appearances can be deceptive.'

'That's definitely true.' Ryan's mouth lifted in amusement. 'For instance, you turned out not to be a real koala.'

I'd known it was only a matter of time before he brought that up, and when I didn't grasp his olive branch, he lowered his gaze and turned away.

'I'll be with the boiler if you want me.'

The next hour and a half flew by as I became engrossed in reorganising Margot's living room, making sure there was plenty of space to move around between the sofa, armchair and coffee table. I positioned a small oak desk underneath the window, which looked out at the garden, so that Margot could be inspired to write here, as well as at the café.

After arranging a group of photos of her with various family members and friends, I moved a collection of glass paperweights to an alcove, making sure they were set well back from the window. I'd seen a news report recently about a house fire caused by a paperweight concentrating the sun's rays onto a pile of books and setting them alight.

Once I'd hung the silky, grey curtains and found a hammer in a drawer in the tidy kitchen and hung up a few pictures, all abstracts in primary colours, I stood back to admire the effect – no love letters lying around this time – and screamed at a sound behind me.

'You really are incredibly jumpy,' said Ryan as I spun to face him.

'I thought you'd gone.'

'The boiler took longer than I thought to fix, and then I made some coffee and started making notes for my next chapter.' He waggled the battered-looking notepad in his hand. 'I was going to make you a drink, but you looked like you didn't want to be disturbed.'

'I forgot the time,' I said, heart palpitating wildly.

He rubbed at his hair. 'Me too.'

'It does feel warmer in here.' I pushed the sleeves of my jumper up. 'Margot will be pleased.'

'She'll be pleased with this room.' He looked past me, eyes widening with approval. 'You've done a great job.'

He sounded more relaxed; the writing must be going well. 'Thanks,' I said, trying to sound cool, but secretly pleased. 'It's just a bit of rearranging, really.'

'You've obviously got a knack for it.' He gave a quick smile. 'My house is a mess. Untidy, not dirty,' he amended, as if keen to make the distinction. 'I think you stop seeing it when it's your own place.'

'That's true,' I said, to be polite. I only stopped 'seeing' a room when things were where they belonged. I tweaked the edge of the curtain, feeling I ought to say more. 'Where do you live?'

'In Marlow, not far from where I grew up. By the river.'

'Nice.' *Expensive.*

'I bought it after my book sold to America.' He tucked his notepad under his arm and leaned against the doorframe. 'I was in London for a few years, earning pretty good money as an accountant, but I missed the countryside.'

'I liked living in Southampton,' I said. 'I had a bit *too* much countryside growing up.' I wondered whether Nicole and the children lived in his river house, but wasn't brave enough to ask. He'd probably either clam up or storm out – or both – and I'd end up in Charlie's bad books. 'I think I've got the city out of my system now.'

'Me too.'

'Will you be going back to Marlow?' *Like, tomorrow?*

'Eventually.' His expression clouded. 'Chamillon's nice, I love it here and it's great to see Charlie and Dolly, but I know I can't hide out forever.' He sounded as though he'd quite like to. 'Once this draft is finished, I'll go.'

Again, I resisted an urge to probe him about his private life, knowing I wouldn't like it if he asked about mine. Instead, I nodded to his notepad. 'Looks like you're getting there.'

'Talking of which, I'd better get back and type it up.' He reached for his coat and put it on, jamming the notepad in one of the pockets. 'I'll leave you to it.'

I followed him into the hall and he gave me a wry look as he opened the front door. 'Checking I'm really leaving this time?'

I opened my mouth to utter something witty and yelped with fright instead, leaping back as a ginger blur shot past and up the stairs.

Chapter Thirteen

'What the hellfire was that?' Ryan spun round, tracking the streak of fur.

'I think it was a cat.'

He headed after it. 'Where did it come from?'

'I've no idea,' I said, hot on his heels, heart pounding. 'Maybe it belongs to Margot.'

'She didn't mention having a cat.'

Ryan slowed and half-crouched, advancing crab-like along the landing. He looked like Sherlock Holmes, hunting for clues. 'Ah, it's Delphine,' he said, a smile in his voice as though spotting a long-lost friend. 'Madame's Bisset's Persian, from the café.'

'Be careful,' I warned, mindful of Holly saying she'd been 'scratchted' by the cat. 'I don't think she's very frien—' The words died on my lips as Delphine launched herself into Ryan's arms and rubbed her furry head against his cheek, purring like an engine. 'Wow, she really likes you.'

'Apparently, I look a bit like Madame Bisset's late husband when he was younger.' Ryan hoisted the cat in the air, grinning as though he'd won a trophy, while Delphine looked deep into his eyes.

'Suits you,' I said as she draped herself over his shoulder. 'My great-gran had a stole like that, only it was a fox fur.'

'She's such a big softy.' Ryan sounded so soppy, I couldn't help a little smile.

I drew closer but stopped short of stroking the cat's head. She looked like she wanted to sink her claws into my face. 'She obviously prefers men.'

'Oh, I don't know.' Ryan rubbed the side of his face along Delphine's back and she closed her eyes in apparent bliss. 'She loves Madame Bisset.'

'OK, well, she hates me.'

'Hate's a strong word.' He reached up to tickle her fluffy chin.

'You know that cats would kill and eat us if they could?' I said. 'I read somewhere they'd start with your face if you died on your own in a room with one.'

'That can't be true,' said Ryan, but he hadn't seen the look Delphine was tossing my way when she thought he wasn't looking. 'I had a cat that slept on my pillow next to me, and Mum swore he used to cry when I went to school.'

I rolled my eyes inwardly. 'I wonder what Delphine's doing here?'

'She must have escaped again.' Ryan tucked her inside his coat and kissed the tip of her ear. 'Where've you been, likkle Delphy?' *Really?*

She snuggled against his chest and gave me a look of triumph. 'Maybe Madame Bisset lives around here.'

'Wouldn't it be weird if all the café customers lived on the same street?'

'It would be odd,' I agreed, taking a step back as I realised I was standing far too close to them both. 'But why would Delphine run all the way from the café?'

'Poor puddy-cat, could have got run over by a bicycle.'

I was starting to feel like a gooseberry. Watching Ryan's openly affectionate cuddling, I couldn't help switching the cat for a baby in my imagination and could suddenly see him as a dad.

'I'll ask Gérard,' I said, pushing the image aside, reminding myself Ryan had actually walked out on his children. 'He might know where Madame Bisset lives.'

'Good idea.'

Still cradling Delphine, Ryan followed me out of the house to Gérard's front door. It was ajar, and I gingerly pushed it open. 'Gérard!' I called, and heard Hamish bark from behind the closed kitchen door. 'It's Nina! Dolly's niece. From the café. By the harbour. *Le Café Belle Vie.*'

'I think he knows who you are,' said Ryan, his voice teetering on laughter.

'Gérard?' I stepped inside and heard movement, then saw Gérard hurrying downstairs looking flustered, his white hair sticking up, his shirt half-untucked. 'Are you OK?' When he didn't answer, seeming stunned by our presence, I turned to Ryan. 'Is he OK?'

'I don't know.' He moved past me. 'Are you OK, Gérard?'

'*Oui, très bien.*' Gérard smoothed his hair with both hands and offered an uncertain smile. 'What 'ave you… Oh.' His eyes widened with alarm when he spotted Delphine peering out of Ryan's coat. ''Ow did…?'

'She came into Margot's house.' The frantic scrabbling and snuffling from behind the kitchen door had increased. 'Do you want to let Hamish out?'

'Hmmm?' Gérard looked oddly vague as he glanced behind me. ''E is not well,' he said and tucked his shirt back into his waistband.

I exchanged a look with Ryan, who raised his eyebrows and shrugged.

'Do you have Madame Bisset's address, so we can take Delphine home?' I said to Gérard. '*Où habite Madame Bisset?*'

His eyes scrunched. 'I think Cécile is at the café, *non?*'

Cécile. Of course, she had a first name. 'Does she live near here?'

He was backing away, and I wondered whether he was allergic to cats. 'I suppose you could take Delphine back to the café,' I said to Ryan. 'Madame Bisset must be frantic by now.'

I started at the sound of creaking stairs, and watched as a ghostly figure appeared and came towards us at surprising speed.

'Delphine!' It was Madame Bisset, a thick mass of pebble-grey hair tumbling to her shoulders, her lipstick worn away and panda smudges underneath her pouchy eyes. She was wrapped in a sheet that barely covered her bouncing, braless bosoms. '*Tu es une vilaine fille!*' she cried. '*Naughty!*'

I glanced at Ryan and could tell he was thinking the same thing. *Delphine wasn't the only one who'd been a naughty girl.*

As Madame Bisset made an attempt to grasp hold of the cat, her sheet started to slip, and Ryan hastily deposited Delphine into her outstretched arms.

Gérard watched with the air of a child caught with his hand in the biscuit tin, while Hamish continued to yelp and scrape the kitchen door.

Outside, a car door slammed and a familiar child's voice pierced the fog in my brain. 'Gérard,' I whispered urgently, remembering Jacqueline's words before she'd left the café. 'Your granddaughter is here with Holly.'

His eyebrows flew up. '*Ils viennent demain.*'

'No, not tomorrow,' I hissed. Delphine's ears twitched. 'They're here now – *maintenant* – to surprise you.' I scratched around my brain for the right words, but could only repeat '*maintenant!*' more loudly, hoping he'd get the message.

His eyes swivelled to the door. Either Delphine had mastered the art of sliding back bolts (it wouldn't surprise me) or Cécile hadn't closed it properly when she arrived for her afternoon delight. '*Maintentant?*'

Gérard's face twisted with horror. '*Mon Dieu*,' he whispered. 'I cannot tell Jacqueline. She will think I do not love Maggie any more.'

Reading the situation, Ryan shoved the door shut and locked it. 'You should probably leave,' he said to Madame Bisset, who seemed frozen to the spot, Delphine now sleeping peacefully across her chest. When she didn't answer, too caught up in murmuring soothing words to the slumbering cat, he turned to Gérard. 'Ask her to leave,' he said gently. 'Unless you're ready to explain to your granddaughter what's been going on.'

'Gérard,' I urged, and as if he'd been prodded with a stick, he sprang to life and spoke in rapid French to Madame Bisset, whose mouth dropped open in a circle of shock.

''Ere.' Without warning, she thrust Delphine into my unsuspecting arms and bolted upstairs, sheet flapping around her calves.

'She's really fit,' I said.

'Must be all the exercise,' Ryan murmured back, while Gérard paced up and down, and Delphine squirmed out of my arms and shot after her mistress.

There was a loud knock on the door and Gérard came to an abrupt halt, as if his batteries had died. '*C'est terrible.*'

I actually thought Jacqueline might be pleased for him, but realised I couldn't be sure, and that it might be better for him to break it gently, when the woman he'd been… *entertaining* hadn't just risen from his bed.

'He can't leave them out there, they'll think he's collapsed,' I said to Ryan. His brow was furrowed, eyes focused as if making a plan. In the kitchen, the barking had reached a crescendo. 'And Hamish *will* collapse if someone doesn't let him out.'

'Look, I'll keep them talking outside for a few minutes while you escort Madame Bisset out of the back door,' he said.

'What will you say?'

'That I've been talking to Gérard about his memories of the area for a future book I'm planning. Or something.'

'That's good,' I said.

Gérard nodded, though I wasn't sure how much he'd understood. 'Ryan has been talking about, er... *la lèvre*,' I said. I was pretty sure that meant *book*.

He looked startled. '*La lèvre?*'

'*Oui.*' I steered him towards the kitchen, a question rising in my mind about the letters, even though it was hardly the time. 'Gérard, what was Maggie's surname before you were married... *nom de famille?*'

'*Quoi?*' He threw me a befuddled look.

'Maggie... *Smith?*' I doubted he'd had heard of the actress with the same name.

He shook his head, frowning. 'Maggie Kendall.'

William Kendall. I filed the name away.

Gérard's smile was filled with regret. 'Maggie would tell me I am being a silly old bugger.'

'No, you're not.' I gave his arm a Dolly-style squeeze. 'You deserve a bit of...' I averted my mind from an image of him shirtless under the duvet with Madame Bisset '...happiness,' I said. '*Bonheur.*'

As he entered the kitchen, he was greeted by an ecstatic leap of wiry fur and glimpse of flapping pink tongue.

'Go on,' Ryan said to me, as there was another, more urgent knock at the front door. 'I'll try and give you a few minutes and then I'll head back to the café.'

'Thanks.' I threw him a quick smile and slipped upstairs to the main bedroom, to find Delphine washing her paws on the bed with the entitled air of a princess, while Madame Bisset pushed her hair inside a big fur hat. Not only had she dressed with miraculous speed, managing to put on tights and button her voluminous coat, she'd even refreshed her lipstick, which was ladybird red to match her scarf and gloves.

Seeing me in the doorway, she nodded to the cat. 'She is always running to the man.' Her English was so much better than my French. 'She 'as got the fancy for 'im.'

'Ryan?' I queried, though it couldn't have been anyone else.

'Like you.' Her smile was knowing as she picked up a canvas bag from the floor by the bed, and I quickly averted my gaze from the messy duvet.

'No, not me and him. We're… I barely know him.'

She pulled down her mouth, shaking her head to say she didn't understand.

'We're friends,' I lied. '*Nous sommes amis.*'

Her softly wrinkled face cleared. 'Like Gérard *et moi*. We are… 'ow you say? *Copains chambre.*' Oh God, no.

'We're really not "bedroom buddies",' I began, when I heard the clatter of claws in the hall downstairs. *Hamish.* 'Listen, we have to go.'

'He cannot see my Delphine.' Madame Bisset scooped the cat into her bag, like a pile of washing and jabbed her gloved finger at the floor. '*Le chien*, he will kill *mon minou.*'

'No animals are going be killed, I promise.' I hoped that was true as I herded her out of the room and down the stairs, willing Delphine to keep her head in the bag.

Luckily, Hamish had trotted into the living room, as if he couldn't keep out now it had been transformed. Gérard peered round the door and I gave him a thumbs up, while Madame Bisset continued through the kitchen to the back door, casting him a last, lingering look.

I accompanied her round the side of the house, keeping hold of her arm so she didn't slip on the snowy surface, and looked round the front in time to see Jacqueline and Holly disappear inside the house. I hoped that Gérard would look suitably surprised – and pleased.

Ryan, who'd pulled up the hood of his coat, spotted me and nodded and gave a thumbs up. I raised my hand in a wave, feeling as if we were in a spy movie – a silly one, featuring Austin Powers.

'Can I walk you home?' I asked Madame Bisset, once Ryan was heading in the direction of the café.

'*Non, merci.*' She checked Delphine was safely tucked away and I caught an evil glint of green from the depths of her bag and shivered. 'My daughter will collect me,' she said. 'I sent her the text message.'

When she'd managed to do that, I had no idea. 'She knows where you are?'

'She likes me to get out of the 'ouse when she is at school.'

I reeled back. 'How old is your daughter?'

'Fifty-one.' Madame Bisset patted her hat, as if checking it was still there. 'She is ze 'eadmistress.' I almost laughed, but stopped when I saw her face.

'That's nice?' Something was telling me it wasn't.

'She is an angry woman.'

'Ah.'

'She think I am under her feet too much.'

Sympathy rose. 'I'm sorry.'

'I 'ave photographs.'

By the time a small blue car had pulled up, I'd seen so many pictures of her angry-looking daughter *and* Delphine that their faces had merged into one, and it was almost a shock when the stern-faced woman at the wheel turned out not to have whiskers – though her expression was eerily similar to Delphine's. As they drove away, the daughter's mouth making angry shapes, and I headed back to Margot's, I couldn't help hoping that one day Gérard and Cecile might end up being a lot more than bedroom buddies.

Chapter Fourteen

Back at the café, I made light work of a bowl of French onion soup and some crusty bread topped with grilled Gruyère cheese.

'Was she pleased?' Dolly said, slipping into the chair opposite. 'Margot?' she added when I looked at her blankly. All the way back, I'd been focused on eating, my stomach protesting loudly at the lack of sustenance.

'She seemed to love it,' I said, recalling her face and murmurs of appreciation as she'd moved from the living room to the dining room, where I'd arranged her table and chairs, filled her white-painted dresser with the best pieces of crockery I could find, and positioned her painting beneath a mounted picture light.

'I did not know what I wanted, but this is it,' she'd finally declared, back in the living room, doing a slow spin to take it all in, a pensive smile on her face. 'I will not be lonely here.' She'd picked up a photo and stroked the glass. 'Not with Raphael.'

'Your son?' I'd asked, having spotted a likeness in their whimsical smiles, and she'd nodded, eyes brimming with tears, before trying to press a wad of euros into my hand.

'Don't let her give you any money for me,' I said to Dolly. 'I refused, and she said she would find a way.'

'It was a job, not a favour,' Dolly said sternly. 'She can afford to pay you.'

'All I did was tidy up a bit.'

'You have to stop calling it that.' She sounded quite ferocious, clearly having forgotten that's what she'd called it in the past. 'What about that woman who's made a million, getting people to throw things away?'

'Marie Kondo? That's decluttering,' I said. 'I just like…' I paused, not sure how to describe the process. 'I like bringing a room to life.' I could feel a blush coming on. 'I know that sounds ridiculous.'

'No, it doesn't.' Dolly brushed her fringe aside. 'I get it, I really do.'

'You told me off when I *tidied* your house when I stayed with you once, remember?'

'Ah, yes, I do.' Her face puckered. 'I felt a bit ashamed, if I'm honest,' she admitted. 'Charlie's dad used to call me a scruffy so-and-so, and I suppose I felt you were judging me.'

'Never,' I said, shocked. 'I should have asked.'

'It's ancient history, and if you remember, I invited some friends from work round for dinner to show it off.'

I hadn't remembered that bit and a smile stretched over my face – then dimmed when I remembered Charlie's dad had taken a fancy to one of the friends.

As if recalling it too, Dolly said briskly, 'Now, how about I show you how the coffee machine works?'

'Really?' I'd been planning to look at the letters again and think about how to source some more information about William Kendall. 'I'm not very technical.'

'It won't take long and you'll enjoy it,' Dolly insisted. 'Come on.'

'I suppose I can't say no, after that delicious lunch,' I said as Stefan moved in to clear the table. 'Where's Charlie?'

'He's on his break,' said Dolly as we made our way to the counter. 'Either talking to Elle or bothering Ryan.'

My heart gave an odd little leap at the mention of his name. 'He's here?'

'Of course.' Dolly gave me a sideways look. 'I gather you bumped into him at Margot's.'

I held her gaze. 'Don't pretend that wasn't your intention.'

'Not at all.' She'd come over all innocent again. 'I thought he'd be gone by the time you got there.'

'Oh?' I couldn't tell whether she meant it, but she'd already turned her attention to the scary-looking machine behind the counter, with its knobs and handles and scary noises.

'Say hello to Annabel,' she said.

I'd forgotten Dolly's tendency to name inanimate objects. 'Hi, Annabel!' I beamed, then stopped when I saw my distorted reflection in the shiny chrome.

Celeste, pouring frothy milk into a jug, gave me a bright smile as she made a cup of hot chocolate, which she placed on a tray with two mince pies before whisking the lot to a waiting customer.

'She makes it look simple,' I said.

'It is.' Dolly launched into a series of words, among them, 'grinding the beans properly', 'use the right coffee-to-water ratio' and 'pull the shot for the correct amount of time', but none of them made much sense. 'Annabel needs at least fifteen minutes to warm up,' she continued, while I watched Stefan carefully arrange a pile of almond croissants in the display cabinet with a pair of tongs. 'It'll give her time to heat the water and build the pressure that's needed to force water through the grounds.'

'Right.' I forced my eyes back to the machine and tried to concentrate as Dolly said things about tamping, beans and temperatures.

'Nina!'

My head jerked back. 'Sorry?'

'Did you get that?'

'Of course I did.' I sounded like I used to whenever Mum asked whether I'd done my homework. 'Go on.'

'What did I just say?'

'Don't worry if the Portaloo overflows.'

Dolly's eyes narrowed.

'Filter,' I corrected. 'Porta*filter*.'

She shook her head and picked up a cloth. 'You have to clean the steam wand before and after using it, to make sure no contaminants get into the milk.'

'Right.'

'Let the steam blow for about five seconds and then close the valve to turn it off.' She demonstrated, the whooshing sound making me jump. 'The bean release gate on the grinder has to be open while you're working to keep the process going.'

'Your job would be so much easier if everyone drank tea.'

Smiling, Dolly put down the cloth. 'It drove me mad at first, latte this, espresso that,' she admitted. 'You soon get used to it, and if a complicated coffee gives people pleasure, where's the harm, when there's so much in the world to feel bad about?'

'True.'

She picked up a cup. 'Go on then.'

'Sorry?'

She nodded at the machine. 'Make me an espresso.'

'Right now?'

She stepped aside and made a sweeping motion with her hands. 'Annabel's waiting.'

I approached, feeling as nervous as when I'd taken my driving test. 'I don't think I can.'

Celeste, back with her tray, gave a reassuring nod. 'You can do it.'

'OK,' I said, eyeing the mess of crockery on top of the machine, feeling an itch in my fingers. 'But can I do something else first?'

By the time I'd rearranged and tidied the area behind the counter, and successfully produced a drinkable cup of espresso ('Third time's a charm,' Dolly had chimed, refusing to let me give in), my temples were throbbing.

'I don't know what that was all about,' I said to Charlie when we crossed on the stairs as he returned from the world's longest break. 'Your mum made me work the coffee machine.'

He grinned. 'She's proud of Annabel. I caught her showing the postman how to use her one morning.'

'I suppose if she taught all the customers, they could make their own drinks and you could have the day off.'

'It might get a bit crowded behind the counter.'

'Fair point.'

'Ryan's busy massaging his prose.' Charlie glanced up, as though Ryan might be standing at the top of the stairs. 'He's obviously broken through his writer's block,' he added. 'I think you've inspired him.'

'Not unless he's dreamt up a particularly grisly murder.'

Charlie looked about to speak again when Dolly called his name.

'I'd better go.' He checked the time on his phone. 'We've a teatime load of elderlies coming in to admire the Christmas decorations.'

'Shame your friend Natalie's not here to write about it for the local paper.'

'She doesn't need to,' said Charlie, assuming a modest expression. 'Word of mouth and TripAdvisor do that job very nicely.'

'You must get the occasional bad review.'

'Not a single one.' Charlie tapped his phone screen and held it up. Sure enough, the Café Belle Vie had over two thousand five-star reviews.

'"Delicious pastries",' I read out. '"Good-looking staff". That can't be you.'

'It's Stefan,' he admitted. 'Everyone loves him.'

When Dolly called him again, he pretended to shrink back and chew his nails in fear, and I smiled as he bounded to the bottom of the stairs.

He turned to look up at me. 'I'm eating with Elle's Aunt Marie this evening, so won't be back until late,' he said.

'That's OK, I'm eating out tonight anyway.'

I spent ages under the shower after discovering it had different settings, opting for Misty Rain, which enveloped me in a gentle cocoon of water, and finally emerged refreshed and headache-free. Back in my room, I sat in front of the Hollywood mirror and dried my hair, tousling it with my fingers to give it some style. Pleased with how it looked, I rummaged for an outfit and settled for another of Dolly's gathered skirts with my favourite blue sweater tucked in, and pulled my furry coat over the top before heading out.

'I'll see you later at Chez Phillipe,' I said to Dolly as I passed the kitchen, where she was fiddling with the temperature dial on the dishwasher.

'That looks lovely on you.' She glanced approvingly at the skirt I was wearing. 'Where are you off to now?'

'I… er… heading to the library, actually.' I'd checked on my phone to see if it was open. 'I've a bit of work to do.'

'On your travel blog?'

I loved how she said it so encouragingly, and felt guilty for lying. 'Mmhmm,' I mumbled, hoping my face didn't give me away. On impulse, I went over and pressed a kiss to her cheek. 'I love you, Dolly.'

Her eyes shone as she squeezed my hand. 'And I love you, gorgeous girl.'

Chapter Fifteen

I made my way to the library feeling buoyed up, partly because it was impossible to stay miserable when walking through snow that was just the right depth and texture, surrounded by fairy lights strung along shop and house fronts, and also because it was exciting to have a project – even one that came with a dollop of guilt.

I told myself that, if I discovered something that cast my great-grandmother in a less than flattering light – such as if it turned out she'd had an affair with William Kendall and passed their child off as her husband's – I'd simply keep it to myself, and neither Dolly nor Mum would need to readjust their memories or rewrite history.

I breathed deeply, enjoying the scents of pine, sea and salted air, as I arrived at the library, a small, municipal-looking building opposite the beach, charmingly called Beach Library. A small fir tree had been planted in a wooden tub by the door and draped with lights, and, as I stepped inside, I was hit by the twin scents of hot chocolate and well-thumbed books – hot chocolate from a drinks dispenser in a cosy reading zone, and books from the well-stocked shelves fixed along the walls and grey carpeted floor.

I approached the desk and was directed in softly-spoken English to a computer in the study area, with instructions on how to log on, and after settling beside a pair of earnest students talking in low voices, I pulled my notepad and pen from my bag, then performed the necessary steps to access Google and typed in *William Kendall + Scottish + Navy + officer* and... *nothing*.

At least, nothing that told me he'd existed. I tried a few more sites, but everything required a lot more information than I had. I roughly knew Augustine's timeline; her dates of birth, marriage and death, as well as the year she'd had her daughter – Dolly and Mum's mum – but no way of intersecting it with William's without access to his records, which there was no way of getting. At least, not without inventing a strong interest in genealogy, which I doubted would convince anyone.

I started again, typing in just his name and *Scotland*, and this time there was a link to an obituary in a Scottish newspaper, which I clicked on and read. *William Norman Kendall aged 84 of Dundee, formerly an officer with the Royal Navy, died peacefully on 28th June 1990. He's survived by wife Margaret and daughter Maggie-Jane. Memorial contributions may be made to a charity of choice.*

I wondered whether Augustine had known – whether she'd kept track of William. She'd had his address, after all, and even if he'd moved, he couldn't have been hard to find, being in the Navy.

At least he'd had a long and happy marriage, as far as Gérard was aware, but it was frustrating, not knowing the details of his break-up with Augustine. Had William spent his marriage pining for her?

Sighing, I shut the computer down, aware the staff were making moves to close the library, and slid my unopened notepad back in my bag.

Maybe some things were best left alone.

*

Chez Phillipe was concealed down a narrow side street lit by lantern-style street lamps, spilling lemony light across the snow.

The restaurant windows were bright and inviting, and my spirits lifted as I entered through the frosted-glass door. The interior was warm, rich with the smell of food, the décor pleasantly rustic: oak beams, chunky tables and woodland-hued upholstery, illuminated by candles in brass holders. It wasn't overtly festive, if I ignored the nicely-dressed tree by the window, with a lit-up star on top – and the Christmas lights twinkling around a pair of ornate mirrors. And the napkin-holders, which were pine cones painted gold.

OK, so it was pretty Christmassy, but in a *French* way. Everything was classy and complemented everything else, and although I'd have created a bit more space between the tables and perhaps cleared the surfaces – there was barely any room for the plates – it was pretty much perfect, and busy enough to create a buzz, but not so packed that I had to wait. I was surprised that Dolly hadn't arrived yet. She prided herself on never being late, but perhaps there'd been a hold-up at the café.

A smiling waiter ushered me to a table for two, slightly tucked out of view, and I swiftly removed my coat and ordered a glass of white wine, wondering whether I should just tell Dolly about Augustine's letters. It would be so wonderful to share them with her; to see her as confounded as I was, that all this time the letters had been in a box, less than five minutes away, and stunned by the link to Gérard, who she treated like a surrogate dad. But while Dolly was normally such an accepting person, emotion ruled when it came to her grandmother (Mum was the same) and I couldn't bear the thought of even slightly tainting her memories of Augustine.

The waiter returned with a bottle of expensive-looking wine '*gratis*', courtesy of the owner Phillipe, and I guessed Dolly must have phoned ahead and ordered it.

'*Merci*.' I took a sip from the glass he'd poured, savouring the delicate flavour, which was neither too sweet nor too dry. '*Délicieux*.'

'May I recommend today's specials, *mademoiselle*?' he enquired hopefully.

'I'm waiting for someone, but thank you,' I said with a smile.

He dipped his chin. 'I will bring you an appetiser.'

'*Merci*,' I said again, wondering how he'd guessed that I was British. Maybe Dolly had briefed him.

As I waited, I discreetly rearranged everything on the table and took a few pictures on my phone. Hardly earth-shatteringly original, but I could compensate with a write-up, providing I could think of something catchy to say once my blog was up and running. As I put my phone down, I wished my blog would up and run itself. Or, just run away altogether.

The waiter was back, bearing a tiny plate. 'Salad of squid, flavoured with Serrano ham,' he explained. 'Enjoy.'

'*Merci*,' I said once more, while he placed the plate in front me as though I was royalty. 'It smells good.'

It tasted good too and I quickly demolished the lot, wondering where Dolly had got to. About to give her a ring, I almost dropped my phone when I spotted a familiar figure making his way to my table, a look on his face I interpreted as 'good-natured but wary'.

'Fancy seeing you here,' I said as Ryan draped his coat over the back of the chair opposite me and sat down, a pleasant scent of cologne drifting over – a mix of lime and mint.

'Makes a change from your usual greeting.' His grin disarmed me and I automatically grinned back, as if my face had a life of its own. There was no denying he looked attractive, clad in black jeans and a moss-green shirt that matched his eyes, and I suddenly wished I wasn't wearing a skirt that belonged to my aunt, and a jumper my gran had knitted for my birthday.

'No, but what *are* you doing here?' I looked pointedly at my watch. 'I'm supposed to be having dinner with Dolly.'

'Oh, she can't make it,' he said. 'Something about a salsa training session with Frank that she'd forgotten about.' This time, his expression read 'sorry, but you'll have to make do with me'. 'She sends her apologies.'

'And sent you in her place.'

He lifted a hand and flattened a maverick curl. 'Apparently.'

I sat back, shaking my head. 'You do know that this is part of her cunning plan?'

'It's hardly cunning, if we know what it is.'

His acknowledgement gave the words an intimacy that sent heat through my body. 'You don't have to stay,' I said, twiddling my napkin ring. 'I can get on with some work while I eat.'

His eyebrows rose. 'Work?'

I thought about saying something lofty, but the waiter was back, pouring wine for Ryan and recommending the steak, which we somehow ended up ordering, medium rare.

'So, what sort of work?' Ryan said, once we were alone again – as if we *were* on a date.

'Oh, I'm supposed to be starting a travel blog,' I heard myself say, directing the words at the table. 'I was meant to be kicking things off by coming to Chamillon, but now I don't know if it's what I want to do, but I can't admit it because I've told people now, and I've spent too long already doing things I'm not cut out for.' My shoulders slumped.

Then I added in a rush, 'Also, I found some letters while I was reorganising Gérard's living room the other day, and it turns out they're from my great-grandmother to his father-in-law, and I think they were having an affair and that Dolly's and my mum's mum might have been their love child.'

'Wow.' It was Ryan's turn to sit back, eyes swimming with curiosity. 'Now there's a plot for a book, if ever I heard one.'

'You're welcome,' I said glumly.

'What's the problem?' He shook out his napkin and laid it across his lap. 'I know Dolly was close to Augustine, she often mentions her. I'm sure she'd love to see those letters.'

'I don't know.' I looked at him properly, noting how dark his eyes were in the candlelight. 'I don't want to upset her by showing her something that might make her think badly of her gran.'

'Would you be upset, if you discovered something similar about someone you loved?'

I tried to imagine finding out Gran had cheated on my grandfather, and that Dad, or one of his brothers, was the result of an affair. 'I think I'd rather not know.'

'Well, maybe that's your answer.'

I let out a sigh. 'I tried to pin down some dates, but it didn't work out.'

'So, it's your little secret.'

'I don't like secrets.'

The waiter was back with our steaks and we ate in silence, lost in our own thoughts. And, in my case, in the perfectly cooked steak.

'This is really good,' said Ryan, catching my eye.

'The best I've eaten,' I agreed.

'I might have to write Phillipe into my book.'

'A murderous chef?'

'Or, murdered by a rival chef.'

We finally laid down our cutlery and drank some wine, and before I knew I was going to say it, I said, 'Did you speak to Lulu and Jackson after you left Dolly's the other night?'

He went very still, and I imagined Charlie dropping his head in his hands.

The waiter reappeared, looking thrilled that our plates were empty.

'I have something to make you smile,' he said, topping up our wine as if sensing a change in atmosphere.

'The steak was perfect,' I said, in case he thought we'd eaten it to be polite, and as he took our plates and headed to the kitchen, my gaze drifted back to Ryan. 'Sorry,' I said. 'I shouldn't have asked.'

'It's heart-breaking, hearing them ask for their daddy all the time.' His voice was so low I had to strain to hear over the chatter of the other diners. 'I just wish Nicole would stop being so stubborn.'

'Aren't you the one being stubborn?' It was hard to believe he was blaming her for trying to maintain contact – was that what he considered high-maintenance? 'I don't think it's unreasonable for her to want you to stay in touch,' I said. 'Whether you like it or not, they need you.'

'No.' He gave me an unflinching look. 'They need their dad, and I'm hoping Nicole will eventually realise that.'

'Wait... *what*?' Had I slipped into a parallel universe? 'That doesn't even make sense.'

'Me being around is confusing for them.' He spoke wearily, as if tired of defending himself. 'I'm trusting my instincts on this.'

We appeared to be talking at cross purposes. '*How* is it confusing?'

He stopped rubbing his fingers along the stem of his wine glass. 'I'd have thought that was obvious,' he said. 'Because I'm not their father.'

For a second, I thought I'd misheard. 'Hang on...' My brain scrambled to pull the threads together. 'You're not their father?'

My voice rose up the scale. 'You're not Lulu and Jackson's *dad*?' In my head, I added a thousand question marks. 'They're *not* your children?' It was as if by saying it several ways, I could get to the bottom of it. 'You and Nicole *don't* have two children together?'

'Wait…' He had one arm extended, as though to help me bridge a stream. 'You thought… you didn't *know*?'

'Oh my *God*.' I cupped my face in my hands. 'I thought you'd walked away from your kids,' I said. 'It really put me off you, you've *no* idea.'

'I think I do.' He looked as dumbfounded as I felt. 'I thought Charlie must have told you the full story and you were being a bit judgemental,' he said. 'I got it, because I felt terrible for leaving after I'd spent time getting to know them, but they didn't want me, at least Jackson didn't, and when I went round there one day, about a month before the wedding—'

'They don't live at your river house?'

'My…' He laughed. 'No,' he said. 'Nicole was hoping John would let her stay in theirs. She didn't like the river house.'

'John's her ex?' I felt as if I was trying to catch up with the plot of a soap.

'Yes, and I ended up having this heart-to-heart with him once, while Nicole was out training for one of her marathons, and it made me realise I didn't love Nic the way John still does, and probably never will.'

I was starting to feel giddy, as if the wine was taking effect. 'I'm so pleased,' I said. 'That you didn't walk out on your children, I mean.'

'I felt as bad as if I had,' he said. 'I'd grown to like them a lot and, like you said, none of it was their fault.'

'*Voilà!*'

I jumped as the waiter slid shallow dishes in front of us, and my eyes opened wide when they landed on our dessert. 'It is the Mont

Blanc,' he said proudly, as if showing off his first-born. 'The best thing you can eat on a cold winter's day.'

I instinctively smiled at the sight of the pastry case, filled with dark chocolate and a golden swirl of chestnut cream, sprinkled with snowy slivers of meringue. 'It looks too good to eat.'

'You must eat,' he urged. 'Phillipe will be most unhappy if you do not.'

'We don't want to upset the chef,' said Ryan. The remnants of our conversation hovered between us, and there was an unexpected twinkle in his eyes. 'We'd better do as we're told.'

I didn't need telling twice and dug my spoon in, closing my eyes in bliss as the creamy softness melted on my tongue, wondering whether Dolly could replicate the recipe for the café – or just for me.

'It's good, isn't it?'

My eyes jumped open. 'Perfection,' I said.

He smiled. 'I couldn't agree more.'

Chapter Sixteen

Fifteen minutes later, I was standing on the snow-covered beach, where the moon had lit a shimmering path of light across the sea. I'd decided to take the longer route to the café, partly to digest Ryan's bombshell – and the meal – and to take some photos as the ones I'd taken before hadn't come out well; the beautiful vista reduced to a murky black.

As if by mutual consent, we hadn't returned to the subject of Nicole or the children –we'd finished eating, declined coffee and requested the bill, which, it turned out, Dolly had paid upfront – but my mind kept circling back, groping for clues. From the start, Charlie had held back from spilling the details about Ryan's break-up and Dolly must have assumed I knew, which was why she kept trying to push us together.

I laughed softly to myself, even as I wondered what it meant – what difference it would make. *That I could like him now?*

'What was happening with you and the waiter?' I said, when Ryan caught up, heart quickening at the sight of him in his winter coat, eyes gleaming in the moonlight.

'He'd apparently read my book and had a copy he wanted me to sign.'

'Get you, Mr Famous Author.'

'He advised me to kill off the parrot, he doesn't like birds.'

I laughed and Ryan joined in, our breath mingling on the cold air. 'Everyone's a critic,' he said. 'You have to develop a thick skin.'

My teeth were starting to chatter as the cold burrowed through my coat, and he fell into step beside me as we began walking back to the café. 'I bet most people are impressed when you tell them you're a writer.'

'I still think my dad would have preferred me to become an architect, but I've compromised by making Grace's dad one in *The Midnight Hour*.'

'It's good that you're writing again.'

He hesitated, as though working out how to define 'writing'. 'I've had a few new ideas,' he said cautiously.

'Like what?'

I felt his eyes on me. 'I'm not being rude, but I don't like to talk about the story until the book's finished.'

'You're not going to kill Grace off, though?'

His tone was apologetic. 'Like I said…'

'You don't want to talk about it.'

'I know it sounds pompous, but trying to explain the story tends to kill creativity,' he said. 'For me, anyway.'

'You're right, that does sound pompous,' I joked.

'You can punch me if you like.'

'Didn't I mention, I'm stronger than I look?'

'You did,' he said. 'In that case have mercy, *mademoiselle*.'

His impression of the waiter at the restaurant made me giggle. 'So, Gérard and Madame Bisset, eh?' I decided to keep the conversation light.

He gave a low laugh, and there was a rustle of material as he dipped his hands in his coat pockets. 'I couldn't believe it when she appeared like a ghost in that sheet.'

'I was more interested in your love affair with Delphine.'

'I can't help it if I'm irresistible to felines.'

'Thanks for keeping Jacqueline chatting outside, by the way.'

'I'm not sure she was convinced by my story.' Ryan shortened his stride to match mine and I noticed the toes of our boots were covered in snow. 'Apparently, Gérard doesn't bolt his door when she's over here so she can let herself in with her key.'

'I hope he's smoothed things over with her.'

We briefly bumped elbows before pulling apart as we left the beach and crunched over the snowy cobbles past the harbour, where the boats jostled on the lapping water. The air was still and clear, everything bathed bright by the moon, and the lights on the tree in the café twinkled like a beacon.

'The travel blog you mentioned,' Ryan said, out of the blue. 'If you don't want to do it, don't.'

He made it sound so simple. 'I think I have to give it a try.'

'Why, if your heart's not in it?'

'It might be, once I get going.'

He puffed out a breath. 'I've given Grace an adversary,' he said. 'Like you suggested.'

I couldn't help a grin spreading over my freezing face. 'That's great!'

'You could say, you inspired me.'

'Like a muse.' I'd always fancied being one; had hoped I might unleash the frustrated artist in Scott, but it had never happened. 'I've got plenty more ideas.'

There was a smile in Ryan's voice. 'I'll let you know if I get stuck again.'

'Thanks for… listening to me about the letters and telling me about Jackson and Lulu.'

'I still can't believe you didn't know.'

'It's quite funny, when you think about it.'

'There was nothing funny about you looking at me as if you despised me.'

'Despised is a bit strong.' I didn't switch on the light, grateful to be inside where it was warm as I stamped the snow off my boots. 'Mild contempt, perhaps.'

'I'd have deserved it,' he said. 'If I had walked out on my children.'

It felt oddly intimate to be talking in the dark at the bottom of the stairs and I was suddenly aware of his proximity, and that we were alone in the apartment.

'I wouldn't mind a coffee,' said Ryan. 'Fancy one?'

'Upstairs?' *Idiot.* My cheeks were probably glowing like plutonium.

'Unless you want to tackle the coffee machine?'

'Definitely not.' Confused by the way my body was reacting, I practically threw myself upstairs and into the living room, where I busied myself with the tree lights, fumbling past the stack of presents for the switch. I accidentally set them to flash on and off, so it looked like there was a disco in progress by the time Ryan came in. I turned to watch him throw off his coat and ruffle his hair, and felt a tipping sensation – as if I'd landed in another life, where we were a couple returning from a night out.

'So, what's she like, this adversary of Grace's?' I said it more to fill the silence, wondering whether some music would be appropriate. I decided against it. Music unleashed emotions and, at that moment, I didn't trust mine one bit. 'OK, I get it, no more questions,' I said, when Ryan gave a reproving shake of his head, and his smile filled me with such warmth I jerked forward, intending to straighten the pile of magazines by the sofa. Instead, I sent them flying and the bowl of fruit on top spilled across the floor.

'Are you OK?' Ryan's amusement was mixed with concern as he stuck out a foot to halt a rolling satsuma. 'How much wine did you have this evening?'

'Hardly any,' I said, though maybe I'd had more than I was used to. 'I'll just…' I gestured to the mess I'd made, knowing I couldn't leave it. 'I'd better clear this up.'

He nodded and took a step back. 'I'll make some coffee,' he said, and once he was in the kitchen, I became a whirlwind, tidying the magazines into a basket by the sofa, then gathering up the satsumas and placing them back in the bowl, which I positioned on the coffee table – once I'd gathered the books there and arranged them on the shelving in the alcove beside the fireplace, careful not to dislodge the tinsel along the edge. Once I was satisfied with how they looked, I straightened the 'Merry Christmas' letters on the wall above the mantelpiece, and couldn't resist realigning the cards on top, moving a snow globe with a robin inside to sit beside a praying glass angel with a halo.

Feeling calmer as my mind emptied out, I hummed as I tweaked the pine-studded garland and nudged the nativity scene into the centre of the hearth, and it was only after I'd turned the Christmas tree lights to static – all the flashing was giving me a headache – and whisked the acrylic polar bear off the table, intending to sit him under the tree, that I became aware of Ryan, watching my movements with interest from the kitchen doorway, just as Gérard had done at the cottage, but with less shock.

'You look like you're having fun,' he observed.

'Not really,' I lied. 'I'm making the place safe, that's all.'

'That's thoughtful of you.' A smile touched his eyes. 'What were you humming?'

My face warmed up. 'What did it sound like?'

'My musical tastes aren't very current. I mostly listen to classical music.' His forehead creased. 'Something by Rihanna?'

I sighed. 'It was "Jingle Bells".'

He nodded, as if reconsidering. 'Now you mention it…'

'Don't.' I rolled my eyes. 'I know I can't carry a tune.'

'But you're exceptionally good at making a room look ten times more attractive.'

'I see the potential, that's all, I can't help it.' I looked at my efforts. 'If there are things packed away that should be on display, bringing pleasure to the owners, I like to bring them out and show them off.' His gaze was unnerving me. 'Or, just rearrange a room so it's nicer to be in, if that makes sense.'

'Perfect sense.' His smile was steady. 'It's a lovely thing to do.'

'That's how I found the letters,' I said. 'You never know what you might find.'

'And sometimes wish you hadn't.'

'I don't wish I hadn't found them,' I said. 'I just wish…' but I didn't know what I wished so I let the words trail off.

'I know,' he said gently.

As his gaze held mine, the air between us seemed to come alive, and something I couldn't put a name to flowed between us. I heard myself swallow and the sound of my heart, beating too fast in my ears. It felt as if the heating had been turned up and I needed to whip off my jumper. And my skirt.

'I've made coffee,' he said, and from the way his voice caught and the look in his eyes, I could tell he too felt whatever it was. 'I'll fetch it through.'

But, before he could move, the ringtone I'd heard during dinner with Dolly and Frank began chiming from his back pocket and reality rushed back in.

'Aren't you going to get that?'

He lowered his head. 'I'm sorry,' he said, and the room temperature seemed to dip as he got out his phone and checked the screen with obvious reluctance.

I could see him wrestle with himself, his teeth clamped over his bottom lip, and knew it was Nicole. 'You should take it,' I said, backing away as though he was holding a grenade. 'I'm tired anyway. I should go to bed.'

'Nina—'

'Goodnight, Ryan.'

I closed the door behind me and heard the ringtone cut off, but couldn't tell whether he'd answered the call or ended it. Either way, it was a reminder that Ryan had unresolved issues with Nicole, and, as I crossed the landing, I gave myself a warning.

Do not get involved.

Chapter Seventeen

I woke early the next morning from a restless sleep – probably due to all the rich food I'd eaten – and met Elle's eyes in the photo on the bedside cabinet. 'It's OK for you,' I said, throwing off the duvet. 'Your life's sorted, now you've met my cousin.' I opened the curtains, heart lifting at the sight of the pale blue sky and view across the harbour.

Climbing back into bed, I picked up my phone and saw a message from Ben.

Mum's decided the donkeys should be in the Christmas play and is 'training' them for their role.

I giggled, remembering last year's nativity play, when six-year old Chloe – the granddaughter of one of Mum's friends – was cuddling Baby Jesus and the doll's head fell off and rolled under a chair, causing stifled laughter from the audience. Taking umbrage, Chloe had snatched up the head and slapped it round the face, prompting a telling-off from her embarrassed mum, and then the 'starry-night' backdrop had fallen down.

Hasn't she learnt not to work with children or animals?

Neither donkey looks keen.

Gran had loved the yearly play, even when things went wrong, as they invariably had, and it was painful to think of her not seeing it this year.

Let me know how it goes x

If I can bear to watch x

Still smiling, I grabbed my pen and notepad off the bedside table, eyes grazing the drawer with the letters inside. I would return them to Gérard, I decided, to do whatever he wanted with them. There was no point me holding onto them now, and I didn't want to risk Dolly coming across them.

I determinedly opened my notepad at a fresh page. There was something inspiring about a blank sheet, waiting to be written on, and I felt I ought to bless it with a sonnet, or some sort of declaration. Instead, I wrote my name in capitals, as though I was ten years old, then drew a picture of a flower with giant petals. Then I doodled a horse's head, wishing the horse-whispering course, as Charlie had called it, had been a bit more successful. I'd thought I might fancy an outdoor life after working indoors for several years – as long as it wasn't farming – and that being used to animals would give me an advantage. Instead, I'd discovered I had no affinity with the equine world at all.

I absently wrote *TidyMinds* in swirly letters on my pad, and underneath it *Clutterfly – let your clutter fly*. Bit obscure. *The Fixer*. Too Olivia Pope. *ClearUp*. Too crime-sceney. *HomeHelp*. Just… no. *The House Whisperer…* I smiled. That wasn't bad.

'Wait…' I threw my pen down. Why was I thinking of 'tidying-up' names, instead of travel blog titles? Tidying up for a living wasn't part of my plan and, even if it had been, I could hardly build a career based on a couple of room rearrangements, one of them accidental. OK, so it felt good that Gérard had reacted so well, but what if he'd just acted politely because I was Dolly's niece – ditto Margot?

Then I remembered the look on their faces. *A gift*, Gérard had said. Why hadn't I been blessed with a gift for travel-blogging?

If you don't want to do it, don't… if your heart's not in it.

Ryan's words echoed in my head and, more confused than ever, I slammed the notepad shut and shuffled off the bed, tugging my dressing gown on over my pyjamas. I was desperate for a cup of tea and wondered whether he was up. I might have resolved not to get involved, but I didn't want to be confined to my room, or forced to go down to the café for refreshments.

His bedroom door was shut when I passed, and I was relieved when I entered the living room to find it empty, the bedding Charlie had used for the sofa bed neatly folded away. I hadn't even heard him come home.

I paused briefly to admire the room, which – thanks to my efforts – now looked classy and cosy, if over-the-top festive, and the tree looked pretty with its twinkling lights and glittering baubles.

I made a cup of tea in the robin mug and sat down on the sofa, huddled into my dressing gown even though the room was toasty. It was still early, but from the sounds downstairs, there were plenty of customers already enjoying their breakfast. It was hard to imagine that this was a normal working day for most people, while I was lazing about with time on my hands.

On impulse, I plucked a magazine from the tidy basket and flipped through. It was the latest issue of *The Expats Guide to Living and Working in France*, which Charlie's friend Natalie wrote a column for. I supposed it wasn't surprising, considering it was the December edition, that she'd chosen to write about Christmas customs in France.

Within minutes, I'd learned that *le Réveillon* is the name of the Christmas Eve feast, that French children put their shoes near the fireplace so that *Père Noël* can find them and fill them with treats and that, traditionally, a Christmas tree is decorated with candies, nuts and small toys. At the end, she'd written, *One of the things I noticed was how Christmas only starts to get going in December over here, which is refreshing after years of seeing Christmas cards and decorations in British stores as early as September.*

'Hallelujah to that,' I said to the room.

I put the paper away and sipped my tea, then crossed to the book-case and scanned it for a copy of Ryan's book, *The Midnight Hour*. I hadn't spotted it during my tidying spree last night, but then I hadn't been looking. I was certain that Charlie would have a copy, and sure enough, there it was, on the top shelf, nestled between a book about French fishing and a novel called *The Girl and the Duke*, which had to be one of Dolly's. I remembered she was a fan of Regency romances.

I pulled out *The Midnight Hour* and took it back to the sofa. Inside, he'd signed it *To Charlie, you owe me £12.99, you bastard*, which made me smile, but it was the bit about the author I was looking for. When I'd first read the book, I hadn't been remotely interested in the writer, but now I was curious about whether Nicole had got a mention.

I turned to the inside jacket at the back and studied the small black and white author photo. It looked like Ryan, but an edgier version. He was wearing a leather jacket, giving the photographer a challenging stare, as if he'd been coerced into posing and couldn't wait to get away. I read the short paragraph underneath, but it only referenced his place of birth, and his previous career as an accountant, and when my eyes landed on the last line, I let out an incredulous laugh. *When he's not writing, Ryan enjoys a game of darts at his local pub.* Darts? Gran had loved a game of darts. She'd installed a board at the farmhouse for family games, but whenever I'd played, I invariably missed the board altogether and once, almost pierced Ben's ear.

Smiling at the memory – Ben claimed it was why he was scared of needles – I slipped the book back on the shelf and was about to go and get dressed when I heard voices drifting up the stairs. Some sixth sense propelled me towards the door and I opened it a fraction, straining to hear who was speaking.

'… she genuinely wants to put things right between them.' It was Charlie. 'She says she's changed and I think I believe her, and she wants to tell Ryan to his face.'

I guessed immediately that he was talking about Nicole. It sounded as if he'd spoken to her.

'From what you've said, it's for the best,' said Dolly. 'It'll be good for them to properly clear the air.'

They seemed to be on Nicole's side now, which was odd. Or maybe it wasn't. Perhaps it was a good thing, especially if it meant Ryan could let go of his guilt about leaving her and the children again. It sounded as if a desperate Nicole had enlisted Charlie's help – perhaps thrown herself on his mercy and begged him to talk to Ryan on her behalf. She must really love him a lot.

The voices drifted away, and the apartment was silent once more. I wondered whether Ryan had heard them talking, but the silence from behind his closed door suggested he was still sleeping. Had he sat up late, working on his novel? Banishing a mental image of him at his laptop, I returned to my room to find all my clothes needed washing, so I rooted through Dolly's drawers for something to wear.

I found a pair of plain black trousers that were a bit short in the leg, but looked OK with my boots, and a crisp white shirt she'd probably bought for work and must have left behind when she moved in with Frank. The whole outfit was a bit 'office manager' (male), but a pink cardigan softened the look, and in the bathroom, after brushing my teeth, I dug a tube of lipstick out of my toiletries bag. It was called Kissable Lips and once I'd swiped some on, I pouted my mouth and made a kissy face in the mirror, imagining my lips meeting Ryan's. *No!* I shut my eyes to wipe out the snapshot, and when my lids snapped open, I met his startled gaze behind me in the mirror.

I swung round, heart banging, wondering whether it was like one of those films where it turned out to be no one there, but there he was – smoothing the air between us with his palms, an apology in his eyes.

'I didn't realise you were in here. The door was half open and I just…' He stopped and straightened. 'I can't believe you didn't scream.'

'It's trapped,' I squeaked, patting my chest. 'It would have been a big one.'

Now he looked as if he was trying not to laugh. 'I'm really sorry.'

'You don't sound it.' He looked attractively rumpled in his navy dressing gown, one side of his hair flatter than the other, and I forced my eyes away from his lips, remembering the call from Nicole the night before. 'Anyway, it's all yours,' I said. 'The bathroom, I mean.'

Not stopping to ponder whether he'd seen my kissing face, I shot past red-faced and headed downstairs, only remembering as I reached the bottom that he had his own en suite, and must have been there because… *oh stop it*, I ordered myself. *He was just passing, that was all.*

Chapter Eighteen

'How was Chez Phillipe?' Dolly greeted me. She was leaning on the central island in the kitchen, her floured hands either side of a mountain of pastry, steam billowing from the open dishwasher. 'I'm sorry I couldn't make it.'

'The food was great,' I said. 'You didn't have to pay for it, or send Ryan to keep me company.'

'But you're glad I did?' She raised an eyebrow. 'Send Ryan over, I mean.'

'Do you know how to make Mount Blanc?'

'*Mont* Blanc,' she corrected with a smile. 'Of course, but it won't be as good as Phillipe's.'

I eyed her meaningfully. 'Did you really have a salsa session?'

'Of *course* I did.' She brushed the back of her hand across her forehead. 'Anyway, it was good to get Ryan away from his laptop, and you had a nice walk on the beach.'

'How do you know?'

'Ryan told Charlie when he got back last night and Charlie told me this morning.'

I wondered what else Ryan had told Charlie. 'You know, I hadn't realised the children weren't Ryan's,' I said.

Dolly's eyes widened. 'You're joking!'

I shook my head. 'I thought he was awful for saying he wasn't ready to be a father and walking away from them, but now I understand.'

Her astonishment gave way to a smile. 'Well, that's wonderful.'

I gave a rueful shrug. 'I'm glad I know, but a meal and a walk on the beach isn't going to make us more than friends.'

'Friends is a start,' I thought I heard her say, but then she was coughing hard, her forearm pressed over her mouth.

'Are you OK?' Looking closely, I noticed that her cheeks were more flushed than usual, her eyes somehow too bright, as if she was running a fever. 'Dolly, you don't look well.'

'Frank has come down with this awful virus that's been going around.' Recovering her breath, she passed the back of her hand across her forehead. 'I didn't get much sleep.'

'Should you even be here?' I said. 'It sounds contagious, and you don't want to pass anything onto the customers, especially this close to Christmas.'

'Oh, I'm fine.' She wafted a hand in front of her face. 'It's a bit hot in here, that's all, and I was up half the night, looking after Frank. He was delirious at one point.'

'That's awful,' I said, alarmed. 'He was OK the other evening.'

'He said he didn't feel well yesterday morning.' Her voice had developed a worrying tremble. 'He normally comes in to help, but was still in bed when I left the cottage.'

'You didn't mention it.'

'I thought he just wanted an excuse to stay at home and hang the doors on my walk-in wardrobe as a surprise for when I got back.'

'But he didn't?'

She shook her head. 'He was still in bed.'

'Poor Frank.'

'He couldn't eat a thing.' She pressed her lips together, as if to stop herself crying. 'He was rushing to the bathroom all night.'

'Sounds grim.'

'Believe me, it was.' She sniffed. 'I've never seen him poorly.'

'I'm sure he'll be fine, Dolly.' I moved round and gave her a hug, hoping I was immune to whatever it was Frank had. 'Why don't you go home?' I said. 'Charlie can manage things here.'

'I can't just leave.' She cast a frantic look around the kitchen. 'Stefan's brother's off sick too, so there's no one to clear tables and wash up and I've got baking to do. We've run out of croissants, and the knitting group's due in later. I always join them for a chat.'

'Could that other lady, the one who used to own the café, come in and do the baking?'

'Mathilde is visiting a friend in hospital today.'

It didn't seem right to ask if she could visit this friend another day. 'But Celeste and Stefan know the ropes.'

'I suppose so.' She hesitated. 'It's just a case of rolling this out.' She patted the dough. I hadn't properly noticed before how small her hands were. Small but strong, like Mum's. 'You need to fold it, shape it into crescents, tuck the ends in and pop them in the oven.'

I took a step back. *Was she actually considering going home?* 'By you, you mean *me*?'

She nodded. 'Remember, I showed you how to make croissants when you stayed before.'

'That was six years ago, Dolly.' And I hadn't exactly taken it in then. 'You know I don't really bake.' *Ever.*

'That's good, because it's not really baking, it's just putting them in the oven for twenty minutes.' It sounded like the very definition of baking.

'But…' I stared at the raw pastry, as if it might magically transform into the required shape. I didn't want to mess things up but my aunt needed me, for the first time ever. 'I mean, if you trust me to help out, I'll do my best.'

'I think I really do need to take care of Frank,' she said. 'I'm a married woman now, in sickness and in health. And I must admit, I've got a stinking headache.'

I knew it must be bad. I remembered Mum being worried when Dolly told her she rarely had a day off, and hadn't been on holiday since buying the café. 'Just like being married to a farmer,' I'd pointed out, which had prompted Mum to book a spa-day with her friend from the village – except, she didn't go because a sheep got milk fever and 'needed company'.

'Go,' I said to Dolly, snatching an apron off the back of the door. 'We'll manage just fine.'

'Really?' The gratitude in her eyes was almost unbearable – mostly because I knew it was misplaced. 'You don't mind taking over?'

'Charlie's here, I'll be fine.' I fastened the apron, then realised it was on back to front. I switched it round, hoping Dolly hadn't noticed. 'Go and look after Frank,' I ordered. 'And yourself.'

'Don't forget to wash your hands.'

'I won't.' I crossed to the sink and switched on the tap to prove it.

'You're a lifesaver.' Dolly came over and gave me a squeeze from behind, and I tried not to breathe in any germs. 'The café practically runs itself,' she said, almost as if she was trying to convince herself. 'You'll be fine.'

I knew that wasn't true. Without Dolly at the helm, the café would be like a ship without a captain. But Charlie was a good second-in-command, and Stefan and Celeste were a great crew and the regulars were understanding passengers… *stop with the sailing comparisons, Nina.* Plus, it was only for a day. What could possibly go wrong?

'What is making the smell of fire?' Celeste appeared through a cloud of smoke as I threw the back door open and slammed a metal tray onto the worktop.

'I've cremated the croissants.' I stared in horror at the charred, misshapen chunks in front of me. 'I don't know what went wrong. They were definitely cooked at the right temperature.'

'Maybe they are not the right size.' Celeste gingerly poked what looked like a chunk of coal. 'They have to be bigger than this.'

I felt like crying. 'I couldn't fold them properly,' I said, unable to look at them any longer. 'I tried to do what Dolly said, but it didn't work.' The pastry had proved impossible to handle, my hands like shovels as I'd tried to mould it. I'd resorted to pulling off clumps and slapping them on the tray, hoping they'd transform as they baked.

'What is this?' Celeste peered with watering eyes at the tray still waiting to go in the oven.

'I thought I'd roll the pasty flat and cook it in one go, then cut it into croissant shapes afterwards.' Saying it aloud made me ashamed. 'Not the best idea I've ever had.'

Celeste kept switching her bewildered gaze from the pastry to my face, as if trying to determine whether I was being serious. Or maybe her English wasn't up to translating my words. They didn't make sense to me either.

'There is some prepared in the freezer.' She moved past slowly, as if afraid I might pounce, and I guessed I looked as wild-eyed and crimson-faced as I felt. 'For emergency,' she clarified, and I was embarrassed that things had apparently become critical when I'd only been left in charge for half an hour. 'Maybe you go round counter and I do this.' She had pulled out some ready-rolled pastry strips. 'There is only almond and cinnamon, but they will make do.'

'Make do.' I nodded gratefully, suddenly reluctant to leave the kitchen, which felt like a sanctuary compared to the café, where actual customers would require my attention. 'I can probably manage those.'

'Is fine, I will do now, for Dolly.' Celeste didn't stop smiling, but I could see the uncertainty in her eyes and felt terrible that I was the cause.

'OK, good idea.' I brushed flour from my apron, which was almost white. I'd tried to emulate Augustine who, when baking at the farmhouse, would liberally sprinkle flour around when rolling out pastry, though I couldn't remember why. I'd thought it might help, but I'd only succeeded in spreading it over myself and the kitchen floor. 'If you're sure,' I said, to double-check.

'I'm sure.' Celeste's smile was crumbling at the edges, so I quickly washed my hands, swapped my apron for a clean one and mumbled my apologies and thanks as I slipped into the café, hoping no one would take any notice of me.

'Nina, you must help!' Far from his usual quiet, self-effacing persona, Stefan looked to be teetering on the edge of a meltdown. 'I cannot do all this on myself.'

Blinking, I looked around. *So many people, where had they come from?* Maybe it was always this busy, but I was seeing it from another perspective – one that was making me wish I'd grabbed the letters out of my bedside drawer and gone straight to Gérard's. 'Where's Charlie?'

'He had to do errands and is not returned.'

Great. Dolly hadn't bothered to mention that. Then again, she'd been feeling unwell, so it wasn't really surprising. 'I'll start by clearing some tables, shall I?'

Stefan nodded so hard his hair shook, and so did the mistletoe sprigs on his Christmas jumper. 'I need you to help here, too.' He switched off the foamer, or steaming device (I couldn't recollect what Dolly had called it), and cast a desperate look at the waiting queue.

'Celeste will be through in a moment.'

'You help.'

The man next in line, who had a thin moustache and a rose tattoo on his neck, raised expectant eyebrows at me and fired off an order in French I had no chance of understanding. 'Back in a minute,' I said, shooting past and picking a cup and plate off the nearest table. I needed a cloth to wipe it – and a tray to put the crockery on. *Damn.*

'Ah, you are Dolly's young lady. *Très charmant.*' A gentleman of around eighty, with swept-back white hair and twinkly eyes, had turned in his chair to offer up a smile, revealing big white teeth. 'I should offer a kiss, but Dolly explained it is not right to be in a young lady's space.' He waggled his hands in the area between us, then swept them grandly over the papers in front of him, which were scattered with musical notes. 'I joined the *Orchestre National de Lyon* in 1969, and played violin with them for many years, and now I am writing a symphony for their fortieth *anniversaire.*'

'How lovely!' I forced a polite expression, not wanting to let the side down. Dolly would no doubt sit and chat to the old man, while managing to stay in control, but I seemed incapable of picking up a cup and smiling at the same time. 'Good to meet you,' I said as pleasantly as my mounting panic would allow, and retreated back to the counter to look for a tray. And a cloth. And an invisibility cloak.

'*Deux chocolat chaud et un tourbillon de cannelle.*' Tattoo-Neck was clearly fed-up of waiting.

'Two hot chocolate and one cinnamon whirl,' Stefan translated as he tipped steaming milk into two mugs for the woman at the front of the queue. 'You know how to do?'

Oh hell. 'Erm…' I eyed Annabel, who looked somehow malevolent with her curvy frontage, steam hissing from one of her pointy things. 'I… I might be able to remember.'

I turned to flash a smile at Tattoo-Neck, whose eyebrows were climbing towards his receding hairline. '*Un instant, s'il vous plaît.*' I had a feeling it would take more than a moment, as I tried to recall Dolly's instructions from the day before. *Why hadn't I taken a barista course, instead of buggering about with bloody horse whispering?* Had Dolly even explained how to make hot chocolate? I seemed to remember espresso had been mentioned a lot. *Milk.* There would definitely be milk.

I picked up a cup and put it down, then looked at the waiting line of people. Most of them seemed happy to wait, scanning their phones, or chatting, but Tattoo-Neck was starting to look pissed off. 'Why don't you go and sit down and I'll bring it over?'

'*Quoi?*'

'Erm… *asseyez-vous.*' I mimed sitting and he scanned the café, then made a pantomime of scratching his head and looking puzzled when it became clear there were no clean tables.

'You like for me to sit on floor?' he said, in a parody of my accent. He'd be giving the café its first one-star review on TripAdvisor next.

'*Non.*' I held up a finger, a rigid smile fixed in place. '*Une minute.*'

I shot into the kitchen, where Celeste was lining up golden pastries, singing softly – it sounded like 'O Little Town of Bethlehem' – as though all was well with the world. As though things weren't about to descend into something resembling mealtime at Ban Kwang Central Prison. (I'd seen a documentary about it once. Although, hopefully, none of the food here was infested with maggots.) 'You have to help Stefan,' I said, feeling closer to hysteria than I could ever remember. I was letting Dolly down on her one day off in… probably since her wedding day. *Where the hell was Charlie?*

'Do not worry, all is good,' Celeste said warmly, calm now that she'd rescued the pastry situation. 'I will go.' She nodded at the tray of cooling pastries. 'Maybe you bring them in?'

'Yes!' I wanted to kiss her cheeks. 'I can definitely manage that,' I promised rashly. 'And I'll come and clear some tables too, I just can't… I can't do the drinks.'

'OK, but I am to go soon, for my hair.' She pointed to her plait. 'It is time for grey ones to leave.'

'What?' *Don't go.* 'I can't see any grey,' I said, scanning her hair. I could, but wasn't about to admit it. 'Could you not go tomorrow instead?'

Her smile faltered. 'I have made appointment with salon. It's for Christmas, I have party to attend.'

'Right, that's fine, it'll be fine, it's all good. I'll bring these cinnamon whirls through.'

'Almond croissants.'

'Whatever.'

As she left, I sagged over the worktop, feeling as though I'd attempted to scale Everest in high heels, rather than failed to make a cup of hot chocolate for a man with a dodgy tattoo. How did Dolly *do* this every day? Her management gene had gone squarely to Charlie, with none whatsoever left over for her 'favourite niece'. It was probably why I'd failed to get my travel blog up and running.

Where was Charlie, anyway?

Deciding to send him a quick text, in case Dolly hadn't had a chance to let him know she'd gone home and left me (*me!*) in charge, I patted my trousers for my phone, before remembering it was charging upstairs in my room.

There was no time to go and get it, so I whipped the tray of almond croissants through to the café, relieved to see that Stefan and Celeste had the queue under control – even Tattoo-Neck had found a table in the corner – and managed to lay out the pastries without too much incident (I dropped one on the floor and Stefan trod on it).

I returned to the kitchen to get a fresh cloth to see Ryan by the fridge and this time, instead of screaming, I said, 'Thank *God* you're here.'

Chapter Nineteen

'Four words I never expected to hear from you.' There was a mildly sardonic edge to Ryan's voice, and I wondered if he was recalling my hasty departure from the living room the night before.

'It's all gone to hell,' I said, restraint dissolving in a sea of panic. 'I'm completely out of my depth.'

He scanned my workman-like outfit. 'Charlie told me that Dolly's gone home to look after Frank and that you're in charge.'

'You've spoken to Charlie?' My voice leapt up an octave. '*When?* What did he say?'

He looked taken aback by my fractious questions. 'I just got a message to say his car's broken down and he can't get back for a while.'

'You're kidding.'

'Nope.' He shook his head. 'He asked if I'd come down and help you out.'

I spun round, a hand clasped to my mouth, aware I was reacting as though the end of the world had been announced. 'I told Dolly she should go home.'

'That's… thoughtful of you?' He seemed puzzled by my tone.

'She's not well and I thought Charlie would be back by now.' I rounded on him. 'I didn't know he'd gone out in the car. He told me he rarely drives these days.'

'I'm just the messenger,' said Ryan, holding up his hands. 'Listen, I'm more than happy to help out, but I've never worked in a café.'

'Me neither.'

'Celeste and Stefan are here, though?'

'Celeste's going soon, she's having her plait dyed, and Stefan's brother usually does the tables and dishwasher, but he's got this virus too.'

'OK.' Ryan took on the barrage of information and braced his shoulders. 'Good job I didn't keep my dressing gown on,' he said, tugging the front of his 'country-singer' shirt.

'That's not the most pressing issue right now.'

'It's fine, we'll manage.' He gave a firm nod. 'I used to work in a bar,' he said. 'It was a long time ago, but they did have a coffee machine, and Dolly gave me a lesson the other morning.'

'You too?' I shook my head. 'She's obsessed with that thing.'

'Just as well, eh?'

'Not really,' I said. 'It took me about an hour to produce one teeny espresso.'

'Maybe leave that to me, then.' He rolled up his shirtsleeves, and I suddenly wanted to hug him, past caring about his complicated personal life. I was just glad to have some help.

The look of relief when Ryan rounded the counter was evident in Stefan's smile. Determined to show I could be perfectly calm and capable of doing something I was good at, I set about tidying tables and straightening chairs, and even swept the floor while Ryan made a pretty good job of dishing out drinks under Stefan's supervision. He looked quite at home behind the counter and I could see he'd attracted interest from most of the female customers – there was a lot of bright, flirty laughter going on – and one man, who kept adjusting his cycle helmet on the table as if to attract his attention.

Celeste came through for her coat and bag while I was loading the dishwasher for the second time. 'You will need to make muffins from freezer into oven, for ladies with needles,' she said, which sounded like a riddle until I realised she was talking about Dolly's knitting group. 'I put oven to correct heat.'

'Thanks, Celeste.'

This time, I managed to produce something that looked edible, without setting the kitchen alight, and left the cranberry muffins cooling on the side as I went out to check whether the ladies had arrived. I was sure they'd be disappointed that Dolly wasn't here, but would do my best to make them feel welcome.

I made some quick adjustments to the Christmas tree – a few of the decorations had been taken off and clumped together on one branch – and stood by the door for a moment to catch my breath, willing Charlie to return. My arms felt stiff from transporting heavy trays, my cheeks ached from constantly smiling and my temples throbbed with the effort of making myself understood. I'd caused some hilarity after mispronouncing *oignon* when recommending Dolly's onion soup.

'You say "fingernail",' Stefan explained, when I asked what they were laughing at. He stuck out his fingers, which were long, like a pianist's, and pointed at his neatly-trimmed nails. '*Ongle*.'

'It's an easy mistake,' said Ryan, dusting a cup of hot chocolate with cocoa powder like a professional. 'Someone asked what I did for a living, and I told them I was a novel.' I gave a splutter of laughter. 'I thought *roman* meant novelist.' He smiled. 'Serves me right for showing off.'

'Sometimes, I say Russian words wrong, but my Spanish, it is very good.' Stefan sounded proud.

'You're wasted here,' I said.

'One day, I will be translator for United Nations.'

'Talk about aiming high,' said Ryan, but I could see he was as impressed as I was. 'In the meantime, could you show me again how to work the grinder thingie?'

I grinned as I turned away, glad I wasn't the only one who couldn't remember all the technical terms – or any of them.

The knitting group ladies were a surprisingly rowdy bunch, who immediately commandeered several tables, where they shook off their coats and unloaded their various works-in-progress, creating a woolly blanket of colour in various shades and degrees of ability. Dolly's absence was greeted with sorry murmurs and sympathetic headshakes, but no one seemed to expect me to sit and chat, so I placed their coffee orders with Stefan and Ryan and returned to the kitchen to fetch the muffins.

For a moment, I couldn't work out what I was seeing. Or rather, *not* seeing. Where the muffins had been cooling, there was just an empty cooling rack and a scattering of crumbs trailing from the worktop to the floor. I rushed over to look more closely, as if they might just have shrunk, and almost fell over a guilty-looking canine by the oven.

'Hamish!' He lowered his head, unable to meet my eye. 'What are you *doing* here?'

'Glad it's not just me, getting the catchphrase,' Ryan said behind me. 'Gérard just came in. He said Hamish had made a dash round the side of the building, and he couldn't catch him.'

'He must have smelt my muffins.'

Ryan's eyebrows flew up, then he followed my gaze and understanding dawned. 'Oh crap.'

'He's eaten the lot,' I said. 'Hamish, not Gérard.'

'How did he get in?'

'I forgot to close the back door when I burnt the croissants.' I was starting to feel a bit weepy. As if sensing my mood, Hamish shuffled over and nudged my hand with his damp nose. 'Don't you dare be cute,' I said. 'Those treats weren't for you.'

'Could you whip up some more?' Ryan looked at the crumbs as if wondering whether it was possible to fashion them into a new batch.

'Whip up some more?' I gave him a withering look. 'Those weren't mine, they were Dolly's. I've never made muffins in my life, I wouldn't know how,' I said. 'I can barely boil an egg.'

'You could follow a recipe, I suppose.'

'Why don't *you* follow a recipe?'

'I wouldn't want to embarrass you with how good I am at baking.'

'Very funny.' I looked at him. 'Are you?'

He nodded. 'I like making cakes.'

'Well, we don't have time.' It was almost a wail. 'The knitters will have to make do with something else.'

As I turned to leave, there was a dreadful retching noise and Hamish regurgitated the muffins all over Ryan's shoes.

'Oh God.' I clapped a hand to my mouth.

Ryan's expression of friendly amusement changed to queasy horror. 'That's…' He stared at the colourful mess. 'That's disgusting.' Hamish whined an apology, then scampered out of the kitchen, presumably in search of Gérard. 'What now?'

I had an urge to giggle at his look of stunned incomprehension. 'You'd better clean up,' I said. 'I've got hungry ladies to feed.'

By closing time, I was ready to collapse. There'd been a rush on Dolly's soup, and I'd had to heat another panful – thankfully, there was plenty in the freezer – and I'd burnt my arm pulling baguettes from the oven.

My feet and back ached, and I never wanted to see another dirty plate as long as I lived.

Managing a café wasn't in my blood, however lovely the location and the customers. And most of them were. Even Tattoo-Neck had nodded a polite goodbye as he left, and no longer looked as if he wanted me sacked, and the knitting ladies had been happy with Mathilde's strawberry and pistachio macarons, which she'd made the day before.

Ryan had returned in cleaned-up shoes, looking a bit peaky, and I'd felt a twinge of guilt that he'd uncomplainingly cleared up Hamish's mess when it had only happened because I'd left the door open. Hamish, none the worse for wear, had snoozed at Gérard's feet, unaware of the chaos he'd created.

'Gérard said thank you for yesterday,' I said to Ryan, as the old man left to join Jacqueline and Holly outside, realising I'd missed an opportunity to give him back the letters, I'd been so preoccupied. 'Apparently, Jacqueline was a bit confused when he told her you'd been discussing your lip with him.'

'My *lip?*'

'I thought I'd said book… *livre*, but it must have got lost in translation.'

Ryan shook his head smilingly. 'I suppose he had other things on his mind.'

Once we'd seen Stefan out and locked up, I checked the kitchen was clean and tidy and Ryan checked his phone.

'Charlie's going straight to Dolly and Frank's,' he said, a crease between his eyebrows. 'Apparently, she thinks she's coming down with whatever Frank's got, so he's going to check on them.'

A surge of worry tightened my stomach. 'Maybe I should go too. She won't be able to cope if they're both ill.'

'Charlie says they're probably infectious and we're to stay here, just in case.'

'He really said that?'

Ryan held out his phone and I read *They're probably infectious so stay there, just in case.*

I tutted. 'What about Charlie? If he comes down with it too, we'll be left holding the fort and I'm really rubbish at it.'

'Oh, I don't know.' Ryan checked the back door was locked and switched off the lights, and as we made our way upstairs I had that strange feeling again, of us being a couple on our way home. 'I think between us, we did OK.'

'Don't you think it's a bit strange?' I said, once we were seated in front of the fire with plates of chicken chasseur and mashed potatoes, which Ryan had rustled up (as well as lighting the fire), while I took another long shower and got into a pair of leopard-print pyjamas.

'Strange?' Ryan poured us a glass of wine each, from a bottle of Sauvignon blanc that Dolly had helpfully labelled 'needs drinking ASAP!!' before sitting once more at the opposite end of the sofa. 'I hope you don't mean my food. I put it in the slow cooker this morning,' he said. 'Dolly's idea, so don't blame me if it's awful.'

'It smells great.' I took a mouthful, savouring the taste. 'No,' I said when I'd swallowed. 'I mean, it's strange that Dolly and Frank both fall ill when they were fine a couple of nights ago, and Charlie has to rush off and look after them, leaving us alone.'

Ryan nodded as he ate, balancing his plate on the arm of the sofa. 'It does seem like another coincidence, now that you mention it,' he said. 'But there has been a virus going around.'

'Who told you that?'

His brow furrowed. 'Actually, it might have been Dolly.'

'There you go.'

'You did say Dolly looked feverish, though.'

That was true, she had. And she *never* took time off work.

'Ignore me,' I said, concentrating on piling chicken on the end of my fork. 'My imagination's working overtime.'

'Mine too, thank goodness.' It took me a second to realise that Ryan was talking about his book.

'How's it going?' I said, taking a few sips of wine. It was cool and grapey and went well with the chicken, so I drank some more. 'The book, I mean.'

'It's... flowing.' He sounded cagey. 'Like I said—'

'You don't like talking about the book,' I chorused. 'I just meant, generally. I thought you might have stayed up for a while last night, writing.' *After the phone call from Nicole*, I didn't add, not wanting to sound as if I was digging for information.

'I did,' he admitted, his gaze fixed on his plate, and I knew he was remembering the phone call too, followed by my swift exit.

'How did you come up with the idea for Grace Benedict?' I asked quickly.

He took a slug of wine, as if he needed fortifying before answering, and I guessed he must get asked that question all the time. 'I don't really know is the boring answer,' he said. 'It was going to be a male detective, but then her voice just came to me with this strong Irish accent, and there she was.'

'It must have been amazing to get a book deal.' It was nice to chat – as long as we stayed away from anything inflammatory, like relationships.

An involuntary smile crossed Ryan's face. 'It was pretty good,' he said. 'I celebrated with a glass of whisky and a bit of twerking.'

I almost choked on my chicken. 'That's something I hope never to see.'

'Your loss.' He put down his now-empty plate and picked up his wine glass again, hoisting one foot on the other thigh and massaging it through his sock. 'I don't think I've ever spent so long on my feet in one stretch as I have today.'

'I'm not going to massage it for you, if that's what you're hinting at.'

'Again, your loss.'

I grinned and fell silent while I finished eating and Ryan poured us some more wine. 'That was delicious,' I said, sitting back and curling my legs beneath me. 'Thank you.'

'My pleasure.' He sat back and gave me a speculative look. 'So, tell me,' he said. 'What sort of wedding were you going to have?'

Chapter Twenty

I almost gasped at the unexpectedness of Ryan's question. 'I thought we weren't talking about our pasts.'

'I've told you plenty about mine, and I'm curious,' he said. There was a looseness to his posture and limbs that I guessed was down to the food and wine. Mostly the wine. 'Was it going to be a big do?' He twirled a hand. 'Cathedral, stately home, honeymoon in Guatemala?'

'It wasn't going to be Lady Gaga at Wembley Stadium big, just medium-sized, I suppose, and not in a cathedral, just an ordinary church, where… where my gran and grandad got married.' I paused. 'On the same date, actually, the twenty-first of December.'

He narrowed his eyes. 'That's tomorrow.'

I nodded and swallowed some wine to wash away the feeling that something had lodged in my throat. 'And not Guatemala, or anywhere exotic like that. Tromsø in Norway, actually, to see the Northern Lights.' I fixed my eyes on the flames dancing in the fireplace. 'It was something my gran had always wanted to see, but never got around to.'

'So, you were going on her behalf.'

His gentle tone made my eyes prickle. 'I'd have been happy for her to come with us, but she had terminal cancer, so…' My voice trailed off and I twisted a tuft of hair around my finger – a habit I'd got out of since having it cut.

'I'm sorry.' Ryan shifted so he was facing me. 'You were obviously very close.'

I nodded, not trusting myself to speak for a moment. 'She was only hanging on to see me get married in that church.' I swallowed. 'And to hear about the honeymoon and see the pictures,' I added. 'I promised to take loads of photos and have them printed out for her. She was old-school like that, liked proper photographs in albums.' I felt the weight of Ryan's gaze, but couldn't look at him. 'She died a week after I called off the wedding.'

He was silent for a moment. 'And you blame yourself?'

'I knew it would have happened anyway, of course I did, but I'd so wanted to give her that *one* thing,' I jabbed my thigh with my finger. 'The thing she'd been looking forward to the most.'

'I'm sure she understood.'

'She said perhaps it was meant to be, but it was the sort of thing she'd say to make me feel better.'

He flashed me a look. 'That's the guilt talking,' he said. 'But you've nothing to feel guilty about.'

'It sounds like you've been carrying some guilt of your own, about Lulu and Jackson.'

'But we're not talking about me,' he said gently. 'Why *did* you call off your wedding, anyway?'

'Oldest story in the book.' I snapped out a laugh. 'He was seeing someone else, and by seeing, I mean sleeping with. Or rather, *not* sleeping.'

'I'm sorry,' he said again, and I had to look away from the intensity in his eyes. 'That must have been awful for you.'

'It wasn't great.'

'And you didn't know?'

I took a shaky breath. *Where was the harm in saying it?* It wasn't as if he was in any position to judge me. 'Actually, I knew he'd been seeing her before, but he promised it was over and asked me to marry him.' I glanced at the space on my finger where, for a short time, I'd worn an expensive ring embedded with diamonds. *To match your eyes*, Scott had said, and even as I'd exclaimed, I'd thought, *how corny is that?*

I wasn't even that keen on diamonds and wished he'd chosen something more personal, but Gran had loved it. *He's a keeper*, she'd said, rummaging out photos of her wedding day, when she'd worn a white lace midi-dress and floppy hat, clutching a bunch of white roses in one hand, Grandad holding the other, the church behind them blanketed white with snow. It had been one of the coldest winters on record. *Happiest day of my life, love.*

'I think Scott proposed out of guilt, and, if I'm being totally honest, I said yes because I knew how much Gran wanted to see me married before she died.' It was the first time I'd admitted it out loud. 'I think, in my heart, I stopped loving him the first time he cheated on me.'

I gulped down the rest of my wine to stop myself talking. I hated that I'd let things get so far, even booking the tickets to Norway – where Gran had hoped to go with Grandad before he died – choosing a hotel that boasted the best view of the Northern Lights. With hindsight, I knew guilt had been the driving force behind Scott letting me have my way. He'd have much preferred a honeymoon in Guatemala. Not that I was about to tell Ryan that. I'd said enough already. He was staring into his empty glass, as if seeing my sorry tale play out at the bottom.

'No wonder you burnt his stuff,' he said.

I thumped my head back against the cushions. 'It was a couple of shirts and a wallet, and a book he didn't even like!'

He laughed in surprise. 'Ah yes, you said. That makes it *so* much better.' I gave him a dead-eyed look 'Seriously,' he added. 'I shouldn't have said what I did when I'd only just met you. I didn't know the full story.' He reached out his hand and rested it in the space between us. 'You should have burnt *everything*.'

My mouth twitched towards a smile. 'The best revenge was leaving him,' I said. 'He came off looking like the bad guy, once word got around, and he didn't like that one bit. The great Scott Mackenzie.'

Ryan jolted upright. 'Scott Mackenzie?'

I bolted upright too. 'You've met him?'

'Tall and…' he swept a hand over his head '…blond hair, looks a bit like that Swedish actor from *True Blood*?'

'Alexander Skarsgård?' Scott would have *loved* that. 'That's him,' I said, shocked. 'How…?'

'My agent invited me to a book launch in London.' Ryan angled his body towards me. 'One of her clients, an artist, had a book out, one of those coffee table type things, and he – Mackenzie – was with her, introducing himself as the guy who discovered her.' He paused. 'I thought they were a couple actually. I think everyone did.'

'Hannah Jepson.' The sting of saying her name had long since faded. 'Scott owns a gallery, he displayed her work, her dad's a friend of his dad, blah, blah, blah.' I waved away the condolences I sensed were coming. 'I had an inkling they were more than friends, even before he went to that launch – without me.'

'I thought he was a bit of a prick, to be honest.'

I smiled. 'Turns out, he was.'

'I'm sorry for thinking… you know.'

'That he'd had a lucky escape?'

He grimaced. 'I'm an idiot.'

'And just for the record,' I added, 'I'm not *unstable* even though I was dressed as a koala and screamed the place down the first time you met me.'

'When did I say that?'

'Remember, I overheard you talking to Charlie.'

'God, I'm sorry again about that.' He rubbed his forehead as if to erase the memory. 'You were right to have a go at me.'

'It's OK,' I said with a grin. 'I think we've put it to bed now.'

The word 'bed' seemed to shimmer between us for a second.

Ryan cleared his throat. 'So, are you any closer to figuring out what you're going to do?'

'About?'

'The letters from your great-grandmother and your travel blog.'

'Ah, right. Well, I'm going to give the letters back to Gérard and forget I saw them, and the blog...' I thought of my scribbled notes the day before that had morphed into possible names for a different kind of business. 'Let's just say, I'm working on it,' I said. 'And that, whatever happens, running a café won't figure in my future.'

'Talking of which...' Ryan glanced at his watch, which looked like an old one with a worn leather strap. 'Do you think there's any chance of Dolly coming in tomorrow?'

I almost dropped my wine glass. 'Are we going to have to do all that again?'

He seemed to find this funny. 'Your face,' he said. 'It's actually not that bad, as long as Stefan and Celeste are here to help.'

'I thought you had a book to write.' I put down my glass and reached for my phone on the table. 'I need to find out what's happening.'

'Don't call Dolly, she might be asleep.'

'I'll send Charlie a message.'

He replied quickly, almost as if he'd been waiting to hear from me. *Doubt any of us will be well enough to make it in.* The tone was unusually gloomy.

I feel as if I've swallowed glass and have a temperature of 1004.

You're technically dead.

Sorry, meant 104. Fat fingers.

Have you had the doctor out?

No need, same thing everyone's had. Need to rest, etc.

'What?' said Ryan, leaning over to look at my screen. I showed him Charlie's message. 'Sounds nasty.'

Are you coming back? I typed.

No, staying here 2nite, try to sleep it off. Things OK there?

I thought about giving him a rundown, but Ryan was right – it hadn't been that bad – or at least, it could have been worse.

Don't worry Chuck, we've got this X

Cheers Nina X

I sighed. 'I still think it's strange how we haven't heard a word about this terrible virus until today and now all three of them have it.'

'Isn't that how viruses work?' Ryan was so close, I could see a tiny freckle on his temple, and the way his eyelashes curled ever-so-slightly at the tips. 'One person gets it, everyone in the family follows.'

'We were with them all the other night, and we're fine.'

I watched as Ryan did an experimental swallow, his Adam's apple sliding up and down. 'My throat feels OK.'

I swallowed some more wine. 'Mine too,' I said.

'Maybe we're immune.'

'I hope so.'

Ryan put down his glass and leant back, legs sprawled, hands folded across his chest. 'You really think they've been trying to throw us together?'

I seemed to be tilting towards him. 'Don't you?'

He thought for a moment, eyes half-closed. 'There *have* been a series of happy accidents as my Aunt Heidi would call it, but they could have been just that.'

'I'm not sure I believe in happy accidents,' I said, but I liked the sound of Aunt Heidi. 'And you know that matchmaking is Dolly's thing?'

'I… yes, I do know that.' He lowered his gaze and, for a second, seemed lost in thought, then his eyes flicked back to my face, filled with firelight and layered with… *something*. My head started to spin. 'You know, if that *is* the case, about Dolly matchmaking, it would be a shame if her efforts were wasted.'

As I scanned his face, warmth sped through me, firing up my nerve endings, and I was suddenly aware of being almost naked beneath my pyjamas. 'What are you suggesting, Mr Sadler?' I'd meant to sound cartoonishly seductive and accompany the words with a dramatic eyelash flutter, but forgot the flutter and ended up sounding seductive. Also, why was I so close to him that I could almost stroke his face?

'I'm saying, we're both single, you're the most attractive koala I've ever seen—'

'Finding koalas attractive is really weird,' I said, trying to block out the word *attractive*, even though my heart rate tripled in response.

He laughed softly, and I realised his hand was round the back of my head, his fingers playing with my hair, and I felt as if my insides were starting to melt. 'You're funny too,' he said.

'Flattery is the lowest form of creativity.' *Why did I still sound seductive?* 'You should know that, being a *roman*.' I giggled at my weak attempt at a joke and wondered whether it was the wine or Ryan that had gone to my head.

'Not if it's true.'

I suddenly couldn't stop staring at his mouth. It was just so… *kissable*. I leant closer so our faces were millimetres apart and I could see myself in his eyes, then closed the gap between us and pressed my lips to his.

He made a sound, like a sigh or a groan as he pulled me closer, his hand still wrapped in my hair, the other circling my waist, and then I was astride his lap, running my hands through *his* hair – there was a lot of hair action going on – and I could feel the firmness of his body as I pressed against him, every cell in mine alive with desire. We drew apart, breathing hard, and I dropped my head to his shoulder, not letting myself think, just feel.

'Have you been at the satsumas?' he murmured, breathing the skin on my neck.

'It's mandarin shower crème,' I murmured back, and we kissed again, as if training for the kissing Olympics, and I'd never felt so much like tearing off a man's clothes and touching his skin.

Ryan held me tighter, hands moving up my back, and there was a split-second when we looked deep into each other's eyes and I felt a shock of recognition – *this* was where I was supposed to be – and had an overwhelming urge to take off my pyjamas.

'Where have you been all my life?' Ryan spoke in a raspy voice as he flipped me onto my back on the cushions and lowered himself on top of me.

'That's so cheesy,' I breathed, sounding like someone in the throes of passion. *Was this the throes of passion?* If so, why hadn't it felt like this with anyone else, including Scott?

As we started kissing again, there was a shift in the air around us, as though the molecules had been disturbed – and not just because of the hormones flying around.

'Ryan?'

We froze and unlocked lips. 'Did you just say my name?'

I shook my head, my heart like a juggernaut in my chest. 'It wasn't me.'

We sprang apart and bolted upright, and I locked eyes with a woman I instantly recognised from the photo I'd seen a few nights ago on Ryan's phone.

'Nicole!' He got slowly to his feet. 'What are you doing here?'

Chapter Twenty-One

On reflection, I probably shouldn't have smirked when Ryan said my 'catchphrase', but I blamed the wine, and the unexpectedness of being thoroughly kissed for the first time in a long time, in a way that I'd never been kissed before.

Thankfully, he didn't notice, his shock at seeing his ex-fiancée was so complete, but Nicole did. Her gaze had swung from Ryan's rumpled appearance to me in my rumpled pyjamas, with my rumpled hair – my face was probably rumpled too – and her smile went tight. 'Looks like I've interrupted… something.' Her eyes skimmed over the dirty plates and glasses and the almost-empty bottle of wine on the table. 'I did knock, but nobody heard.' *And now I can see why.* The words hung in the air, but remained unspoken.

'We were having dinner,' I said redundantly as Ryan continued to stare, clearly unable to believe what he was seeing. There was no way of telling whether he was pleased, angry or somewhere in between, but I wished he'd had time to flatten his hair and button his shirt. *Had I unbuttoned it?* I supposed I must have and my face flamed when Nicole gave me a knowing smirk of her own.

She was incredibly pretty in the flesh, with thick blonde hair cascading from a centre parting, framing a symmetrical face. Her eyes were a

nicer shade of grey than mine, her nose smaller, her full lips coloured
an eye-popping shade of red I'd never be able to pull off.

Ryan clearly didn't have a type because she was my opposite in
every way.

He ran a hand over his face, and his gaze briefly touched mine.
'This is Charlie's cousin, Nina,' he said, and she gave me a brief nod
before throwing down her leather bag and slipping her hands into the
pockets of her swingy, scarlet coat. 'How... when did you get here?'
He sounded as if it was an effort to get his words in the right order.

'About half an hour ago, the usual way.' She gave a toss of her
amazing hair, as though the details weren't important. She was tiny, I
realised, and it gave her a vulnerable air. I remembered how she'd kept
calling Ryan, and Charlie advising him to ignore her. *Could Nicole be
unstable?* It seemed an impulsive act, to jump on a plane and fly out
this close to Christmas, to talk to a man who'd apparently made his
feelings crystal clear and walked away months ago.

'How did you know where to find me?'

'I spoke to Charlie,' she said, and I remembered the conversation
I'd overhead between him and Dolly. *She says she's changed and I think
I believe her.*

I wondered whether Charlie had any inkling Nicole was planning
to come over. If so, he clearly hadn't said anything to Ryan, unless he'd
forgotten, with his car breaking down and then becoming ill.

Ryan was shaking his head, whether annoyed with Nicole, or the
situation, it was hard to tell. 'How did you get in?'

'The back door was open.'

Bloody hell. I was sure I'd locked it, after the muffin disaster earlier. I
could see myself turning the key and testing the door, but it obviously
hadn't worked.

Judging by his concentrated expression, Ryan was seeing it too. He'd watched me do it. 'Where...?' He hesitated. 'Where are the children?'

'With my mum and dad.' Nicole gave me a quick look that said plainly that she didn't want to talk in front of me. 'They're fine.'

I got to my feet, which were pale and clumpy next to her shiny black spiky-heeled boots (not suitable for snow) and I wished I wasn't wearing pyjamas. Compared to Nicole's delicate beauty, I felt like a giant, over-tired toddler, though – looking closer – even in the subdued glow from the Christmas tree lights and the dying fire, I noticed smudges of tiredness beneath her eyes. 'I'll go,' I said, as if I had a choice. 'You've come a long way and must be tired.' I looked at Ryan and caught his small, helpless shrug of apology. 'Your children look lovely, by the way. Ryan has a photo of you all on his phone.'

'He does?' She sounded pleased, and I wondered with a clench of horror whether I'd made things worse by suggesting he was far from over them. 'That's so cute,' she said.

Ryan lowered his head and kneaded his eyebrows, as if trying to conjure some words that would change what was happening.

'Nicole, I—'

'I just need to talk to you face-to-face.' She spoke gently but with feeling, and I realised what had been obvious from the moment she appeared, in her scarlet coat and high-heeled boots, with perfect hair: she was here to win him back. Her gaze shifted. 'This is a really nice room,' she said as if noticing it for the first time. 'I really tried with the Christmas tree at home, but Lulu keeps pulling off the baubles.'

Her words brought the ghost of a smile to Ryan's face, and seeming heartened by the sight of it, Nicole moved closer and touched his arm with her French-manicured fingertips. Even with two children under five to look after, she'd found time to take care of the details. 'Just give me half an hour,' she said, with the sort of beguiling smile that must have drawn him to her in the first place, and I realised that, although he knew the details of my break-up with Scott, I knew next to nothing about his relationship with Nicole. 'You really do need to hear what I have to say,' she said softly. 'I promise you won't be disappointed.'

It was painful to watch the way Ryan was looking at her – as if now she was in front of him, in all her tiny glory, he was wondering how he could ever have given her up.

Taking my cue to leave, I didn't look at him again as I gathered up our plates and glasses and dumped them in the kitchen, before pouring myself a glass of water and closing the door firmly behind me as I left the room.

If there was going to be a reconciliation tonight, I didn't want to hear it.

My bedroom felt cold and uninviting and I roamed around it, moving things about, then gazed out of the window at the star-scattered sky, going over and over the kiss with Ryan, wondering what it had meant, trying to convince myself it hadn't meant anything – it had been a moment of madness brought on by the wine. Things had got out of hand, that was all. *But, that kiss.* How could I go back to everyday life after that? It had released something inside me I hadn't known existed. I didn't even know what it was, only that I was now filled with an even bigger, restless yearning I didn't know what to do with.

After replaying our conversation for the tenth time, I finally settled into bed and read Augustine's letters again, feeling the longing she'd had for William, as though she was reaching out to me through the years. Had she felt like that about Dolly's grandad, or was it a pale imitation of her *real* love?

Frustrated, I switched off the light and read some more of *The Midnight Hour* on my Kindle, losing myself for a while in Grace Benedict's life, which included a complicated relationship with her alcoholic sister, seeing everything differently now that I knew (and had kissed) the author. I pictured Ryan sitting at a mahogany desk, overlooking the river in front of his house, half an ear open for what might be going on behind the living room door.

At one point, I slipped out of bed on the pretext of going to the bathroom and held my breath, listening for sounds of voices, or even crying, hoping I wouldn't hear anything that hinted at a passionate reunion.

Charlie's bedroom door was open, no light on inside, so at least they weren't in there. I had a peep inside, jumping when I was faced with a poster of Max Weaver on the wall, looking disapproving. How did Ryan feel about the handsome actor watching him sleep? I tried to picture Ryan asleep, then realised I was hovering like a phantom waiting to be discovered and shot back to bed.

I couldn't even message Charlie because I'd left my phone in the living room – though he'd probably be sleeping anyway.

I flumped back on the pillows and closed my eyes, willing sleep to come. I hoped Dolly was OK. I'd missed her presence today as without her around, things felt less solid somehow – as if chaos could break out at any moment (which it almost had).

Much later, I thought I heard whispered voices on the landing, but they merged into a dream where Ryan and I were walking a Great Dane along a cycle path, our arms wrapped around one another, and when I woke, daylight was poking around the curtains.

I squinted at Dolly's digital clock and saw with a shock that the alarm I'd set hadn't gone off and it was nine o'clock. From the sounds downstairs, it was obviously business as usual, but I shot out of bed and hastily dressed in yesterday's discarded clothes (I really must put a wash on) before stepping onto the landing, pulling back quickly when I spotted Ryan and Nicole at the top of the stairs.

Had she stayed the night? Of course she had. Where else would she have gone? As I spied through the gap in the door, I wondered whether Ryan had slept on the sofa and given Nicole his bed. She was wearing her coat, as if she'd never taken it off (I hoped she hadn't) and I tensed when she moved into Ryan's arms. They closed around her, as they must have done hundreds of times before, and she nestled against him for what seemed like ages, before they pulled apart and went downstairs together.

So, a reconciliation, after all.

I waited until I was sure the coast was clear before leaving my room, feeling as if I'd swallowed something heavy that was weighing me down.

'Looks like they've sorted things out,' said Dolly, beaming widely as soon as I entered the kitchen.

'You spoke to them?'

'Just briefly,' she said. 'They're going to have a bite to eat in the café and take a look around before heading to the airport.'

Nausea swirled in my stomach. 'That's great,' I said with forced brightness.

She nodded. 'It's good for those kiddies,' she said, and I wondered what had happened to Ryan's insistence that he wasn't ready to be a father, that the children needed their *real* dad. Perhaps he'd be hands-off, leave the fathering to Nicole's ex, or was he keen to play a big role in their lives – John, the biological one, and Ryan the father…

Perhaps Nicole had come up with some solution that would work for them all – though I couldn't imagine what it would be. That the children live full-time with John, while she moved in with Ryan? Either way, it wasn't my concern.

'Feeling better?' I said drily.

'Top of the world, thank you, love.' Dolly certainly looked in peak condition, her fringe extra glossy, her cheeks glowing, but no longer in a feverish way. 'Frank's on the mend too.'

'That's good, considering how ill he was yesterday.' Her gaze remained steady, as innocent as a child's. 'And Charlie?' I looked around, wondering whether he was in the café, where I recognised Margot's distinctive voice, asking for her 'usual'.

'He had a very sore throat last night.' Dolly prepared to roll out some pastry, and I hoped she hadn't looked in the bin outside and seen my burnt offerings from yesterday. 'He said he was going to try and sleep it off. He wants to be better for when Elle gets here.' Her eyes twinkled at me. 'Sounds like you and Ryan did a great job yesterday.'

'I wouldn't go that far.' My gaze strayed in the direction of the café. *Was he still wearing the shirt I'd unbuttoned yesterday evening?*

My face grew fiery hot.

'Sure you're OK?' Dolly pinned me with her all-seeing eyes. 'You're not running a fever?'

'I'm fine.' I injected my voice with a smile. 'Ryan's great with the coffee machine.' *And a world-class kisser.*

'He's a natural.' *Unlike you*, she didn't add as she nodded to Stefan's brother, who was approaching the sink with a tray of plates in each hand.

'Looks like *he's* recovered too,' I said. 'What a coincidence that everyone's healthy and the café's fully staffed once more.'

Dolly looked round. 'Oh, Sacha,' she said. 'Yes, he's fine.'

'I've never known people get better so quickly from the flu.' I studied her face for a tell-tale tic or twitch, but Dolly gave nothing away.

'Sacha's was just a twenty-four-hour thing.' She took the lid off a jar of fragrant mincemeat and dug a spoon inside with an expertise borne from years of practice. 'You sound suspicious, Nina.' She cocked her head. 'Don't you believe Sacha was ill?'

Hearing his name, Sacha looked up from the dishwasher, big brown eyes wide with alarm.

I shook my head. 'Of course not,' I mumbled, tugging at my crumpled shirt. I must look a state in the trousers I'd managed to cover in flour the day before, with just a clean dark square where my apron had been. 'I'm glad everyone's feeling better.'

'Apart from Charlie.'

'I'm sure he'll be fully recovered by lunchtime.' I looked away from Dolly's reproachful stare. 'Did he know Nicole was going to turn up?'

She didn't flinch at the abrupt change of topic. 'He spoke to her on the phone yesterday morning,' she said. 'He thought it was likely, but didn't want to tell Ryan in case he tried to put her off, or did a runner.'

Odd, when he'd been the one telling Ryan to ignore Nicole in the first place. 'I don't think he'd have done a runner, Dolly, he's not a teenager.'

'She said she wanted to tell him something he needed to hear.'

'But she didn't say what?'

Dolly's hands stilled. 'You sound very interested.'

'It's just we were having… dinner and she walked in.'

'You and Ryan were having dinner together?'

I had no idea why she sounded so pleased when it didn't matter any more. 'He'd made a chicken chasseur in the slow cooker.'

'Oh, how lovely!' she said as if it hadn't been her idea in the first place. 'He's really quite domesticated, you know.' As if seeing something in my face, she began cutting circles out of the pasty and pressing them into a tart tin. 'The knitting ladies thought you were lovely,' she said, knowing when to switch topic. 'Dee said Margot told her what a splendid job you'd made of her front room.'

I remembered Dee was the florist with red, spiky hair, who'd eaten the most macarons and whose knitting was the most puzzling: a jumble of mismatched colours that stretched to the floor, wide at the top and gradually narrowing. When Madame Bisset came in and sat nearby, giving me a conspiratorial smile, Delphine had leapt under the knitters' table and clawed at the end of whatever Dee was making.

'It is fine, she will not notice,' Madame Bisset had assured me, once Delphine had returned to her lap, keeping one eye on me. I hadn't dared touch her, in case I activated her attack button.

'That's nice,' I said to Dolly, coming back to the moment.

'She'd like you to do her bedroom.'

'Oh?' I brightened. 'When?'

'Any time.' Dolly spooned mincemeat into the pastry moulds. 'She lives above the shop. You can go up and do it whenever you like.'

'Word travels fast around here.' I indulged a quick fantasy of me advertising my services: *Nina Bailey: The House Whisperer. Let me bring out the beauty in your home.* So many houses, so many rooms – it was almost irresistible. I clenched my tingling fingers and tried to push them in my pockets, but the trousers were too tight.

'Chamillon's a small place,' said Dolly. 'But there are other villages on the island. You'd never be short of work.'

'I can't stay here, Dolly.'

'I don't see why not.' She placed the tray in the oven. 'But it's the sort of business you could set up anywhere.'

Before I could respond, she turned and said brightly, 'Breakfast?'

'Could I take some coffee upstairs? I'm feeling a bit...' My words petered out as I imagined Ryan and Nicole, heads together over whichever table they were sitting at, catching up on the past few months, probably riddled with lust. After everything he'd said, all it had taken was for her to literally turn up on the doorstep, wearing a swingy coat, to bring home to him exactly what he'd lost, his resolve swept away with one blast of her dewy eyes and a gentle touch on his arm. 'I'm a bit tired.'

'I know what day it is, Nina.'

I jolted. 'What?'

'It would have been your wedding day today.' Dolly's voice was gentle.

'That's right, it... it would.' *How could I have forgotten?*

'If you need some time alone, I understand, but remember, love, if it was meant to be, you'd still be together.' Augustine and William leapt into my head, and I wondered whether that was true, or whether other forces had kept them apart. 'And not all men are like him.' She was obviously referring to Scott. She never got to meet him after his no-show at the café, which I knew even then she'd felt spoke volumes about his character.

'I know that, Dolly, but thank you.' All of a sudden I was very near to tears. I wondered whether to tell her it was more about Gran than Scott, knowing she'd understand, but now I'd told Ryan, I didn't feel the need to say it again. Telling him how I'd felt had put it into perspective, I realised. I would always be sad that she hadn't lived to see me get married, and a part of me still believed that calling off the wedding had precipitated her death – but I knew in my heart she wouldn't have wanted me to marry a man who'd cheated on me, a man who didn't love me the way I wanted to be loved. 'I think I might go for a bike ride,' I said instead. 'Blow away the cobwebs.'

'That wind will blow *you* away.' She turned to the window, and I saw it was snowing once more, flakes hurtling past the glass. Elvis was singing 'Blue Christmas' on the CD player, which Dolly had placed on the windowsill, and she was baking mince pies in her reindeer jumper. It was almost like being back home.

'Maybe I'll go for a walk later on, instead.'

Chapter Twenty-Two

Dolly made me some coffee and fetched me a couple of pains au chocolat, which I took upstairs and stuck my head around Charlie's bedroom door. The room was empty and as tidy as ever, with no sign of any activity – even sleeping. Ryan's suitcase was lying at the foot of the bed, so he'd have to come back to collect it before going to the airport. Unwilling to examine my feelings about him leaving, I went through to the living room and placed my coffee and pastries on the table, before looking in the kitchen to see it was clean and tidy in there too. I wondered whether Ryan or Nicole had done the washing-up. Perhaps they'd done it together, falling into old habits.

I went back to my room, gathered my dirty clothes and put them in the washing machine, then sat at the dining table, scanning the sofa for evidence that it had been slept on as I drank my coffee. The sofa-bedding was in the same neat pile it had been when I left the room, the cushions squashed in places, where Ryan and I had— I snapped off the memory, and wondered what would have happened if Nicole hadn't turned up.

I also wondered what had possessed me to kiss Ryan in the first place. I'd known his life was complicated, and I was supposed to be focusing on my career, not snogging men while I was here. Even if he had the most kissable lips in the universe.

Stop it, Nina. It was over – whatever 'it' was – before it had barely begun.

I picked my phone off the coffee table and messaged Charlie. *How's the invalid this morning?* He was probably still sleeping, so I didn't expect an answer right away.

I ate a pain au chocolat without really tasting it, then took a photo of the tree and sent it in a message to Ben. *What do you get if you cross an apple with a Christmas tree? A PINEapple!! X (pine as in pine tree, pine as in pineapple… the fruit.)*

You're hilarious he replied, seconds later. He was never far from his phone even out in the fields, or supervising milking time. *How's it going?*

Surprisingly eventful. How's life on the farm?

He sent an image of a dog 'driving' a tractor.

I miss Tess! I replied.

She's been going to the farm shop with Mum, the customers love her.

How's the donkey training going?

She's been trying to teach Barney to sit down.

???!!!

What have you bought me for Xmas?

I sent an image of a black hole and he responded with a crying emoji.

Say hi to Mum and Dad for me.

They hate you and don't want to see you again X

Hate you too XXXXXX

Feeling cheered, I put down my phone and finished my coffee, then looked at Ryan's laptop, which was open in front of me, the screen black. I pressed a key, not expecting it to come on, or to at least be password protected this time, but just like before, a document sprang up. He really was careless about security. What if I was a rival novelist and pinched his ideas? Or I found his email inbox and sent an embarrassing message to everyone on his address list. Not that I would. Anna had once sent a picture of a cat dressed as the Cookie Monster to everyone at work and nearly got the sack.

I pushed my plate aside and looked more closely at the page. He'd stopped typing mid-sentence, as though he'd been interrupted – probably by me.

I scrolled back a bit, feeling furtive, but also excited, just as I had reading Augustine's letters to William. I couldn't resist a glimpse of the new Grace Benedict novel before anyone else saw it. Only one page, I promised myself, pulling the laptop closer. Anything more would be a total invasion of privacy.

...Noah was a force of nature; funny, sweet and kind, with a sense of humour that made people warm to him. He was Grace's opposite in many ways and she wondered whether that was why she found him intriguing, even if his approach to police work was somewhat unorthodox. She'd heard that on one occasion,

Noah had turned up to a job wearing a one-piece sleepsuit – a onesie – designed to look like a penguin, complete with a yellow beak. An icebreaker, he'd said, executing a funny penguin dance, arms clamped to his sides...

I stopped, mouth falling open and read the paragraph again. The character was clearly based on me. Ryan had taken my advice to heart and given Grace an adversary, but not the hard-bitten, gum-chewing, smart-mouthed female I'd had in mind, someone for Grace to lock horns with. Instead, he'd used my onesie as inspiration, and turned me into a *man*.

I scrolled down and read some more.

...Noah was adept at catching criminals, his record was a testament to that, and he never looked happier than when doing the thing he loved most, but he was no great shakes in the kitchen – could barely boil an egg, in fact. He did love tidying up though, and took great pleasure in rearranging his surroundings – releasing their potential – a trait that Grace admired and found endearing. In fact, murder was on her mind less and less these days. She almost wished she didn't find Noah Dailey so attractive...

'You've got to be kidding me!' I couldn't work out whether I was flattered or outraged by Ryan plundering my life for entertainment. What next? Was he going to write in what I'd told him last night? Would *Noah* suddenly confess to having called off his wedding – a wedding he'd only agreed to in order to make his dying grandmother happy? Or maybe he'd change it to *grandfather*, because that would be original. Would he find some ancient love letters and uncover a passionate affair that he had to stay quiet about?

I felt winded. Was this why Ryan had been suddenly keen to talk to me? Perhaps he'd decided I was a rich source of material. It would have been more flattering if he'd written me in as a sassy but sexy redhead (I'd always fancied having red hair), who was brilliant at kick-boxing, and could speak Japanese and had a Pomeranian called Sushi.

Still unsure how I felt, wishing I hadn't looked... *what was the visual form of eavesdropping called? Snooping, I supposed...* I closed the laptop and felt the walls closing in; I needed to get some air, snowing or not.

I threw on my coat, dragged on my boots, grabbed my purse and phone and ran downstairs. Dolly wasn't in the kitchen, but I didn't want to go through to the café and anyway, she didn't need a rundown of my whereabouts. I was a grown woman (apparently).

I let myself out of the back door and almost screamed when I bumped into Mathilde coming in, shrinking back from her thunderous glare as she passed.

The wind was bracing, blowing flurries of snowflakes that blurred my vision as I headed away from the harbour, but it didn't stop me from spotting the swish of Nicole's scarlet coat in the distance, her hair cascading from a black knitted hat with a furry pom-pom on top. She was walking beside Ryan, her arm through his, her cheek pressed to the sleeve of his coat as if trying to draw warmth from him. It was such a loving gesture, I felt my insides drop.

Picking up pace, I followed them through the streets to a medieval-style square which had been transformed into a winter wonderland of wooden huts and market stalls, strung with coloured lights and displaying gifts, crafts and food. It was surprisingly busy, considering the weather, and people seemed in good spirits as they browsed.

There was a tall pine tree, wrapped with winking lights and topped with a flashing star, and a small, glistening ice-rink in the middle of the square, dotted with warmly dressed children on wobbling blades, trailed by smiling parents. If I'd still hoped to avoid signs of Christmas, I'd definitely come to the wrong place, but found myself soaking up the atmosphere, and taking some photos just because I wanted to.

I lost myself among the shoppers, keeping track of Ryan and Nicole's progress as I took in the array of goods around me: handcrafted candles and soaps, wooden toys and fine crystal, handmade glass and Angora sweaters. There were plenty of local specialties on offer too – fresh bread, pralines and fudge – and a stall heaped with fresh seafood: eel, shrimp and trout.

I paused as Nicole stopped to admire a nativity scene in an open stall, complete with straw and a baby Jesus in a wooden crib. She seemed enchanted as she exclaimed and pointed, but I thought Ryan's smile looked rather fixed. Perhaps he was thinking about his book (maybe I'd get written out, now they were back together) or even our kiss last night… I cut off the thought before it grew wings. It was more likely I'd misread his expression and he was simply feeling the cold.

As the icy air bit at my cheeks, I shuffled closer to a stall selling Mirabelle plum liqueur and drank one of the tiny samples, which tasted like warm honey, then bought a bottle, which I tucked inside my coat. I could give it to Dolly for Christmas – she deserved something nice. It was selfish to not buy gifts, just because the season was a reminder of my non-wedding and of losing Gran.

Returning my gaze to Ryan, I saw that he'd taken his phone out and was poking at the screen. His hair was sprinkled white with snow, giving him a distinguished air, and I imagined what he might look like when he was older. For a moment, I thought he was going to take a photo of Nicole, who was holding up a toy polar bear wearing a Christmas hat, but he carried on prodding his screen, not seeming to notice. I caught the roll of her eyes as she put down the bear, and felt a bit sorry for her. Maybe she'd thought about buying the bear for Lulu or Jackson, and wanted Ryan's approval. *What was wrong with him?*

Then he stuffed his phone in his pocket, said something that made her laugh, and she nodded and picked up the bear again and handed a note to the stallholder, which she fished from a tiny purse in her pocket.

They ambled to the next stall, and Nicole picked up a gingerbread heart with 'Noël' piped in icing. She waggled it at Ryan, who shook his head, and put it back with a shrug.

I trailed them through the market to the shops skirting the square, which were ablaze with lights and festive decorations, stopping when they entered the boulangerie and Ryan turned, as if sensing he was being followed. *What was I doing, sneaking after them?*

Turning away, I inserted myself into a throng of chattering Germans and feigned interest in the nearest stall, heart banging against my ribs. If I'd wanted to see what they were like together, well, now I knew. They were like any other couple out exploring. Nicole had expressed a desire to see the island where her ex had been hiding out, and do a bit of Christmas shopping before they headed to the airport. Perfectly normal.

It suddenly struck me that she might have been to the island with Ryan before – after all, he'd visited Charlie in the past. The thought was unsettling, as though Chamillon, the café and everyone in it belonged to me, and Nicole was an intruder. *What was happening to me?* I looked down to see I was holding a pair of *charentaises* – traditional woollen slippers with crêpe soles that looked just the right size to fit Ryan.

I remembered his bare feet in the kitchen as he'd cleaned up the milk I'd spilled when he made me scream, and before I knew it, I'd paid for the slippers and they were in a paper bag with string handles in my hand, along with the bottle of Mirabelle liqueur. They'd probably fit Charlie, I reasoned, as I scurried away, boots slipping a little on the fresh fall of snow. Not that I'd ever seen Charlie wearing slippers, but there had to be a first time for everything.

I looked round, as if Ryan might be advancing, ready to accuse me of stalking, but could only see people enjoying the festive ambience, unaware of the crazy woman in their midst.

As the snow fell harder, I decided it was time to leave.

Chapter Twenty-Three

I couldn't face going back to the café and thought of Dee, the florist. Dolly had mentioned I could go round anytime, and sorting out Dee's bedroom was a task guaranteed to keep my mind off everything else.

The shop wasn't difficult to spot, the greenery in the window vivid against the whiteness all around, and if Dee was surprised to see me again, she didn't show it as she emerged from behind the counter, this time followed by a little white dog.

'It's Bon-Bon,' I said, bending to pat her soft head as she sniffed my feet.

'I look after her now my sister has moved away,' Dee said.

'I saw her being walked on the beach the other morning.'

'Ah, yes.' Dee made a gentle shooing motion, and Bon-Bon retreated politely to a plush, padded dog bed by a pewter bucket of big-headed purple flowers. 'Dolly, she was very kind to offer her visitor, the writer, to take her out when my dog walker was ill.'

I knew it was a set-up. 'Very kind,' I murmured as Dee led me up to her bedroom without question. It was easily the untidiest I'd ever seen – more of a storeroom than a bedroom.

'The untidier the better,' I said, when she offered an apology, blaming a busy workload. 'I really don't mind.'

'I want it to be like…' She made a wafting motion with her long, thin arms and did an impression of sinking into sleep, pressing her hands together and resting her cheek against them, eyes fluttering shut behind her narrow glasses.

'Relaxing,' I said. '*Relaxant?*' It sounded almost the same in French and I blushed a little as I looked for a place to put my bag down, settling for a dressing table crowded with floral paraphernalia.

Dee smiled and nodded and disappeared, returning as I was shedding my coat with a mug of blue-tinted water that gave off a flowery scent. 'Blue tea,' she explained. 'Oolong, blended with blue butterfly pea flowers.'

It looked as if it should have a paintbrush in it, but when I took a sip it tasted like walking through a meadow. '*Délicieux.*' I smiled my appreciation, even as a scene from Ryan's book popped into my head, where a shop owner offers Grace some Chai tea that turns out to be drugged. '*Merci.*'

'You do not have to speak French. My English is very good.'

There was no disputing that. 'How's the knitting?' I said, putting my mug on the cluttered dressing table.

She prodded her glasses onto the bridge of her nose, a cloud crossing her narrow face. 'When I came home, I saw it was badly damaged,' she said. 'It was a scarf for my husband – a Christmas gift – but maybe I will buy him one from the market.'

From what I'd seen of the 'scarf', Delphine had done Dee's husband a massive favour. 'It can't be rescued?'

Her eyes brightened. 'Maybe I could ask my friend, Marie,' she said. 'She is very good with the wool.'

Oops! Maybe I shouldn't have said anything. Poor Marie was going to have her work cut out. 'Good idea.'

Downstairs, the doorbell tinkled, heralding the arrival of a customer, and once Dee had insisted nothing was off-limits and to let my imagination 'be free', she left me to it. I finished my flower tea and poked around, examining the contents of various boxes, reminded once more of the letters at the apartment. After visualising how the layout would work best, I rolled up my shirtsleeves and set about transforming the room into the relaxing space Dee craved.

It was surprisingly easy, once I'd moved most of the clutter down to the little storeroom at the back of the shop, but when I'd finished, I was amazed to see that several hours had flown by, and I hadn't thought about anything but the job. It was like therapy, but free, and I didn't have to talk to anyone – apart from disturbing Dee a couple of times to ask for picture hooks, and a hammer and a screwdriver (I really needed my own toolkit).

She endearingly covered her eyes when I was done and let me lead her upstairs, and I realised my heart was racing, adrenaline flooding my body. This was the best bit – waiting for her response. I knew it could go either way (though I hoped she wouldn't burst into angry tears), but the buzz of anticipation was almost worth it.

Luckily, when Dee dropped her hands from her eyes, her expression was one of surprised joy – just as Gérard and Margot's had been. I almost wanted to take a picture – then realised I should, for my blog. Not my travel blog, but the house-whispering one I clearly needed to start. I almost laughed aloud as the realisation crystallised.

Of course this was what I wanted to do for a living. I just had to stop fighting it. 'Do you mind?' I said to Dee, taking out my phone.

'Of course,' she said, and as I snapped away, I explained how I'd moved the bed so it wasn't directly in line with the door and had easier access from both sides, and that I'd rehung the mirror on the opposite wall to the window to spread the light around, making a mental note to write up the tips on my blog.

'It looks so *different*,' she breathed, taking in the cleared surface of her dressing table, her floral accessories back in the shop where they belonged. '*Maman!*' she exclaimed, spotting the pair of pictures above the bed I'd found stuffed in a box underneath, of a smiling woman surrounded by buckets of bright flowers outside an older, sun-bathed version of the shop. 'I had forgotten all about them.' Her eyes shone as she moved to examine them more closely, and I felt an ache in my cheeks from smiling as I put my phone away and retrieved my bag and coat.

'I'm so glad you like it,' I said.

She turned, eyes sweeping from the newly-attached light shade to the small pile of books on the nightstand, down to the clear stretch of gleaming floorboards. Sliding her hand into the oversized pocket of her apron dress, she took out a handful of notes. 'I'm *very* happy.' There was an emotional catch in her voice. 'I think I will sleep well in here tonight.'

I didn't ask what her husband would think – it was clear that this was Dee's room, regardless of who she shared it with. 'I don't want payment.' I waved her money away. 'It's practice for me,' I said. 'You're happy, I'm happy.'

'This is not a good way to run a business.' She reluctantly tucked the money back with a frown. 'You must set a tariff.'

'I will.' It sounded like a promise, and the irony of those two words, which should have been spoken in an entirely different context today, wasn't lost on me: 'When I have more experience.'

'I will recommend you,' Dee said. 'My friends, they will be very happy for you to do this.' She looked back at the room, which was awash with light filtering through the muslin curtain at the window. 'I will show them.'

'You don't have to do that,' I said. 'I'll be returning to England after Christmas.'

'Ah.' She nodded, looking as if she didn't quite believe me – as though people who came to Chamillon never left. Then I remembered that was what had happened to Dolly and Charlie, and even Elle was returning to live at the café. 'You are lucky you have a calling,' Dee said. 'I did not find mine, but I am good with the flowers, thanks to *Maman*.' Her smile returned. 'Let me make you another bouquet.'

I nodded, chewing over her words as I followed her downstairs. It was sad to think she was a florist because she felt she'd had no choice, and I hoped that wasn't my brother's view about working on the farm, though he seemed to be enjoying it so far. Not all jobs were instant cures for sadness. I knew that from working at the pub and then the gallery. It was so easy to fall into doing something just to earn a living – it was what most people did, after all. I supposed anyone who had a *calling*, as Dee had put it, was one of the lucky ones, like Dolly with the café, and Ryan and his writing, although – recalling the frustrated outburst I'd read on his laptop the day I arrived – even that had its moments.

As my thoughts landed back on Ryan, the sense of peace I'd felt in Dee's bedroom began to evaporate. He was probably at the airport now, and I'd let him go without even saying goodbye.

It was for the best, I decided, fondling Bon-Bon's ears as I watched Dee expertly hand-tie a bunch of winter-white roses and some other white flowers I thought might be irises but didn't like to ask. I'd only just started getting to know him, and one amazing kiss didn't compare to a relationship that had almost led to a wedding – still could, if he and Nicole managed to work things out. I imagined his reunion with Lulu and Jackson and felt an almost melancholic twist, as if I was mourning something that had never even happened. Thank God they were young enough to adjust to all these changes – at least, I hoped they would, once things had settled down.

'You don't like them?'

I realised Dee was holding out the flowers, while I stared at the space above her head, imagining Ryan, Nicole and the children on a fairground ride, her fantastic hair whipping across her face, the children's laughter streaming out and Ryan… I couldn't quite place him in the scene, probably because I'd inserted myself into the picture, and now there was just the two of us, on Dolly's orange sofa, locked in each other's arms – *I was a terrible person.*

'Oh, I'm so sorry, I was miles away! They're *magnifique.*' I took the flowers from Dee and pressed my nose into the velvety rose petals before arranging them in the bag with the slippers and bottle of liqueur. It was starting to look a lot like Christmas shopping. On impulse, I pointed to a pretty cut-glass vase on a shelf. 'I'll take that too, *s'il vous plaît.*'

Looking pleased, Dee wrapped it in layers of white tissue paper and refused to let me pay. 'You have earned it,' she said, kissing me on both cheeks. '*Merci*, and *joyeux Noël.*' She tilted her eyes to the ceiling. I could tell she was waiting for me to go, so she could run upstairs and admire her room once more, and I left the shop feeling happy that I'd brightened her day.

I still wasn't quite ready to return to the café and ducked into the gift shop next to Dee's, where I checked to see if Charlie had replied to my message. *Nothing.* I called the number and it went straight to voicemail. Maybe his phone battery had died and there wasn't a charger at the cottage. Unless he'd turned it off and was still sleeping through whatever lurgy Dolly was insisting he had. *Poor Charlie.* He must have had the usual childhood ailments, but I couldn't remember him ever being ill when he was staying at the farm – not counting the time he disturbed a wasp's nest and got badly stung and reacted as though he had the plague, demanding Mum call out a doctor because of 'anaphylactic shock and poison'.

Thinking back, it was the only time I'd seen him really grumpy, ordering me to fetch him drinks and make him toast and check his stings to see if they were getting worse. 'He's scared, that's all,' Mum had said when I complained that he was being 'nasty'. 'He's frightened he's going to die.' She was blunt about death – most people in the farming community were – but Charlie had heard the words 'going to die' and started sobbing hysterically, and Ben had to let him have a go on his new Nintendo.

'*Allez-vous acheter?*' Back in the moment, I realised I'd been fingering a keyring in the shape of a fluffy ginger cat that reminded me of Delphine, and instantly recalled how Ryan had pressed his face to the grouchy cat's fur and looked as if he was in love.

'Yes, I'm going to buy.' I handed the keyring to the snooty assistant, who eyed me suspiciously, as if unused to seeing visitors daydreaming in her shop. 'These too,' I added, grabbing some novelty pink braces and a souvenir pen, as if to show her I wasn't a shoplifter.

'Thirty euros,' she said in perfect English, raising her neatly pencilled eyebrows.

I raised my natural eyebrows. 'Thirty euros?' I pointed to the label on the box. 'It says two euros ninety-nine here.'

'Twelve euros ninety-nine.' She said it in a tone of such contempt that I made a point of counting out the exact amount of money, practically curtseying before leaving the shop.

Outside the snow had stopped, leaving an untouched stretch of pure white on the quiet street, which was tucked away from the busy market square.

I crossed the road, my boot prints joining the bike tracks left by a couple of cyclists, who seemed to be taking great pleasure in making a pattern of tyre marks in the snow, looking back dangerously to admire the trail they'd made.

On a whim, I made up my mind to visit Frank and Charlie at the cottage. It was a risk, if they really were ill and contagious, but it must be miserable being cooped up. I could make them something to eat, if they felt up to it. Even I could manage to make a sandwich or some eggs. As long as the eggs were scrambled. I was hungry too, now I thought about it, having only drunk a flowery tea at Dee's since my pain au chocolat hours ago.

I pushed my phone into my pocket and walked back through the square, where a pair of teenage girls were gliding expertly around the ice-rink, jumping and twirling to the delight of the watching crowd, and rounded the harbour to the row of white-fronted cottages facing the café. The sky had darkened, lights twinkling across the water, the snowy rooftops glistening, and I suddenly wished Mum and Dad were here to appreciate the view, instead of the usual vista of muddy fields. It was ages since Dad had been anywhere, and I knew Uncle Hank would be only too happy to take charge of the farm for a few days. It would be good for Dad to take a break, especially one with Mum.

Then I remembered I'd wanted to escape all reminders of home and Gran, and they could hardly come away anyway with all Mum's Christmas preparations coming to the boil.

I tapped on the cottage door and when no one answered, tentatively opened it, mindful of the sight that had greeted Ryan and me at Gérard's house. Not that there was any chance of seeing a half-naked woman parading around here. Even if Frank wasn't crazy about Dolly, he probably wasn't up to much more than blowing his nose right now.

I'd half expected to find him in front of the TV, maybe wrapped in a blanket, a pile of scrunched-up tissues beside him, but the living room was in darkness. I glanced at the table where we'd eaten dinner, the vase of flowers still there. Had it really only been a few nights ago that Charlie had told Ryan to ignore Nicole's call and I'd asked him about 'his' children? It was hard to believe how much had happened in the short space of time since.

And now he was flying back to England.

Fighting an urge to run all the way to the airport and… *what?* Wish him luck? Beg him to stay? Wrestle him to the floor and clamp my mouth to his? I checked the kitchen area, in case Frank had collapsed by the cooker, and jumped when I heard a sound from upstairs, like the whine of a drill.

I moved to the bottom of the stairs and glanced up. There was light slicing from under one of the doors off the landing, and I was about to call out when I heard something else. *Music.* A faint, but familiar salsa beat drifting from the bedroom.

Chapter Twenty-Four

My heart dropped as I imagined Frank in bed, a buxom woman stroking his forehead – or something else – thinking the coast was clear because Dolly wasn't around. Unless she'd come home early. But there was no sign of her; no coat, no bag, no shoes in the entrance. No *sense* of her in the house.

I wondered whether to creep out, go back to the café and pretend I hadn't been here, then remembered Charlie. Surely Frank wouldn't have a woman on the premises when his stepson (*that* sounded weird) was in the spare room asleep. Unless it was Charlie up there with a female. *No.* His short-term flings were a thing of the past now that he'd met Elle, and he would hardly bring someone here, even if he wasn't unwell.

And where did the drill fit in? It was going again in quick bursts, and when it stopped there was a groan, followed by a thump on the floor as though something heavy had been dropped. Ruling out a female presence, I risked a hesitant, 'Frank?' My voice sounded too weedy, so I tried again, 'FRANK!'

There was another thud and some muffled cursing, then the music went off and the light on the landing grew brighter as the bedroom door flew open. Frank appeared at the top of the stairs, his hair awry, one of his red braces flopping over his trousers. *Thank God he was fully-clothed.*

'Nina!' He snapped on the overhead light, looking like he'd seen a statue come to life. 'What are you doing here?'

His words immediately made me think of Ryan – *again*. Everything seemed to circle back to him. 'I came to see how you are.' I climbed the next few stairs, pausing when Frank stepped back as if I was primed to attack.

'That's very kind of you.' He smoothed his hair down in a nervy gesture as though remembering his manners. 'I'm feeling much better, thank you.'

I tried to look past him. 'I thought I heard a drill.'

'Oh, *that*.' He shot a look into the bedroom and seemed to make up his mind about something. 'I thought I'd finish Dolly's walk-in wardrobe as a surprise.'

'That's great.' I climbed another couple of steps. He *must* be feeling better if he'd been busy with his drill. 'Can I have a look?' I told myself I wasn't double-checking that there wasn't a woman in the room, and felt a rush of relief when Frank nodded and said, 'Come on then.'

Despite a slight air of resignation, I could tell he'd been dying for an excuse to show off his handiwork. 'I've been having a bit of trouble getting the doors on,' he explained as I joined him on the landing. He had dust on the knees of his trousers and a bruise on his forearm. 'It's really a two-man job.'

'I suppose Charlie's not up to helping.' I looked at the closed door on my left, surprised the noise hadn't brought him out to see what was happening, but he'd always been a deep sleeper.

Frank was shaking his head. 'He's got it pretty bad,' he said, and I was pierced with guilt for having doubted that Charlie was really ill. He was too straightforward to make up something like that. 'I don't suppose you could give me a hand?'

Frank sounded so hopeful I couldn't bring myself to refuse. 'Sure,' I said, following him into the bedroom, which was decorated in typical

Dolly fashion: blush pink walls, grass-green accessories, French-style furniture and lavishly framed photos scattered along the surfaces. There was one of her and Frank in a salsa clinch, and an unposed shot of their wedding day, Dolly in her powder-blue dress, her head thrown back in laughter as Frank smiled alongside her, smart in his stone-coloured suit.

There were several photographs of Augustine at various ages, and I found myself scanning her face for clues to her feelings, as if *I'm in love with another man* might be written in her eyes, but she looked the same as she always did in pictures: not quite smiling, but with an air of contentment that suggested she was happy with her lot.

There were some of Charlie and Elle in various settings, glowing with newly discovered feelings, and one of Charlie as a boy, leaping to head a football, and I was touched to see a photo of Ben and me as children with gappy grins, and one of Mum in her pre-farm days, wearing a figure-hugging dress, ankle bracelet and four-inch heels, her silky hair glinting with highlights. Back then, she used to steal Dolly's boyfriends (according to Dolly), until she met Dad at a barn dance she'd been dragged to by a friend who knew his brother and instantly fell in love (according to Dad).

There was a smell of new wood in the room, and a door lying flat on the plush cream carpet where it had fallen. As Frank bent to pick it up, I peered inside the wardrobe, which was really more of a walk-in cupboard with two rows of railings for Dolly's clothes. Frank had fitted downlighters and plenty of shoe shelves, which Dolly would struggle to fill unless she developed a serious passion for footwear. 'There's a cupboard for your aunt's handbags,' Frank said, with touching enthusiasm. 'And I'm making his and her drawers for our belts and gloves.'

I wondered how many belts and gloves they had (or needed), then spotted several belts coiled like snakes on one of the shelves and a row of the sort of black leather gloves that TV killers wore to murder people. I made a mental note to tell Ryan about them – perhaps he could work a scene into his book – then remembered it was unlikely I'd ever see him again.

'You've done a good job,' I said, putting my bag on the floor to help Frank shift the door. 'Dolly will love it.'

He looked pleased, his healthy colour deepening. There was no sign that he had a cold – if anything, he looked fighting fit. 'Where will you put your clothes?'

'Oh, I've got a couple of drawers in the chest over there, and I only need half a rail for my suits.'

I hid a smile as we manoeuvred the door into place, and as Frank sank down on one knee, I could easily imagine him proposing to Dolly, which he'd apparently done on their fourth date, after their first salsa lesson. He retrieved his screwdriver and I braced my shoulders and in a few minutes the door was where it should be. He opened and closed it a couple of times, nodding his satisfaction when it closed with a pleasing click. 'I think that's it,' he said. 'A coat of paint, and that's your aunt's Christmas gift sorted.'

'You shouldn't really be doing this when you've just been ill,' I said as he began to gather his tools.

He paused for a fraction, then nodded too vigorously. 'I enjoy doing things. I'm like Dolly in that way, I can't be doing with sitting around.'

'Yes, but when you're *ill*, you're supposed to take it easy.'

His movements had sped up, as if he wanted to fast-forward the next few minutes and find me gone. 'I'm good at fighting infections.' He hoisted his braces into place. 'And your aunt took good care of me yesterday, which helped.'

'Were you really ill, Frank?'

He breathed in deeply and then let it out with a sigh: 'No.' I was surprised by how quickly he caved, but admired his honesty. 'Your aunt has very firm ideas about some things.'

'Romance things?'

He pulled out his shirt tail and polished one of his screwdriver handles with great attention to detail. 'I knew straight away she was the one for me, and after my wife died, I didn't think I'd ever love anyone again.'

My throat tightened. 'That's lovely, Frank, but—'

'She's always right.' He gave me a direct look. 'About love.'

'Sorry?'

'She knew that Charlie and Elle were meant to be together from the get-go.'

I wanted to argue that if it had been meant – as Dolly had said to me about Scott – it would have happened anyway, but from everything Mum had told me after the wedding, Dolly had played a big part in Charlie and Elle getting together. 'Did she invent your flu virus as an excuse to spend the day here, so Ryan and I had to run the café together?'

He levelled his gaze to mine. 'Yes.'

'And was she ill herself?'

'No, she doesn't get ill.'

'But she looked feverish.'

'She said she put her face in the dishwasher so that it would turn red.'

Wow. 'And has she been setting us up dog walking and furniture moving, hoping that Ryan and I would bond?'

He nodded.

'You'd make a great informer, Frank,' I said. 'MI5 should snap you up.'

'I don't think I'm telling you anything you don't already know, love.' His expression was sympathetic. 'Hasn't it worked out?'

I thought about saying it had – in a way – but that in a twist of fate, whatever had begun to grow between Ryan and me had been snatched away. 'No,' I said, and felt bad when the smile that had started to brighten his face dropped away. 'His ex turned up and spent the night, and they've flown back to England today.'

'They have?' He sounded surprised. Dolly couldn't have got around to relaying this latest development.

'So, I'm afraid her efforts were wasted.'

'Nothing's ever wasted, love.' I thought about landfill and plastic in the ocean, and all the time I'd wasted doing personality quizzes online when the gallery was quiet, to find out which Disney animal would be my perfect pet (young Simba from *The Lion King*), and which TV character I resembled (Bart Simpson, worryingly), but guessed Frank wasn't talking about the environment or my old work habits. 'There's something to be learnt from every experience,' he said, and I tried to appreciate that he was trying to help. 'I'm sorry if you feel we deceived you.'

I wished Frank had always been my uncle. 'You *did* deceive me.' I cracked a smile to show there were no hard feelings. 'But I'm glad you're not really ill.'

'Your aunt didn't know what to do with herself when she got back here.' He swept a hand over the dressing table and checked it for dust. 'She had a pair of binoculars on the café at one point, checking it hadn't caught fire.'

'It's like her second child,' I said. 'Talking of children, I can't believe that cousin of mine is still sleeping.'

'He *is*?' Frank shot me a look of concerned surprise, as if he'd forgotten that Charlie was in the house.

'I might just go and check on him.' I crossed the landing, glimpsing a busy mosaic of blue and white in the bathroom, and lightly knocked on his door.

'Chuck, are you OK?' I pressed my ear to the frame, but couldn't hear any sounds of him stirring inside.

'What are you doing?'

I turned to see Frank watching with a puzzled stare, his tool bag in his hand.

'I know I shouldn't wake him, but he's been out for hours,' I said. 'Don't you think it's strange?'

'That room's empty.' He came closer, slippers padding softly on the carpet. 'We haven't got round to doing up that room yet. There isn't even a bed in there.'

'So, he slept on the sofa?' *Poor Charlie.* He must be longing to be back in his own bed. 'When did he leave?' *And where has he been all day?*

'About half nine, I suppose.'

'This morning?' I frowned.

'Last night.'

'Last *night*?'

Frank looked taken aback by my tone. 'He said he was going to spend the night at his friend Natalie's house on the rue de Forages.' His eyebrows pinched together. 'Your aunt told him to take the day off today, because he'd got a terrible sore throat, and he said he'd make sure he got a good night's sleep there.'

I'd clearly only got half the story from Dolly – either that, or our wires had become crossed. 'I just assumed he was here,' I said, thoughts racing. When Charlie had sent his message the night before, I'd suspected he was in on Dolly's plan and was staying at the cottage to leave Ryan and me alone. Why not just say he was spending the night at Natalie's house, because he was feeling unwell? Maybe he'd known we'd feel bad if he admitted there wasn't a bed for him at his mum's and would have insisted he come home. 'He's not answering his phone,' I said, returning to the bedroom to fetch my bag.

'Maybe he's back at the café. I'll give Dolly a call.'

I followed Frank downstairs and waited while he found his phone, unease circling in the pit of my stomach. I still hadn't eaten and my insides felt hollow.

'He's not there,' he said moments later, a note of worry in his voice. 'She hasn't heard from him all day.'

My heart began to race. 'Is there a landline at Natalie's house?'

'I don't know, but Dolly will have the number if there is, so let me—'

'It's fine, I'll go round there now,' I interrupted. 'Do you know what number the house is?'

'I do,' he said. 'It's a few streets away from the café, next door to Dolly's friend Marie Girard, who runs a guest house. We went there for dinner the last time Natalie was over with her parents. Her father's a retired police officer, very funny, and Marie's a wonderful cook, though not as good as your aunt, of course, but—'

'Frank!'

'Sorry, sorry, it's number twenty-one. Shall I come with you?' He was reaching for his coat.

'No, it's OK.' I already had the front door open, cold air snaking in. 'I'll call Dolly from there.'

'I'm sure Charlie's fine, but let me know,' Frank said, and the doubt in his voice echoed the one in my head, telling me to hurry, and I didn't look back as I left.

Chapter Twenty-Five

The air was cold and clear, the navy sky scattered with darker clouds, and snow flattened underfoot as I hurried round the harbour, the lights from surrounding buildings guiding my way. The café was still open, the Christmas tree in the window like a guiding light, and I imagined Dolly trying to call Charlie, telling herself she was being overprotective, that he was a grown man who didn't need his mum checking up on him. *Who was I kidding?* She'd be desperate to close the café and look for him herself – then I remembered it was Margot's book launch this evening, and she'd be preparing for that.

I tried to speed up, but there were icy patches where the snow had started to melt and then frozen as the temperature dropped. I'd be no good to anyone if I fell and broke my ankle.

I imagined Charlie in the grip of a fever, staggering, delirious, out into Natalie's garden and getting hypothermia. Was it possible to have a fever *and* hypothermia, or would one cancel the other out?

I checked the street names on each corner, and stumbled across the rue des Forages at the end of a long row of whitewashed houses, their shuttered windows and doors a stark contrast to the snow. Most of the shutters were closed, giving the impression of sleeping eyes, but light spilled from a few, brightening the road outside. There were a couple of parked cars, roofs piled with snow, and I guessed one must be Charlie's.

Approaching, I saw his practical estate car parked halfway between number twenty-one and the house next to it, which must be the guest house Frank had mentioned. I hurried closer, stiff-legged to stop myself sliding, wishing I'd left my bag of shopping behind; my fingers felt frozen around the handles. The house shutters were open, but I couldn't see any light inside, and my heart bumped up a gear as I rapped my knuckles hard on the front door and waited a few seconds.

Nothing.

'Charlie!' I pounded the door with my fist.

No answer, or any sign of movement from inside. Maybe he wasn't here. I moved to the window and pressed my forehead against the icy glass as I attempted to peer inside but the room was in darkness, no sliver of light filtering in from anywhere.

I took my phone from my pocket, remembering I could use it as a torch, swearing when my fumbling fingers brought up a photo of Steven the seagull. *For God's sake.*

I finally found the light and angled the beam so I could see the room, which now had an eerie, haunted house appearance. I was reminded of a film I'd seen with Anna called *Paranormal Activity* and half expected to hear a whooshing sound and a figure to move past the window.

I swung the phone around, heart jumping when I spotted an open paper and a tumbler of half-drunk liquid on a low table in front of the sofa. Charlie had definitely been here at some point. I slowly moved the beam, which picked out his boots on the floor, one tipped on its side as though he'd kicked them off prior to sitting down. He was still here, he *had* to be. His car was outside and had clearly been there overnight, so where else could he have gone? Had he self-medicated on whisky and drunk himself into a stupor? It was hard to imagine, but I should hammer on the door once more, in case he was so deeply asleep he hadn't heard it the first two times.

As I moved my phone, the glare snagged on a set of glowing eyes on the staircase and a scream, bigger than any I'd experienced before, attempted to fly out of my mouth. It got trapped in my throat and I could only stare, open-mouthed with terror.

The eyes moved, and a familiar, fuzzy-edged cat-shape emerged, a paw lifted in readiness for grooming. *Delphine.* 'What the *hell?*' I muttered through chattering teeth, my heart slowing to a gallop. Maybe the cat was staging a protest at her owner's liaison with Gérard by running away. Or, she'd gone looking for her new love, Ryan, and ended up here.

I moved to the door and knocked again, then tried to open it. When it swung inwards, I nearly laughed out loud. Charlie hadn't locked up before going to bed – or passing out, delirious in the garden. Dropping my bags and bunch of flowers on the floor, I felt the wall for a switch and slammed on the light, blinking in the flood of brightness. 'Charlie!' Delphine, who'd frozen mid-paw-lick, shot me a look of intense dislike and disappeared upstairs, and I hurried to the kitchen at the back of the house and stared out of the window.

Light from next door cascaded over the garden, but there was no sign of Charlie. Unless he was in the shed, but the snow on the lawn was thankfully free of footprints – just a set of bird tracks leading to the wall at the end. I opened the back door just in case. 'Charlie!' My voice sounded dead on the air, and I came back inside and took the stairs two at a time.

It was colder up here, and in the first bedroom I came to a plume of icy air funnelled out, even though the window inside was shut. 'Charlie?' The duvet on the brass-framed bed looked like a drift of snow, and was indented in the middle as though it had been lain – or sat on – recently. Pulse fluttering, I darted out and snapped on the landing light. The next room was empty, a tartan blanket neatly folded at the end of the bed, no sign of life other than the faded scents of perfume and men's cologne in the air. In the bathroom, there *were* signs of life – a tube of toothpaste with the lid off, and a towel flung on the laundry basket, and there was a pair of socks on the sparkling quartz-tile floor, as though Charlie had been about to take a shower but was interrupted. Or maybe his feet had been hot and, in his delirium, he had thought the tiles were snow. I wasn't sure why I'd fixated on him being delirious, but it seemed the only explanation for him not being where he should be.

A frustrated sense of panic rose as I ran downstairs and checked the living room again – a nice room, I could see in proper lighting; cosy and inviting, everything where it should be. I ran to the kitchen, jumping slightly when I spotted a photo on the windowsill of an elderly couple, sitting on spread-out coats on a grassy hillock. Probably Natalie's grandparents.

Unbidden, I thought of Gran. 'Where's Charlie?' I said out loud, and as if she'd heard and sent a sign, I detected the faintest noise directly above me; a slight scraping sound that triggered a rush of adrenaline. I took the stairs more cautiously, half-expecting to see Delphine arranging herself on top of a wardrobe, ready to jump on my head, but when I looked in the first bedroom, she was standing by a door I hadn't noticed before.

It was slightly open, and I realised where the draught was coming from: an en suite bathroom. The window in there must be open. I darted across the room, stumbling over Delphine, who'd chosen that moment to wind herself through my legs in a figure of eight, tail lashing with pleasure – or anger. As I toppled, I shot out my hands, falling into space as the door slammed open, sending me crashing to my hands and knees on the floor inside. 'Jesus *Christ*!' *That cat!*

I sucked in a breath, waiting for the pain in my knee to subside, shivering with cold in the darkness. I lifted my head, looking for the light-pull, when I noticed a shadowy outline on the floor by a claw-footed bath, and felt all the breath leave my body. Not only was one foot awkwardly twisted, a dark stain was spreading from under his head.

'*Charlie*!' I crawled forward, fighting an urge to be sick. 'Charlie, wake up!' I lifted his arm, scrabbling my fingers down to his wrist. His skin felt dry and hot, in spite of how cold the room was, which at least meant he couldn't be dead. 'Charlie!' I couldn't make out if it was his pulse I could feel, or the rapid beat of my heart in my fingertips.

'Chuck, wake up,' I pleaded, as if this was one of our childhood games and he was pretending to be dead to scare me. Any second now, he'd rear up, howling like a wolf, and I'd scream loudly enough to bring my parents charging into the room.

When he didn't move, I rested my hand on his chest and felt a faint rise and fall. *He was breathing*. 'Charlie.' His name came out on a sob and he groaned and twisted his head.

'Elle?'

'Charlie, it's me, Nina.' I took his face gently between my hands, tears spilling over. 'You mustn't move your head,' I told him. 'You've had a fall.'

'Whereami?' It came out as one word, thickened by pain, or maybe his painful throat. 'Wha… ithurts,' he slurred.

'Where?'

'Everything.'

'Don't try to talk.' I kissed his forehead. *Too hot.* He smelt strongly of citrus, as if he'd recently sprayed himself with strong deodorant. 'You're at Natalie's house,' I said, wiping a hand over my face before feeling for my phone. 'I'm going to get help.' As I said it, I realised I didn't know the number for the emergency services. I'd have to call Dolly and get her to ring them – only, I didn't have the number for the café. Or Frank's number, or anyone else's in Chamillon. I thought about asking Charlie, but I didn't want to worry him – plus his eyes were closed once more.

Whimpering, I brought up Google, but had only got as far as typing in *whatis ebergency bumbers fro frannece* before my battery gave up and died – probably in protest at my trembly-fingered spelling mistakes.

'*Shit!*'

'Wassup?' Charlie tried to move again and let out a bloodcurdling yell, hand shooting to his leg. 'Think s'broken, Nina.'

I felt a fresh twist of panic. 'Charlie, what the hell happened?' I said, forgetting I'd just urged him not to speak. But he'd slumped back into semi-consciousness before I could ask where his phone was. 'Keep an eye on him,' I ordered Delphine, who was sitting Sphinx-like on the toilet seat, eyes gleaming like headlights. 'Do NOT eat his face.'

I didn't want to leave him, but couldn't wait around on the off chance that Frank or Dolly would be worried enough to turn up. I got to my feet and yanked the window shut, then grabbed the duvet from the bed and laid it over Charlie. I wanted to put a pillow under his head to make him more comfortable, but daren't risk moving him. He was twitching and muttering as though in the grip of a nightmare, and I decided against pulling the light on. I couldn't bear to see the bloodstain in all its grisly glory.

I raced back downstairs and flew outside and hammered on the door of the guest house. There was the sound of footsteps on floorboards and a latch being lifted, then the door opened slowly, releasing a cooking fragrance of wine and herbs that made me feel fainter than I already did.

'Marie?'

'Ah… *oui*.' The woman sounded wary. I must look a total state. '*Qui es-tu?*'

'Nina,' I said and swallowed. 'Charlie…' I pointed next door and the woman stepped closer, silhouetted by the light in the entrance behind her.

'Charlie?' Her tone sharpened with alarm. '*Que c'est il passé?*' she said. 'What has happened?'

'I need you to call an ambulance,' I gasped. I'd never gasped before. '*Ambulance.*'

The woman gasped too, a hand flying to her mouth. As she backed quickly to a narrow table and picked up a handset, I hurtled next door, willing Charlie to be back to his usual self. He was lying where I'd left him, murmuring incomprehensively, while Delphine looked on from the toilet lid, purring loudly. Glad to be in the cocooning effect of shadows once more, I filled a glass with water at the sink. Falling to my knees, I gently lifted Charlie's head. 'Help's on its way,' I murmured, trickling some water between his lips.

Hearing rapid footsteps on the stairs, I put the glass down and turned to see the neighbour outlined in the doorway.

'Charlie!' she cried, her hand reaching for the light pull.

As the room flooded with brightness, I turned my head and covered my eyes, terrified of what I would see.

'How is he hurt?' Marie was on her knees beside me, and I looked at her through my fingers, glimpsing silver-threaded dark hair, escaping a clip at the back of her head, and dark eyes brimming with tears.

'I think his ankle might be broken.' She caught her bottom lip between her teeth, as if to stop another cry escaping. 'He's got a head injury too.' My voice wobbled. 'It looks pretty bad.' I slowly lowered my hands, steeling myself to see just how bad it was, eyes travelling from Charlie's bare feet over the thick duvet shrouding his body, up to his neck and… I shunted backwards and screamed so loudly, Delphine shot past as though fired from a canon. 'It's green,' I croaked, clasping my cheeks, looking at the fluid seeping from Charlie's head. His eyes had snapped open, staring unseeingly at the ceiling, adding to the sense that I'd landed in a nightmare. 'Why is it green?' I whimpered. 'What's happening?'

'Elle?' Charlie whispered.

Marie, who'd been staring at me with wide-eyed shock, looked down and touched the liquid. '*Citron vert*,' she said, bringing her fingers to her nose. 'It smells like limes.'

'Limes?' That was the smell I'd assumed was Charlie's deodorant.

'There must be a…' Marie cast her eyes round. 'Look, it has spilled.' She pointed to a plastic bottle without its top, lying under the bath. 'I think it is shower gel.'

Trance-like, I reached past Charlie, who'd flung his arm across his eyes as if to block out the light, and picked up the empty container. The words 'Lime Sensation, 100% Natural' were written on a leaf-shaped logo on the front and the bottle was almost empty. 'Shower gel,' I murmured.

Thank God, Charlie wasn't bleeding. He must have planned to take a bath, and in a delirious state (definitely delirious) had slipped and fallen, knocking the open bottle to the floor, where the gel had oozed out. I nearly giggled, then choked out a sob of relief.

'You're such an idiot, Chuck. Why didn't you just come home?'

He was trying to sit up, grabbing for the rim of the bath, and Marie gently pressed him down, making shushing noises as she tucked the duvet around him. 'Who are you?' she said to me.

'I told you, I'm Nina.'

'You are his friend?'

'His cousin.' Crouching, I picked up the glass of water again and tilted Charlie's head so his lips met the glass. He took a couple of sips, wincing as he swallowed.

'We do not know that he did not bang his head,' Marie said, and my relief gave way to another wave of worry. 'I think he is feeling a lot of pain.'

'He wasn't well yesterday.' I dabbed his mouth with the edge of the duvet. 'His throat was hurting.' A siren was approaching, getting louder as it turned into the street. 'It's the ambulance.' Relief flowed in once more.

'I will go and let them in,' Marie said.

There were two paramedics, one with equipment, the other in charge, and after Marie explained in French what we thought had happened, Charlie was gently checked over, a tiny torchlight beamed into his eyes and down his throat.

He kept trying to talk, but wasn't making any sense and I caught the word *délirant* from one of the paramedics. *Delirious*, I knew it. He also had a suspected broken ankle, possible concussion, inflamed tonsils and was running a temperature.

'I must make a call,' Marie said, her face pale beneath a light layer of make-up. 'Elle will want to be with him.'

I looked at her properly for the first time. She was a young-looking fifty-something, with a neatness about her movements, dressed in a belted jersey dress and low-heeled shoes.

'You're her aunt,' I said, the penny dropping. 'The one she didn't know she had.'

'I am.' Her whole face softened as she said it. 'Elle is my niece.'

While Charlie was being carefully transported downstairs on a stretcher, I heard him say Delphine's name. 'She's fine,' I told him, tears springing to my eyes as I touched his hand. I'd never seen him so helpless. 'Don't worry about anything except getting better.' I turned to Marie. 'I need to call Dolly.'

But she was already at the front door, a coat thrown over her work trousers and apron, the reindeer on her Christmas jumper peering through the gap, watching as her son was slid into the back of the ambulance, like one of her trays of croissants into the oven. I moved to hug her, and explained as fast I could. 'He's going to be OK,' I said. 'They're taking him to the hospital in La Rochelle.'

'I have to go with him.' She looked stricken. 'Can you go back to the café, love, and help Frank with the launch?'

'Launch?' I imagined a rocket shooting into the sky, then remembered what she was talking about.

'Margot,' she said, giving my arms a squeeze. 'It's her book party tonight.'

Chapter Twenty-Six

Thankfully, Frank was on host duty when I returned, cleaned up and dapper in royal blue braces with matching pinstriped trousers, listening intently to a woman with a jet-black bob and a Yorkshire accent, talking loudly about reconnecting with an old lover on a recent trip to the UK. Because of her accent, I wondered whether Frank was a relative, but when he saw me, he pulled away and said in a low voice, 'That's Mimi Carruthers. She's sex-obsessed, I'm afraid.'

'Too bloody right I am!' she boomed, with a cackle that made her considerable bosom bounce. 'I'm making up for lost time.'

With a comical grimace, Frank hustled me away and said, 'Thank heavens you went to find him, Nina.'

'Did Dolly call you?'

'From the ambulance.' There was a layer of anxiety beneath his smile. 'It's a good job you found him when you did, love.'

'I'm sure you or Dolly would have, if I hadn't.' A wave of tiredness crashed over me as the enormity sank in. Just another hour or so, falling in and out of unconsciousness in a freezing cold bathroom with a broken ankle, could have seen Charlie's condition deteriorate fast. I could still see the tail lights of the ambulance disappearing down the street, and hear Marie's concerned voice, checking I was OK, only retreating to call Elle when I'd assured her that I was fine to walk back to the café on my own.

Frank's hand cupped my elbow. 'You go up and sort yourself out, I've got this,' he said. 'We've plenty of pairs of hands, and you look like you need a lie down.' Stefan eased past, a black bow tie at the collar of a fresh white shirt, a tray of champagne flutes balanced on both hands. 'Margot's all set up and Celeste's sister's helping out.' He nodded to a taller, broader version of Celeste, but with the same warm, open smile.

Margot was easy to spot among the assembled guests. She was by the Christmas tree, presiding over a table piled with copies of her book, resplendent in a black and green floaty dress, hair teased high, with tendrils curling around her cheeks. The dark-haired man, smiling proudly at her side, could only be her son, Raphael. She kept casting him little looks, as if checking he was really there, and he had a similar way of holding his head, as if listening to something no one else could hear.

'I see Dolly couldn't resist adding some festive touches,' I said, spotting all the Christmas crackers laid out and several guests wearing foil party hats. One was making a racket with an old-fashioned party blower – the sort Mum would eventually confiscate when Ben and I got carried away and gave her a headache.

'It's going down well,' Frank said.

'I'll just get changed and come back down.' I raised my voice over a blast of laughter from a group of women I recognised as the knitting ladies, Dee among them, a finely-knitted shawl draped around her shoulders that I was certain she couldn't have knitted – it looked too perfect.

'If you're sure, love.'

I nodded. I didn't want to be in the apartment alone, wondering what Ryan was doing, and knew I wouldn't rest until I'd had an update about Charlie. Pushing aside an image of his anguished face, and Dolly's brave one as she climbed into the ambulance, I slipped through to the kitchen, to see Mathilde putting the finishing touches to a spaceship cake, complete with sugarpaste lovers draped in a sheet of icing.

'That's amazing,' I said, then remembered she was deaf. '*INCROY-ABLE!*' I roared, riveted by the sight of her gnarled fingers delicately tweezering tiny silver stars onto the cake board. *Did she know about Charlie?* Knowing they were close, I was wondering whether to mime what had happened, with appropriate facial gestures, when she raised her head and gave me a smile so venomous, I quickly backed away and headed upstairs.

I couldn't resist looking in Charlie's bedroom as I passed, my heart sinking when I saw that Ryan's suitcase was gone. How could he have upped and left without waiting to at least say goodbye to Charlie? I imagined him hanging around for a bit, hoping his friend would come back, Nicole growing increasingly impatient as their flight time drew closer, finally firing off a text and asking Dolly to pass on a message, with no idea that Charlie was ill.

I checked my room too, with the ridiculous notion that he might have left a note on my pillow – some tiny acknowledgement of what had passed between us the night before – but my pillow, and every surface in the room, was note-free. Even if he'd thought about it, I supposed it would have been tricky with Nicole here, desperate to get him back to England.

In my imagination, she was morphing into a pinch-faced crone, her hair straggly and dry (and shorter) than in real life, hawk-like eyes tracking Ryan's every move, adamant he'd never escape her clutches again. *Eurgh!* I needed a slap. Nicole was a mother, and the woman he'd once asked to marry him – and he had a mind of his own. She hadn't exactly had to twist his arm to tempt him back.

I scoped the room once more, angling the bedside light to make sure a note hadn't fluttered to the floor when I opened the door. Remembering the letters in the drawer, I took them out and laid them on top of the chest to remind me to return them to Gérard, before making my way to the living room, where the dining table looked oddly bare without Ryan's laptop there.

The E in Merry Christmas had slipped sideways above the fireplace, and I automatically straightened it, then let it slip again. What did it matter, when there was no one but me to see it? I straightened it again. *It matters to me.*

I bashed the cushions on the sofa into shape, trying not to think about the activity that had taken place there less than twenty-four hours ago, but my brain was already pulsing with the remembered feel of Ryan's lips, the pressure of his hands in the small of my back, the feel of his body against mine – the smell and taste of him, and his intense expression as I talked, absorbing my words as though they mattered to him. It was part of his job as a writer to be a good listener, I reminded myself. Even as we'd kissed, he was probably storing up the experience to put in his novel. Remembering Noah Dailey and his penchant for nightwear, I hardened my heart and stalked into the kitchen, where I pulled my washing from the washer dryer and wolfed down the leftover chasseur and half a baguette with unnecessary force.

Back downstairs, the launch was in full swing, a queue of customers waiting to have their book signed by Margot, who looked to be in her element, writing messages with a flourish of an old-fashioned fountain pen, while her son watched, looking rather like a politician's bodyguard in his dark suit.

The classical music switched to Dolly's Christmas CD, Slade belting out 'Merry Christmas Everybody' reminding me the big day was looming and I was going to be eating the turkey-with-all-the trimmings dinner that Dolly had planned, as if I'd never left England.

I'd assumed she no longer followed the old traditions, and the day would involve a soup-kitchen vibe, attending to regulars who had no family of their own (Mum had mentioned it being Dolly's new thing) and that we'd take a walk on the beach, where I would sit on a sand dune and look at the sea while remembering Gran, before returning to the café to drink one – or two – of Charlie's cocktails.

'I like your pantaloons,' said Stefan, offering me a glass of bubbly liquid from his tray, and I glanced down at the gold, velour jumpsuit of Dolly's I'd wriggled into after taking a shower that had made me think of Charlie, collapsing before he could get into the bath – and had also made me wonder why he'd bothered to open the window (perhaps the delirium) and why he'd removed his socks in the main bathroom (maybe he'd fancied a bath instead of a shower).

'Thanks,' I said with a self-conscious smile, wishing half a dozen people hadn't overheard and were looking me up and down, nodding their approval. At least, I thought it was approval and not pity. My curves weren't quite as generous as Dolly's, so I'd had to cinch in the waist with a cowgirl-style belt, and put on some lipstick because apparently, gold made me look like a vampire had drained my blood.

'*Ah, c'est magnifique!*' For a second, I thought the symphony writer (composer?) with the mad-professor hair was referring to my breasts – his eyes had been firmly fixed in that area since I'd appeared – but as more appreciative cries went up and the small crowd parted, I saw Mathilde carrying through Margot's cake in the style of a contestant on *The Great British Bake Off*. She was listing to one side so that Frank had to do a goalkeeper-leap to stop it sliding to the floor, his face paling when her eyes shot sparks of fury – I was glad it wasn't just me she despised – and as she shuffled closer to Margot, I felt my partly charged phone start to buzz in my jumpsuit pocket.

Moving back to the kitchen, I pressed it to my ear: 'Dolly?'

'He hasn't broken his ankle, love.' Her voice was hearty with relief. 'It's just a bad sprain, but he's got mild concussion, a nasty throat infection and he's dehydrated, so they've got him on a drip and are pumping him with antibiotics.'

'Thank God for that.' I sagged against the worktop, which was littered with Mathilde's silver stars and an inch-thick layer of icing sugar. 'I mean, thank goodness it's not much worse,' I said, a wave of relief tearing through me.

'I thought you'd want to know.' Dolly's voice quivered with emotion. 'I can't thank you enough, Nina. If he'd been lying there much longer—'

'His hair would have been nice and clean,' I said to lighten the mood, then had to explain about the shower gel (not mentioning I'd mistaken it for blood until Marie put the light on). 'And it was Frank who pointed me in the right direction. I had no idea he was there,' I added pointedly. 'It's a good job I called round to see how Frank was, after his *terrible virus*.'

Still not taking the cue, she said, 'We haven't even got a bed for Charlie at the cottage, isn't that awful?'

'Dolly—'

'He had to go to Natalie's house to get a good night's sleep and could have died.' Her voice cracked. 'Sod my walk-in wardrobe,' she sobbed. 'I should have got Frank to make him a bed.'

'Dolly, this is not your fault.'

'I should have known when Elle called this afternoon to ask how Charlie was because his phone was going to voicemail that something wasn't right, but I told her he likes to sleep when he's ill – not that he's ill very often. He hates being ill.'

'You couldn't have known,' I said firmly, but from the tear-filled sigh at the end of the phone, it was obvious she felt she'd failed him in some fundamental way. 'He probably didn't know himself how unwell he was and he's going to be just fine.'

'Oh, it's awful,' she fretted. 'I feel terrible.'

'Does he know Ryan's not here?'

For once, Dolly didn't jump on my comment. 'He's still sleeping,' she said. 'I haven't been able to talk to him yet, but Ryan told me before he left for the airport that he'd talk to Charlie soon, and to say goodbye if I saw him.'

Say goodbye if you see him.

It sounded so casual, after Charlie and Dolly had welcomed him into their home and given him space to write his book and recover from his break-up with Nicole. Charlie had even given up his bed, without a word of complaint. *Say goodbye if you see him.* I tried to picture Ryan saying it, his lips forming the words, his suitcase in one hand, Nicole holding the other, and hardened my heart a bit more.

'...stay here for a bit in case he wakes up,' Dolly was saying as I tuned back in, aware of my fingers clenched around my phone. 'How's it going over there?' she added, as if she'd forgotten the café, which had to be a first.

'Everything's fine.' As I said it, a volley of excited barking broke out, followed by a bloodcurdling yowl. Gérard and Madame Bisset had obviously arrived with their respective pets, which meant... I hurried out to see Delphine squirming in her mistress's arms as Hamish danced on his hind legs. It was hard to tell whether he was trying to impress or bite her.

'I don't believe it,' I said. 'After all that, she managed to find her way home.'

'Who did?'

'Delphine was in Natalie's house,' I explained. 'She was standing outside the door where Charlie had fallen.'

'That cat's got a sixth sense.'

It was such a Dolly thing to say, I couldn't help smiling as I rolled my eyes. Then again, Delphine *had* alerted me to the open door where Charlie was, so maybe there was something in it. I'd looked for her after Marie went back inside, but it had been so cold, and I'd felt too shaken to search for long. 'Anyway, Frank's being a great host,' I said, watching him distract Hamish with a macaron.

'He always is,' said Dolly fondly, and I promised her I'd tell him that Charlie was going to be OK, and that she would call him later, and agreed that, yes, Frank was an absolute rock and she'd been right to 'put a ring on it'.

'You know, your life is only as good as the man or woman you marry – *if* you marry,' she said, becoming sentimental. 'And my life couldn't be any better right now, love. At least, it will be, once Charlie's out of hospital.'

I smiled, her words reverberating in my head. How good would my life have been if I'd married Scott Mackenzie? Filled with anxiety, regret and self-loathing, probably. And what about Ryan's life if he'd married Nicole? No doubt he'd find out soon. *And what about if Augustine had married William?*

Twisting my mind away, I decided to give Dolly another chance to come clean. 'Do you think Charlie caught his throat infection from Frank?'

'I doubt it, love. Frank's was a virus while Charlie's is bacterial.'

She was really good. I thought about telling her Frank had confessed, right before I helped him hang the door on her walk-in wardrobe, but suspected she'd simply gloss over it. And anyway, the wardrobe door would be a nice surprise for her when she got home.

'I'd better go,' I said, watching Margot positioning herself behind her sponge-and-icing spaceship, ready for a photo, a Christmas party hat parked at a jaunty angle on top of her piled-up hair. 'Mathilde's taken Margot's cake out. It's pretty spectacular.'

'Just don't let her cut it,' warned Dolly, sounding more like her usual self. 'She can't be trusted with a knife.'

Chapter Twenty-Seven

By the time I crawled into bed just after eleven, after helping to clear up and seeing everyone off the premises – reassuring Frank I'd be fine on my own – I felt as if I'd lived through several lifetimes. I could barely summon the energy to send more than a clapping emoji when Ben messaged to say it had been snowing over there.

How's things? he persisted, clearly in a chatty mood.

I replied with the emoji of a monkey covering its eyes.

That bad?

Yawning, I sat up and switched on the bedside light, immediately spotting the letters I'd forgotten to return yet again. I put them back in the drawer and tucked the duvet around me. The heating had gone off and it was cold.

Charlie in hospital, throat infection, badly sprained ankle.

Ouch.

Found him collapsed, thought he was dead.

Shit!! Are you OK? Is Charlie OK? Is everyone OK??

All fine, just shattered. Helped host a book launch at the café.

Sounds fancy.

There was a spaceship cake and champagne and mulled wine and I learnt a French song called Petit Papa Noël.

Tell me you didn't sing.

I hadn't, despite an overwhelming urge to, invoked by a couple of glasses of mulled wine and the relief of knowing Charlie was being looked after and would soon be home.

It was a shame he and Dolly hadn't been there to listen to Margot give a reading from *Tempêtes de Pluto* – I hadn't understood it all, but gathered there was a galactic power struggle and a sinister conspiracy, and Brigitte, the main character, was a mercenary in love with her (Zac Efron lookalike) pilot – or to see Gérard and Madame Bisset exchanging smiles when they thought no one was watching. (Jacqueline was and didn't seem to mind.) At least I'd managed to record Mathilde cutting the spaceship cake for Margot, under Frank's guiding hand, and sent the clip to Dolly.

I mouthed the words I replied to Ben.

He sent a string of laughing emojis. *Mum's Christmas play was a disaster, by the way.*

NO! What happened?

One of the donkeys pooed on the stage, Mrs Danvers forgot her lines and started quoting Shakespeare and there was a power cut halfway through. He attached a photo of a chaotic stage scene, partially lit by torchlight, a donkey's tail just visible in the corner. I was laughing so hard, I didn't have time to reply before another bubble of text appeared.

I'm not supposed to say anything but I know you don't like surprises, and you went there to escape all the madness, but Mum and Dad are on their way to you for Christmas.

I was so shocked, I dialled his number. 'What the hell?'

'I know,' he said, and I was surprised at how nice it was to hear his familiar Somerset twang. 'Mum said it wouldn't be right to have Christmas without you *or* Gran.'

In my tired, emotional state, I felt the approach of tears. 'I thought she was preparing for the Bailey Christmas feast, and they were going to do toasts to Gran and play her favourite games.' The idea had been unbearable a few weeks ago, but now didn't seem so bad. 'Mum bought a new Pictionary game, and what about all the cousins?'

'She's sacked everyone off,' said Ben. 'Reckons she deserves a break and so does Dad, and she wants to see Aunt Dolly.'

'What about the farm?'

'I'll be here, and Uncle Hank has said he'll help out.'

'I thought you were having Christmas dinner with Lena's family this year?'

'They're coming here instead,' he said. 'It'll be fun playing Farmer Bailey.'

'You *are* Farmer Bailey, get used to it.'

'I'll sit in Dad's place and raise a slice of goose.'

'I can't believe they're flying out.'

'Sorry,' he said. 'I thought you'd want to know, so you can find somewhere else to stay if you want to avoid all the... you know, the Christmas stuff.'

But now the initial surprise had worn off, I realised I didn't mind. In fact, I was looking forward to seeing my parents, even though I'd been away for less than a week. It would be fun to see what Dad was like without his farm props and routine – lost, probably.

'I suppose Dolly knows?'

'Actually, no,' said Ben. 'They want it to be a surprise.'

I smiled, imagining Dolly's face when her sister rocked up. I might not like surprises, but Dolly did.

I slept as though sedated, only stirring when the alarm beeped me awake at six thirty. I dressed quickly and crept downstairs, not sure why I was being quiet when there was no one there but me, to find Dolly coming in through the back door, bringing a cold draught and a flurry of snowflakes with her.

'I thought you'd be at the hospital,' I said, returning her fierce hug and helping her out of her coat. 'How's Chuckleberry Finn?'

'His temperature's down, his sats are good, blood pressure's normal.' She sounded like an ER doctor. 'He's sleeping like the dead.' She pressed a hand to her mouth. 'I shouldn't say that,' she said, 'it's tempting fate.'

'It sounds like he's out of the woods.' My whole face was a grin of relief. 'When's he coming home?'

'Hopefully, later today.'

'You didn't have to come in,' I said. 'I was going to open the café, and Frank said he'll be here at seven.'

'When Charlie woke up, he told me to come home, so I thought I'd have a shower and a nap and a change of clothes and pop by to see how my baby's doing.'

'Aw, that's nice,' I said. 'I slept really well, actually.'

'I was talking about the café.'

I smiled. 'I know you were.'

She was already speeding around the kitchen, firing up the oven and ferreting in the freezer for supplies. 'Frank's finished my wardrobe,' she said. 'He's done a wonderful job.'

'*Really?* What an *amazing* surprise for you to come home to, especially as he was still recovering from his *virus*.'

She looked at me from under her fringe. 'Put the kettle on, love, I'm parched.'

By eight the café was fully staffed and in full swing. Dolly was showing no signs of leaving, even though Frank had turned up as promised and was cleaning tables efficiently.

'Have you talked to Ryan?' Dolly asked as I nibbled an almond croissant by the fridge, trying not to get in anyone's way.

'No.' I wondered why she thought I would. 'You?'

She nodded. 'He called to say he couldn't get hold of Charlie, so I explained what had happened. He was pretty upset,' she said. 'He's going to try and get hold of him this morning.'

If he can be bothered. 'I'd like to go and see Charlie. Is he allowed visitors?'

'That would be lovely.' Dolly's smile was bright enough to power the village. 'Any time from ten.'

'Will Elle be there?'

'I doubt it.' Her smile wound down. 'There's been heavy snowfall since yesterday evening so all flights from Gatwick were cancelled. We're waiting for an update.'

'Well, I'm happy to keep him company until she arrives.'

'He'll be so pleased to see you, love.'

Frank offered to drive me to the hospital, but I could tell he really wanted to stay and help Dolly, so I said I'd get a taxi.

Driving over the bridge away from the island felt strange – as if I was leaving before I was ready to face the big wide world. I hadn't realised how much I liked being in my little Chamillon bubble and already wanted to return.

The snow had stopped temporarily, and the roads had been cleared, but around us the rooftops and streets were carpeted white. Beyond some halting exchanges about the weather ('It's the same in England apparently,' was the best I could do), the driver wasn't talkative, which suited me, and I tipped him generously when he dropped me off outside the Hôpital Saint Louis, a sweeping building with lots of tiny windows that could have been an office block if it wasn't for the ambulances, and the patient with a cast on his leg in a wheelchair outside the entrance.

Hospitals made me think of Gran, but I reminded myself that this was a happy visit that would end with Charlie being released today (I hoped).

I was directed to the ward by an English-speaking nurse in a pale-blue uniform that accentuated her shiny dark hair, which swirled in a thick ponytail down her back. 'He is very much better this morning,' she said, pointing me to a bed by the window with a view of snow-coated tree branches against a goose-grey sky. He was sitting up, reading a magazine, a blanket covering his lower half, and looked like his normal self – apart from the hospital gown.

'Hey, Chuckster,' I said, doing a hip-shaking dance to his bedside to make him smile, overcome at the sight of his lovely, friendly face – the face that had been present during some of the best bits of my childhood. 'Nice threads.'

'You'll never be a salsa champion.' He'd put down the magazine, breaking into a smile. 'And you're just jealous because you're not wearing something that shows your bare bum when you get up to go to the loo.'

'How do you know I'm not?' I glanced round at my bottom and gasped. 'Oops!'

'I don't like this conversation.'

'Me neither.' I stifled a giggle as the man in the next bed strained to look at my behind.

I wanted to hug Charlie, but we'd never been the type, so I gently punched his upper arm instead. 'How's your throat?'

'I'm on antibiotics and heavy painkillers so can't feel any part of my body at the moment.'

'And your ankle?'

'I'll let you know when the painkillers wear off, but it's fairly swollen this morning. I might need a crutch for a bit.'

'You gave me such a shock,' I said, removing my coat and pulling up a chair. 'Lying around like that, looking dead.'

'Sorry about that.' He stuck out his bottom lip. 'I was lying on the bathroom floor, planning what to wear to Margot's book launch, and woke up in here.'

I punched his arm again, less gently. 'You could had *died*, you idiot.'

He grabbed my hand and gave it a quick squeeze. 'Mum said you found me,' he said. 'Thanks, Nina.'

I was on the cusp of tears again. 'It was actually Delphine,' I said, blinking madly. 'I hadn't realised there was an en suite, but she was just standing outside the door.'

He lowered his head to his chin and moved it slowly from side to side. 'What?'

'It was the bloody cat that nearly killed me,' he said, meeting my gaze with a look of mild outrage.

'*What?*'

'I still felt really, really rough when I got up yesterday morning, so I thought I'd have a shower and go back to bed, but I heard a noise.'

'Delphine?'

He nodded, then winced. 'I need to stop moving my head.'

'She was in the other bathroom?'

He shook his head and winced again. 'She was actually outside, sort of tapping on the window with her claws,' he said. 'She'd climbed up on the roof and got stuck, so I stood on the bath to open the window to let her in, and she kind of slithered past – you know how fast she moves – and—'

'You slipped and fell and bashed your head,' I finished. Now *my* head was swinging from side to side. 'I *knew* that cat was evil.'

'Well, at least she hung around to let you know where I was.'

'It was the least she could do,' I said grimly. 'You must have knocked the shower gel off as you fell.'

He nodded. 'There was a bottle on the side of the bath.' A frown settled on his forehead. 'I kept half waking up and realised I couldn't swallow properly, and thought I smelt limes, and it was really cold, and I started having weird dreams and couldn't move my ankle – God it hurt – and it was really, really cold, but I was kind of boiling hot as well.'

He paused, looking so comically helpless a giggle escaped. 'I expect when the pain kicks back in, you'll start feeling angry.'

'Probably,' he agreed. 'Elle will run a mile when she sees what I'm like.' But even as he said it, I could tell he didn't believe it.

'Your mum's been really worried,' I said. 'She sent these, in case they're not feeding you properly.' I pulled the bag of mince pies she'd given me from my coat pocket. 'I had some flowers too, but apparently they're not allowed.'

'They'd only make me sneeze,' he said, with his old Charlie grin. 'And I'm not sure I can eat mince pies just yet.' He pointed to his throat.

'Oh, yes. Sorry,' I said with a wince. 'What were you reading?'

'An old edition of *Expats*.' He picked it up. 'Funnily enough, it was one of Natalie's old columns, about healthcare in France, before she started being herself and writing funny stuff.' He picked it up and read in a monotone: *After being admitted to a French hospital, you will need to show proof of your health insurance card (carte vitale), and you may be asked to show a notice certifying you are entitled to public healthcare (attestation). You should bring proof of private health insurance if applicable, your CMU-Complémentaire or CMU-C.*

I pretended to jerk awake. 'I must admit, it wouldn't make a good book,' I said. 'Talking of which,' my heart did a leap, 'have you heard from Ryan?'

'We've exchanged a few messages.' He nodded to his phone on his locker. 'It was in my jeans pocket and it's nearly out of signal, but I got a message from Elle too. She'll be here shortly.'

'That's brilliant,' I said, and ate half a mince pie. 'About Ryan—'

'It's great, isn't it?' he interrupted, shuffling further up in the bed. 'It was a bit underhand of me, but you know I did it for the right reasons, don't you?' A plea for understanding shone from his eyes. 'And it worked, so you have to let me off the hook.'

I lowered my hand, crumbs scattering across my jeans. 'Sorry?'

'I hated not saying anything, but I thought the element of surprise would be best, so Ryan wasn't on his guard.' His fingers pleated the sheet. 'I'd never have agreed to pick Nicole up from the airport, or let her into the apartment, if I didn't think it would work.'

'*You* let her in?'

'I know.' He sighed. 'I hate being sneaky like that, asking Marie for the spare key to Natalie's so I could spend the night there, but I knew you'd all need some space to let things sink in.'

'You planned that whole visit with Nicole?' I sat back in disbelief. 'She never said a word.'

'She's actually quite nice, when she's not being clingy and demanding,' he said to my sheer disbelief. 'And it worked, didn't it?'

There was a look on his face I couldn't decode, and I didn't bother trying as anger and disappointment rolled through me. Charlie had engineered that whole scene with Nicole at the apartment, and then stayed at Natalie's to let it all play out.

'You know your mum had arranged for Ryan and me to be alone to "get to know each other"?' I said. 'Nicole walked in on us... on the sofa.'

'Oh, God.' Charlie closed his eyes. 'That must have been a bit awkward.' He looked at me, and I could have sworn there was a shimmer of amusement in his eyes. 'I didn't think things would progress that far, in spite of Mum's... well, you know what Mum's like.'

'Yes, I do.'

'Look, Nina, I thought you'd want to know what was happening because I could see you were starting to have feelings for Ryan, in spite of everything you said when you got here.' He was smiling hopefully, and I didn't have the heart to vent my true feelings – to tell him how much it hurt; that even if he thought he'd done the right thing and saved me from future heartbreak by exposing Ryan's true feelings, knowing what I'd gone through with Scott, I hated that he was the one to have done it.

'Are you OK?' Sensing my mood change he tried to sit forward and flinched. 'Shit, Nina. Did I get it all wrong?'

'No, no, it's fine.' I wished my voice hadn't trembled. 'I must admit though, it was a surprise to find out he's not Lulu and Jackson's dad.'

He made a baffled face. 'No one said he was.'

'No, but I… oh, it doesn't matter,' I said. 'Charlie, did you ever hear Augustine talk about someone called William?

'What?' He waggled his head, as if clearing it of debris. 'Why are you asking about Great-gran?'

'Oh, it's nothing. Don't move around like that, you'll hurt your ankle and I'll have to get the nurse. Talking of which…' I looked around, hoping for an excuse to escape. 'Isn't it time for your bed bath?'

'I don't think they do that sort of thing any more.' He sank down, a little paler than before. 'I'm just waiting to be released.'

'You're not in prison, Chuck.' It was an effort to regain my bantering tone, and I was flooded with relief when I saw someone approaching at speed, blonde hair lifting from a heart-shaped face, a luggage bag over her shoulder, her royal blue coat flapping open to reveal the sort of comfy outfit celebrities advised wearing on flights – the sort I'd live in, if I could get away with it. 'I think your girlfriend's here.'

But Charlie had seen her, and was wearing a look akin to the one I'd seen the first time he held a newborn lamb (after getting over the shock of seeing it born) only better, and I knew that they were going to be together for life.

Chapter Twenty-Eight

Once they'd finished kissing and Charlie reassured Elle he was going to be OK, and once she'd apologised for taking so long to arrive, and he'd introduced us, and I'd fully explained what had happened and admired Elle's loungewear ('Oh God, it's so comfy,' she said, and I knew we'd get along), the doctor appeared and declared Charlie fit to go home after lunch. He would need to complete a course of antibiotics, keep taking painkillers for his ankle and generally take it easy for a while.

'I'll call Dolly and let her know,' I told him, burying my brief surge of resentment as I impulsively pressed a kiss on his messy hair (which still smelt strongly of limes). This was Charlie, my favourite cousin, and he'd done me a massive favour where Ryan was concerned – even if it didn't quite feel that way just yet.

'See you back at the ranch,' I said, dropping crumbs on the floor as I stuffed the bag of crushed mince pies in my coat pocket and pushed my arms in the sleeves. 'Nice to meet you, Elle.'

'You too.' She gave me a dazzling smile, before returning her anxious but loving gaze to Charlie. 'See you soon.'

I broke the good news to Dolly over the phone, and when she said she'd get his room ready before driving over to pick him up, I felt a twist inside, knowing that Ryan wouldn't be sleeping in there any more.

I was even less inclined to talk on the taxi ride back to Chamillon, but this time the driver was friendly, and wanted to discuss the vagaries of the English language.

'Why do you say, I broke my arm, as if you are blaming it on yourself? You should say, my arm got broken in the motor accident.'

'I really don't know,' I said, hoping he wasn't familiar with motor accidents as I leaned my head against the window, longing to be back at the café.

'And, when you ask, "are you sure you don't want to have cake?", do I reply "yes" because I am sure, or "no, I do not want to have cake"?'

'Who doesn't want to have cake?' My brain was too frazzled to figure it out.

He laughed appreciatively. 'I do love the wit of the British,' he said and continued driving in silence, punctuated by the occasional chuckle.

It was business as usual back at the café, where a mother-and-toddler group was in full, noisy swing. Holly was sharing a gingerbread reindeer with Hamish, while Jacqueline helped Gérard with his crossword, and I wondered why I hadn't realised they were related on my first day, when Holly had made a fuss of the dog and compared her grandfather to Santa Claus.

'Margot came in for her usual, but she's writing from home today since you sorted out her room,' said Dolly, seeing me glance at the table where Margot had done her book-signing the night before. 'I looked in upstairs earlier and hardly recognised my living room.'

'Oh God, I'm sorry.' I hid my face behind my hands. 'I just thought I'd—'

'Tidy up a bit, I know.' I peeped out to see Dolly beaming. 'It looks amazing,' she said. 'I love it.'

'Really?'

'Really. And I've had a couple of customers ask if you can do theirs after Christmas.' She untied her apron as I followed her into the kitchen. 'Dee's been spreading the word, apparently. Like I said, if you want to stay a bit longer, you'll have plenty to do.'

'I don't want to outstay my welcome,' I said. 'You must be fed up with me.'

'Never,' she said and I smiled. I didn't want to think about leaving just yet.

'I've changed Charlie's bedding, and just need to run a cloth round the bathroom and then I'll get over to the hospital,' Dolly continued. 'Frank's going to hold the fort here.'

'I'll sort out the bathroom,' I said. 'You must be shattered.'

'Oh, I'm on top of the world!' She seized Celeste as she came through from the café and danced her round the kitchen, and the action seemed to sum up perfectly how Dolly always grabbed the good things in life and ran with them.

It was quiet upstairs, everything as I'd left it, and although the pillows in Charlie's room looked freshly plumped, it didn't look that much different to when Ryan had slept in there. He'd gone without leaving a trace.

My phone buzzed with a message.

Mum and Dad took off at 10 this morning.

On an aeroplane?

Ho, ho, ho. They'll be with you just after 2. You'd better look surprised.

I'll start practising. I sent a shocked face emoji. *Thanks Benjamin Button x*

May the force be with you Nee-naw X

I grabbed a cloth and a bottle of cleaning fluid from the kitchen cupboard and found some rubber gloves. I wasn't just cleaning the bathroom for Charlie's return – Mum and Dad were going to be staying here too and Dolly didn't even know. Although, she wouldn't be too interested in cleaning the apartment even if she did. *Take me as you find me* had always been her motto. Mum's too, actually. I used to think that if people took *me* as they found me, they'd be sorely disappointed.

I realised I'd have to sleep on the sofa so my parents could have Dolly's room, and I needed to change the bedding, but first, I threw open the bathroom door and half-heartedly moved the cloth around the sink – which wasn't exactly filthy to start with – then succumbed to the temptation of a shower, setting it to Relax, which felt like standing in warm drizzle.

In my bedroom, dressed in the freshly washed and dried koala onesie – I wasn't planning on going downstairs any time soon – I tried not to think about Ryan telling me that koalas had the smallest brain-to-body-size ratio of any mammal. Then found myself wondering whereabouts in Australia his sister and nephew lived, and thinking of all the things I didn't know about him and never would – not without grilling Charlie and coming across as really weird.

Sighing, I turned to strip the bed and noticed a pale brown envelope lying on the bedside cabinet, just as Dolly shouted upstairs, 'Nina! I meant to say, Gérard left an envelope for you. I've put it by your bed. He said to tell you he found it after you left the other day and he thought you'd like it.'

'Thanks!' I called back. 'I've got it!'

The envelope had been stuck with Sellotape and I ripped it open, hoping I wasn't going to find money inside. Instead, there was a single sheet of paper, and I pulled it out with clumsy fingers, immediately spotting Augustine's signature and four kisses at the bottom.

When I saw the date at the top, I sank down on the bed: *4 February 1928.* I was certain she hadn't been married to Charles then, and she didn't give birth until 1932. According to Mum, there'd been a heatwave that year and her mother had been born during a severe water shortage.

Breathing quickly, I read the letter, eyes skipping over the words.

Dear William,

I can't tell you what it meant to finally hear from you, and to know you understood that being apart so frequently made it hard for me to consider a future for us.

With so little time together and only occasional letters, and the constant worry about your job – I can't stop thinking about the loss of U.S. Navy ships at Honda Point, though I know you'd say that nothing like that could happen over here – it's impossible to keep the flame burning, for both of us, and I'm so pleased to have your blessing. I love Charles with all my heart and know he's the man I want to have a family with – to spend the rest of my life with, and it's thanks to you, dear William, for showing me what true love is. I could never settle for anything less and Charles makes me happy, as you once did.

I wish you all the best, and if you decide to settle down one day, she will be a very lucky woman. Know I will always hold you dear in my heart, and I shall raise a glass to you, and the times we spent together, every New Year's Eve!

Maybe you will do the same for me.
Take care, William.
Augustine xxxx

I raised my eyes and stared in a daze at the wall. *Augustine didn't have an affair. William wasn't the father of her child. She'd truly loved my great-grandfather.*

A smile found its way to my lips, and I sent up a silent thank you to Gérard, in lieu of the real thing, when I would tell him about the link between our families that Maggie had unknowingly kept hidden all these years.

Dolly was going to *love* this.

I was on the verge of grabbing the rest of the letters and charging downstairs to show her, but something stopped me: I had a better idea.

After reading the letter once more, I placed it with the rest and carefully bound them together with the pink ribbon, before returning them to the drawer.

It would be the perfect Christmas gift for Mum and Dolly.

After dashing a tear from my cheek – I had *no* idea why it was there – I turned my attention back to the bed and after I'd stripped it, I tipped out the items I'd bought at the market the day before.

I'd intended to give the slippers and cat keyring to Ryan, but now I knew Delphine had almost killed Charlie, I thought about throwing the keyring away – then remembered she'd helped me find him and decided to keep it. The Mirabelle liqueur would be an extra present for Dolly, and Mum would love the vase I'd brought from Dee's. Dad could have the gift-shop pen for his secret poetry scribbles that we all knew about, and I could easily see Frank wearing the pink braces I'd bought on impulse. Only Charlie didn't have a gift. Then I remembered the giant bar of chocolate that I had hidden in the bedside drawer. *It was Charlie's favourite.* And, with any luck, he'd share it (with me).

I wondered whether Dolly had some wrapping paper tucked away. Given the number of gifts I'd seen under the tree, and her hoarder-like tendencies, it was highly likely there'd be a raft of sheets stashed in a drawer in the living room.

I checked the time: nearly an hour before Mum and Dad arrived. Still buzzing from reading Augustine's final letter to William, I gathered my booty in my arms and headed down the landing. I nudged open the living room door with my forehead and edged inside, and let go of the lot when I saw Ryan, leaning over his laptop at the dining table.

Hearing the clamour, he turned, a smile breaking over his face. 'Ah, it's my favourite koala.'

Frozen to the spot, I could only stare for what felt like an hour, wondering if I'd finally run out of screams.

'What…?'

'…am I doing here?' His smile seemed to fill his whole face, but I simply couldn't compute why he was here, in the apartment, and not on a plane with Nicole.

'Where…?' My gaze swivelled around painfully. *Was she in the kitchen, making tea?*

Ryan scrunched up his face and strummed his chin. '…are the satsumas?' he said, pointing to the empty bowl as he finished my sentence. 'I ate the last two this morning.'

Why was he being so jokey? My heart was going berserk and my eyes felt too big.

'Nicole,' I managed to force out. 'Where's Nicole?'

'On her way back to Gatwick.' He stood up and stretched – a sight that felt oddly familiar – before drawing his hands down his face. 'Every flight last night was cancelled,' he added, miming a weary look. 'Have you ever tried sleeping in an airport?'

Unable to even contemplate what he meant by that, I said stupidly, 'Your laptop wasn't here.'

He did a big frown and a full-body swing to look at it on the table, before swinging back again. Why was he being so swingy and light-hearted? So… *happy*. But, of course, why wouldn't he be happy now the pieces of his life were slotting into place? 'I take it with me, wherever I go,' he said. 'In case there's an opportunity to do some writing, which – as it happened – there was. I was typing half the night, actually, and had an idea in the taxi on the way back for my next chapter. I thought I'd get it down while it was fresh in my mind.'

He swiped his arm across his body, finger aimed at his screen, with that same jokey attitude. 'I heard you in the shower,' he said, then laughed. 'I don't mean I *heard* you, you weren't singing or anything, but I heard the water running and guessed you must be in there.'

Was he actually *teasing* me? In spite of our incredibly passionate kiss, I'd clearly been relegated back to the role of Charlie's cousin. I supposed I should be grateful he didn't seem awkward, or regretful, and was at least being friendly. *Very* friendly. 'But why aren't you on the plane with Nicole?'

'What?' He tucked in his chin.

'Are you getting another flight?' That must be it. He hadn't been able to get a ticket at such short notice and would be joining her later today.

'There wasn't a flight in the first place, so I can't get another,' he said, and I was reminded of the taxi driver, puzzling over meanings and felt as if I was losing the plot. His eyebrows drew together, as though my responses weren't making any sense. 'Why would I get a flight in the first place?'

'Because you and Nicole are back together,' I exploded. 'I saw you both, at the market—'

'You followed us?'

'I was Christmas shopping, and that's not the point.' I ignored the arch of his eyebrows. 'Charlie told me he'd picked Nicole up from the airport yesterday, because she wanted to say something you needed to hear and that I needed to hear it too, because I was getting too close to you – or something.' I was becoming confused. 'And Dolly said you'd worked things out, and you left without saying goodbye.'

'Only because you weren't here.' He took a step towards me with an expression I couldn't fathom. 'I told Dolly to tell you I'd speak to you soon, and I had no idea that Charlie had picked Nicole up from the airport, or that he'd ended up in hospital until I got hold of Dolly this morning. I've been in touch with him since.'

I felt as if *I* was on a plane, experiencing turbulence. I was missing something crucial, but couldn't work out what it was. 'You and Nicole… you looked good together,' I said, which apparently wasn't the right thing to say at all.

He recoiled slightly. 'I think I was relieved to have finally sorted things out, that's all.' He gave a quick shake of his head. 'I'd spent so long apologising for not wanting to marry her, trying to explain myself, feeling guilty and fielding her phone calls because all she wanted to do was shout and swear and beg me to come back, because she couldn't cope.'

I tried to picture it – a single mother with two young children, deserted instead of married with a loving partner. It was hard to blame her for being mad with him.

'I don't blame her,' he said, as though he'd read my mind. 'But…' he nodded slowly, 'since cutting off contact a couple of months ago and coming here, where she was unlikely to just turn up, things have changed. She's had time to think and realise what's really important.'

Something was happening to my insides. It felt like a flock of doves was trying to take off, wings beating against my ribcage. Was Ryan… was he saying that he and Nicole *weren't* getting back together? 'So… you and Nicole *aren't* getting back together?'

He shook his head, eyes soft as they roamed my face. 'I'm honestly surprised you thought that was even a possibility after… you know.' His gaze moved to the sofa and back to my face. 'That kiss.'

I tried to remember how to breathe. 'I thought you might have spent the night together. Here, I mean.'

His head lurched back, as if the idea was as remote as life on Venus. 'She slept in Charlie's bed and I crashed on the sofa,' he said. 'I don't know how Charlie's managed on there, to be honest. It's fine for the first hour, then really uncomfortable. I feel terrible.'

'Your suitcase isn't here.'

'Sorry?'

'Your suitcase had gone.'

His face cleared. 'Nicole must have put it in the wardrobe,' he said. 'She's a bit of a neat freak.'

I started pacing, thoughts crashing through my head. 'Why did you propose in the first place, if you didn't love her enough?'

'Nicole was on the rebound when we met,' he said, combing his fingers through his hair, seeming as stunned as I was. 'It was all a bit of a whirlwind actually. I was at a birthday do in a pub—'

'Playing darts?'

'What?'

'Sorry, go on.'

He took a second to regroup. 'Anyway, Nicole was there with friends, we got chatting and she said she was organising a hen do, so I asked if it was hers and she said, "Is that a proposal?" and I said something cocky like, "Not now, but give me a few months and it might be".'

I folded my arms. 'That's unbelievably cheesy.'

'There might have been drink involved.'

'And then you fell for her?'

'I suppose I did, but I never meant it to get serious,' he said. 'My book was coming out and I was trying to buy a house, but things were moving fast. Nicole was really intense and by the time she told me she had children, I was in too deep.'

'She didn't tell you right away?' My estimation of Nicole plummeted.

'Don't judge her,' he said, telepathically. 'John was working abroad and she was struggling with the children, so she told him to leave for good. She was basically looking for a replacement, but didn't tell me about Lulu and Jackson right away because she wanted to know I really liked her before introducing me to them.'

Privately, I thought this was a terrible way to start a relationship, but there didn't seem much point in saying so.

'Not a great start to a relationship, but they were really cute, and she started telling them they'd have a new daddy soon, and… I don't know, I felt like I couldn't back out.' There was a haunted look in his eyes. 'I started to feel responsible for them, like I said.'

Like I had, with the lamb who'd lost his mother, keeping him in my wardrobe/stable, thinking I could be a substitute mother. But totally different.

'I didn't want to just leave, like their dad did, but it turned out he hadn't left of his own accord, Nicole had kicked him out. But because he loves her and the kids, he decided to take a job in England so he could be around all the time, but by then, Nicole was set on us getting married. She'd booked the venue, the hen night, you name it. Then I had the big conversation with John and knew I couldn't go through with it, and I knew it wasn't fair to keep seeing the children. I wanted them to forget me and start seeing their dad again.'

I hadn't thought him capable of saying so many words in one go, but as I drank them in, I realised they were beautiful words – words that showed his true character, one I liked very much. 'I wish I'd known all this before we met.' He was looking at me closely, gauging my response. 'I probably wouldn't have had you down as an arsehole.'

His mouth began to smile. 'I called you unstable.'

'I know.' But I was smiling too. It felt like a natural expression to be wearing now everything was out in the open. 'I'm glad it's worked out for Nicole,' I said, secretly feeling a bit sorry for John. She definitely sounded high-maintenance, especially with all that marathon training. 'And I think you were right to call off your wedding, even if it was at your stag party.'

'You know, Charlie was at that party. We talked for hours after I'd been to see Nicole…' He paused and swallowed, and I could only imagine how difficult that conversation must have been – unlike mine with Scott, when I'd simply said, *I don't want to marry you* and he'd said, *OK then* and went to stay with a friend (probably Hannah) until I'd cleared my stuff out of his house. 'Anyway, we got a bit drunk, and he said he'd always meant to introduce us, because he thought we'd be great together, but the timing was never right.'

'Really?' I thought of my conversation with Charlie at the hospital and realised, in technicolor hindsight, that we'd been talking at cross purposes. He hadn't facilitated Nicole's visit to show me she and Ryan were meant for each other at all – he'd wanted me to know she was reuniting with the father of her children, and that the path was clear for Ryan and me. 'That's… I had no idea.' My chest felt tight. 'He never mentioned it.'

'Yeah, well, I might have said something about staying away from relationships in future and concentrating on my writing career instead.'

'Talking of which,' I said, when we'd searched each other's eyes. 'I'm not sure I approve of you writing me into your book.'

He slid a sheepish look at his laptop. 'Have you been snooping again?'

'I wasn't snooping the first time,' I protested. 'I just nudged it and it came on.'

'Riiiight.'

'Noah Dailey?'

'You should be flattered,' he said. 'If you read it properly, you'll know that Noah is a very appealing character – warm, quirky…' His eyes sparked. 'Extremely attractive.'

'He's a man.'

'But I was thinking of you when I wrote him.'

'That's not weird at all.' I was still smiling. 'Can he at least have a secret cool side? Be a champion athlete, or good at picking locks, or a computer genius?'

Ryan's gaze didn't waver. 'I prefer him as he is.'

I realised we'd had this whole, life-altering conversation with me dressed as a koala and he'd still taken me seriously. 'You'd better give me a mention in the acknowledgements.'

'I've done better than that.' He held out a hand and mine slotted into it, perfectly. He tugged me past the spilled presents on the floor to the dining table.

'If you nudge the screen again, it'll probably come on,' he said, maintaining a straight face.

I nudged his shoulder instead. 'I'll let you do it this time.'

He sat on the dining chair and touched the keyboard and a document appeared with some words typed in italics halfway down. 'See?' His arm wrapped around my waist and pulled me close, and as I bent to read what he'd written, happiness bolted through me.

For Nina, who inspired me to keep writing and is a fine example to koalas everywhere.

I turned so that our foreheads touched and he drew me tighter.

'It's another perfect Christmas gift,' I managed.

'Another?'

'I'll tell you later,' I said. 'Thank you for this.'

Our faces were close and it felt so right kissing him, as though this was what I'd been missing my whole life. As he gently pulled me onto his lap and I wound my arms round his neck, I knew this Christmas was going to be a good one after all.

'What are all those?' Ryan murmured, when we finally broke from our third – maybe fourth – long kiss, casting his gaze to the items I'd dropped on the floor.

'I was going to do some present wrapping.' My lips felt twice their usual size. 'A couple of them are for you, so you'd better not look.' I pressed my nose to his neck and breathed him in. Even after a night at the airport, still wearing the clothes he'd left in, he smelt totally delicious with an underlying tang of satsuma.

'Talking of presents…' He loosened his grip on my waist and shifted slightly, fishing his phone from his pocket. 'I don't want to embarrass you in front of everyone, so I'll show you now.'

'Honestly, the dedication is enough.'

'I hope you'll like this more.' He prodded the screen and turned it to show me, but all I could see was a barcode and a jumble of letters.

'I don't get it.'

'It's a plane ticket to Norway, for New Year's Eve,' he said. 'To see the Northern Lights.' I hadn't thought it possible to feel any more emotional than I had a minute ago. 'Two tickets, actually. Grace Benedict has never been to Norway, so I thought I could do some research for my next book, if you don't mind me tagging along.' My heart was so full, I couldn't produce any words. 'I thought it would be a nice way to say a proper goodbye to your gran.' Doubt crowded his face. 'I haven't booked a hotel, so if you don't fancy it—'

'Shut up, Ryan.' I took his face between my palms and kissed him fiercely and we didn't pull apart until there was an eruption of noise from downstairs.

'Charlie's back.' I was so croaky-voiced, I sounded a lot like Margot.

'We'd better go and welcome him home.' Ryan's voice was seriously gruff. 'Though I'd rather stay right here for a few more hours.'

'Serena!' Dolly's shout of delight shot a smile to my face. Mum and Dad were here too, and I suddenly couldn't wait to see them. 'What are you *doing* here?' Dolly cried.

I grinned at Ryan's expression. 'It's not really a catchphrase,' I said. 'It's just something everyone says.'

'We'll have to invent a new one.' He stroked a hand through my hair, as if he didn't mind that it wasn't long enough to toss about, and I got to my feet unsteadily and held out my hands.

'Come on,' I said as our fingers entwined and tightened.

'Do we have to?'

'We do.' I smiled into his eyes. 'I want you to meet my parents.'

Epilogue

'We're not going to see them, are we?' I dropped my suitcase by the door and sat beside Ryan on the sofa. 'Almost a week, and nothing.'

He wrapped a comforting arm around my shoulder. 'There's still time before we leave for the airport,' he said, but I could tell he was as disappointed as I was that there'd been no sight of the Northern Lights since our arrival in Norway, six days ago.

'So much for us being in an aurora borealis hot spot,' I said, referring to the boast on the website that our cabin, located just outside Tromsø, afforded a perfect view of 'nature's celestial ballet' from the balcony, thanks to the 'Arctic latitudes and clear, unpolluted skies'.

Make sure you have your cameras charged and ready!

Not that I was too worried about taking pictures of views these days; just photos of the rooms I'd been revamping since Christmas for my blog *The House Whisperer*, which was gaining new followers every day.

'We were unlucky to pick a cloudy week,' Ryan admitted. 'It's the first time it's been like this in ages.'

I nodded. 'Probably something to do with climate change.'

Since our first evening, when we'd spotted a grey streak arcing across the sky and rushed to the balcony just as it disappeared, there hadn't been a glimpse of any 'celestial' activity at all, and I wished the clouds would clear off – or at least part for ten minutes and give us a flash of… *something*.

'They're supposed to appear at least two hundred nights of the year,' I said, for about the hundredth time.

'We've still had a brilliant time.' Ryan kissed the top of my head. 'Your gran would have loved it.'

I smiled as I nestled against his chest, feeling the reassuring thud of his heart through three layers of clothing – despite the crackling fire in the log-burning stove, we weren't built for arctic temperatures. 'It's been amazing,' I said, keeping an eye on the ink-black sky beyond the glass wall of the cabin, just in case. 'I've loved every minute.'

'Most memorable moment?'

I lifted my head. 'You mean apart from…?'

His gaze drifted towards the bedroom door. 'Apart from that,' he said, and the heat in his eyes shot my temperature up several notches. It still felt exciting to touch each other whenever we wanted – which was most of the time, when we were alone together.

'In that case, it has to be the sleigh ride.'

His mouth curved into a grin. 'I agree.'

It had been as magical as I'd hoped, snuggled together beneath fur blankets, wearing thermals and boots to protect against the cold, driven through the frozen beauty of the snow-swathed mountains and iced fjords by a friendly guide and a pack of beautiful, blue-eyed huskies. We'd been allowed to cuddle the friendly dogs afterwards (my personal highlight) before eating a traditional Norwegian fish dish, and sipping hot coffee around an open fire to warm us up.

Sadly, the amazing light display the guide informed us had manifested every night the previous week had failed to put in an appearance. Even so, we'd thrown ourselves into making the most of our trip, learning to master a snowmobile, attending a midnight concert at the Arctic cathedral, with its floor-to-ceiling stained glass window, and had marvelled at the ethereal beauty of the scenery all around us.

We'd feasted on crabs, tried a seaweed cocktail that wasn't as delicious as one of Charlie's, and eaten a meringue, vanilla-cream and almond-packed sponge called *kvæfjordkake* that I was going to beg Dolly to replicate the second I returned to Chamillon.

We'd been whale-watching, seen reindeer and arctic foxes, but the aurora borealis had remained stubbornly hidden behind a thick veil of cloud, and now it was almost time to leave, and for Ryan to head to London for a catch-up meeting with his agent now that he was well underway with *The Rising Dawn*.

'I don't think Gran would have had a better time, even without seeing the lights,' I said, quashing a spike of disappointment as I disentangled myself and stood up, knowing I was going to miss the cosy cabin that had been our home for the past week. 'I promise I won't mention them again.'

'I won't hold you to that.' Ryan gave me a lazy grin as he got to his feet and stretched – a sight I knew I'd never grow tired of seeing. 'The taxi will be here in a minute,' he added, reaching for his coat on the back of the sofa. 'Have we got everything?'

'I think so.' Hearing a message alert on my phone, I picked it up off the table where we'd drunk coffee, and eaten local flatbreads slathered with butter, sugar and cinnamon that morning, before a final hike to look at the mountains, smiling as I read the message. 'Apparently, Dad enjoyed Christmas at Dolly's so much, Mum says he's suggesting they go again this year.'

'Wow,' said Ryan, who'd found common ground with Dad after a slightly awkward introduction by proving surprisingly knowledgeable about farming and rural affairs. Later, he confessed he'd done some research after hearing me talk about the farm over dinner at Dolly and Frank's, and had become engrossed in the topic. Mum, by contrast, had taken to Ryan before he'd even opened his mouth, giving Dolly a wink and a thumbs up when she thought I wasn't looking. 'It *was* an amazing Christmas though.'

My smile grew. 'It really was.'

It had been better than I could have imagined, and not just because I appeared to have fallen in love when I'd been least expecting to. The day itself had been magical from the start: we awoke to falling snow and the glorious smell of breakfast cooked by Dad. Dolly and Frank arrived and we piled into the living room to open our presents around the tree. Even Ben had been there with Lovely Lena, via Skype, and although we'd all felt Gran's absence, it hadn't been the sad affair I'd dreaded. Instead, we'd reminisced over our roast turkey dinner, recalling our favourite memories, played a riotous game of Pictionary in her honour, and raised a glass of her favourite brandy, with a mince pie, and although there'd been plenty of tears, most of them had been happy.

After lunch, I took out the letters and handed them to Dolly and Mum. My heart was beating overtime, and my hands shook as I explained what I'd found. Despite Augustine's final letter to William making it clear that she had really loved Charles, I couldn't help worrying about their reaction. But to my relief, they were both delighted. Dolly read and re-read the letters: at first in disbelief – *I can't believe these are her words, Nina. It's like seeing her as a young woman* – then again with grief – *I still miss her, you know* – and finally, happiness, that she'd been wrong to assume her gran had been wishing she'd spent her married life with someone else.

'Look, Serena, she really did love Gramps,' she'd said, showing the letters to Mum, who'd read them, glossy-eyed, fingers pressed to her lips, slowly shaking her head as she took it all in. '*William*,' she murmured. 'I can't imagine her with a William, can you?'

They kept reading out snippets to each other, and blurting, *do you remember...?* and Charlie had said with a twinkle, 'Thanks a lot, Nina. My Christmas gift is going to look really rubbish now,' which made everyone laugh, then Mum had noticed Ryan and I holding hands and burst into tears.

After lunch, Ryan called his parents to wish them a Happy Christmas and to tell them about me, and Ben called later to say he'd proposed to Lena, prompting more tears from Mum and Dolly, who'd become horribly over-emotional, and when Charlie and Elle exchanged a look that suggested it would be their turn next and more tears started flowing, Dad had suggested a walk on the beach so everyone could 'calm down'.

A couple of days later, Dolly had invited Gérard for dinner to tell him about the letters and he'd been astonished, and touchingly moved.

'All this time,' he kept saying. 'We did not know. Maggie, she did not know.' He kept shaking his head, eyes bright and blinking. 'I did not even read the letters. Maybe I would have known the name. You have told me about your Augustine,' he said to Dolly, seeming suddenly stricken, but she'd assured him he couldn't possibly have made the connection, it was too extraordinary, and it was only thanks to my nosiness that it had ever come to light.

'It was meant to be, as Nina's Gran would have said.'

'And now we are... we are *famille*.' Gérard had spoken with an air of wonder, and Hamish barked an agreement, and even though it wasn't strictly true, it had felt right somehow.

'Don't forget your hat,' said Ryan, bringing me back to the moment. 'You know you don't like having cold ears.'

'I've got it.' I pulled it from my coat pocket and over my hair, and couldn't resist a final glance through the window.

'I think… are those stars?' I said to Ryan. 'Look, I'm sure I can see some stars.'

'I doubt it, the forecast was for more snow tonight.' He was preoccupied, picking up our cases. 'I'll take these out, shall I?'

'I can help.' I tried to grab mine. 'Stronger than I look, remember?'

'Really?'

It was heavier than I remembered. 'OK, maybe not.' I relinquished my grip, just as the taxi drew up outside, wheels crunching over the snow. 'Are you sure it's OK to leave the fire burning?'

'The owners said it was fine, they'll be along to clean the place shortly.'

'Seems wrong to think of anyone else staying here.'

'I know what you mean.'

Ryan turned off the light and we stood for a moment and I knew I'd remember this week as the start of the rest of my life, then the taxi blasted its horn and I almost shot out of my skin. Chuckling, Ryan carried our cases out, and I followed with a pair of smaller bags, boots squeaking on the snowy path away from the cabin.

As he loaded the boot, I felt in my pockets for the key. 'I'll just lock up,' I said.

'Don't forget to put the key in the…'

'…little black box,' I said. We often finished each other's sentences these days. Charlie found it funny, even though I'd heard him do the same with Elle.

As I reached the door, I remembered something. 'I left my phone on the table,' I called to Ryan, feeling a lurch that I'd nearly forgotten it. 'I won't be a minute.'

Inside, the air was warm with the scent of woodsmoke and pine. I crossed to the table, aware the darkness from earlier had lifted, and a luminous white glow was spreading through the room, as though the moon was rising, and something was happening at the edges of my vision – the light taking on a greenish tinge, as if...

I flew back to the door. '*Ryan!*' I yelled. 'Ryan, it's happening!'

Back inside, I ran to the balcony doors, slid them open and stepped outside, my breath catching as ribbons of emerald began to shimmer and dance between the stars, then Ryan was behind me, drawing me close, his arms wrapping tightly around my waist.

'Either we're about to be abducted by aliens, or we're finally getting our light show,' he murmured, and I gave a choking laugh, the view blurring momentarily as tears filled my eyes.

'It's so beautiful.'

As the sky erupted in a dancing, swirling mass of light over the winter landscape, the neon-green merging into violet, I twisted to look at Ryan and saw that his eyes were misted with emotion too. 'If I hadn't come in to get my phone, we might have missed it,' I whispered, and heard Gran's voice, as clearly as if she was standing next to me. *Maybe it was meant to be.*

'Good job you did,' said Ryan. 'This is definitely going in my next book, by the way.'

I blinked away my tears. 'What about the driver?'

'I'm not putting him in the book.'

I gave him a nudge. 'I mean, he'll wonder where we are.'

There was a smile in Ryan's voice when he said softly, 'Oh, I think he'll understand.'

For a long while after that, the only sound was our breathing in the cold night air, until the colours eventually began to fade and the stars reappeared, glittering like tiny diamonds, and Ryan kissed my frozen cheek tenderly.

'Ready to go home?'

I turned, holding him close. 'I'm already there,' I said.

A Letter from Karen

I want to say a huge thank you for choosing to read *I'll be Home for Christmas*. If you did enjoy it, and want to keep up-to-date with all my latest releases, just sign up at the following link. Your email address will never be shared and you can unsubscribe at any time.

www.bookouture.com/karen-clarke

It was such a pleasure to revisit the Île de Ré in winter for my Christmas tale and tell Nina's story. She has her reasons to want to escape the festive season, which – being a lover of Christmas – is hard to understand, but I think anyone who has lost someone they love – as Nina has – can find it a very difficult time of year. I was keen to explore what home really means and how, often, it's so much more than a place or a building – it's being with people you love, who love you in return, whether that's in Chamillon, England, or even the Arctic Circle, hoping to catch a glimpse of the Northern Lights!

I hope you loved *I'll be Home for Christmas* and if you did, I would be very grateful if you could write a review. I'd love to hear what you think, and it makes such a difference helping new readers to discover one of my books for the first time.

I love hearing from my readers – you can get in touch on my Facebook page, through Twitter, Goodreads or my website.

Thanks,
Karen

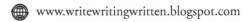 www.writewritingwritten.blogspot.com

 karen.clarke.5682

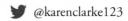 @karenclarke123

Acknowledgements

A lot of people are involved in making a book, and my heartfelt thanks go to Oliver Rhodes and the brilliant team at Bookouture for making it happen. Enormous thanks to my brilliant editor Maisie for her patience and clever guidance, to copy editor Jane for all her hard work, proofreader Jane, cover designer Emma (this is my favourite!) and Noelle Holten, Kim Nash and the marketing wizards, who work so tirelessly to spread the word.

As ever, I'm enormously grateful to my lovely readers, as well as the blogging community, whose reviews are a labour of love, and to Amanda Brittany for her feedback and friendship.

And last, but never least, thank you to my family and friends for not getting fed up with me talking about my books, my children, Amy, Martin and Liam for their unwavering support, and my husband Tim, for not getting fed up (especially when things are frenzied!) and the cups of tea – I couldn't do any of it without you.